Lawrence Block

The Burglar
Who Thought
He Was Bogart

A Bernie Rhodenbarr Mystery

No Exit Press

1996

No Exit Press,

18 Coleswood Rd

Harpenden, Herts, AL5 1EQ

A CIP catalogue record for this book is available from the British Library.

ISBN 1 - 874061 - 55 - 6   The Burglar Who Thought He Was Bogart

9 8 7 6 5 4 3 2 1

Printed and bound in Great Britain by
Cox and Wyman Ltd, Reading, Berks

For Otto Penzler

The author is pleased to acknowledge the contribution of the Ragdale
Foundation, in Lake Forest, Illinois, where some of the preliminary
work on this book was done, and of the Virginia Center for
the Creative Arts, in Sweet Briar, Virginia, where it was written.

ONE

At a quarter after ten on the last Wednesday in May, I put a beautiful woman in a taxi and watched her ride out of my life, or at least out of my neighborhood. Then I stepped off the curb and flagged a cab of my own.

Seventy-first and West End, I told the driver.

He was one of a vanishing breed, a crusty old bird with English for a native language. "That's five blocks, four up and one over. A beautiful night, a young fella like yourself, what are you doing in a cab?"

Trying to be on time, I thought. The two films had run a little longer than I'd figured, and I had to stop at my own apartment before I rushed off to someone else's.

"I've got a bum leg," I said. Don't ask me why.

"Yeah? What happened? Didn't get hit by a car, did you? All I can say is I hope it wasn't a cab, and if it was I hope it wasn't me."

"Arthritis."

"Go on, arthritis?" He craned his neck and looked at me. "You're too young for arthritis. That's for old

farts, you go down to Florida and sit in the sun. Live
in a trailer, play shuffleboard, vote Republican. A fellow your age, you tell me you broke your leg skiing,
pulled a muscle running the marathon, that I can
understand. But arthritis! Where do you get off having arthritis?"

"Seventy-first and West End," I said. "The northwest corner."

"I know where you get off, as in get out of the cab,
but why arthritis? You got it in your family?"

How had I gotten into this? "It's posttraumatic," I
said. "I sustained injuries in a fall, and I've had ar-
thritic complications ever since. It's usually not too
bad, but sometimes it acts up."

"Terrible, at your age. What are you doing for it?"

"There's not too much I can do," I said. "According to my doctor."

"Doctors!" he cried, and spent the rest of the ride
telling me what was wrong with the medical profession, which was almost everything. They didn't know
anything, they didn't care about you, they caused
more troubles than they cured, they charged the
earth, and when you didn't get better they blamed
you for it. "And after they blind you and cripple you,
so that you got no choice but to sue them, where do
you have to go? To a lawyer! And that's worse!"

That carried us clear to the northwest corner of
Seventy-first and West End. I'd had it in mind to ask
him to wait, since it wouldn't take me long upstairs
and I'd need another cab across town, but I'd had
enough of—I squinted at the license posted on the
right-hand side of the dash—of Max Fiddler.

I paid the meter, added a buck for the tip, and, like a couple of smile buttons, Max and I told each other to have a nice evening. I thought of limping, for the sake of verisimilitude, and decided the hell with it. Then I hurried past my own doorman and into my lobby.

Upstairs in my apartment I did a quick change, shucking the khakis, the polo shirt, the inspirational athletic shoes (*Just Do It!*) and putting on a shirt and tie, gray slacks, crepe-soled black shoes, and a double-breasted blue blazer with an anchor embossed on each of its innumerable brass buttons. The buttons—there'd been matching cuff links, too, but I haven't seen them in years—were a gift from a woman I'd been keeping company with awhile back. She had met a guy and married him and moved to a suburb of Chicago, where the last I'd heard she was expecting their second child. My blazer had outlasted our relationship, and the buttons outlasted the blazer; when I replaced it I'd gotten a tailor to transfer the buttons. They'll probably survive this blazer, too, and may well be in fine shape when I'm gone, although that's something I try not to dwell on.

I got my attaché case from the front closet. In another closet, the one in the bedroom, there is a false compartment built into the rear wall. My apartment has been searched by professionals, and no one has yet found my little hidey-hole. Aside from me and the drug-crazed young carpenter who built it for me, only Carolyn Kaiser knows where it is and how to get into it. Otherwise, should I leave the country or the planet abruptly, whatever I have hidden away would probably remain there until the building comes down.

I pressed the two spots you have to press, then slid the panel you have to slide, and the compartment revealed its secrets. They weren't many. The space runs to about three cubic feet, so it's large enough to stow just about anything I steal until such time as I'm able to dispose of it. But I hadn't stolen anything in months, and what I'd last lifted had long since been distributed to a couple of chaps who'd had more use for it than I.

What can I say? I steal things. Cash, ideally, but that's harder and harder to find in this age of credit cards and twenty-four-hour automatic teller machines. There are still people who keep large quantities of real money around, but they typically keep other things on hand as well, such as wholesale quantities of illegal drugs, not to mention assault rifles and attack-trained pit bulls. They lead their lives and I lead mine, and if the twain never get around to meeting, that's fine with me.

The articles I take tend to be the proverbial good things that come in small packages. Jewelry, naturally. Objets d'art—jade carvings, pre-Columbian effigies, Lalique glass. Collectibles—stamps, coins, and once, in recent memory, baseball cards. Now and then a painting. Once—and never again, please God—a fur coat.

I steal from the rich, and for no better reason than Robin Hood did: the poor, God love 'em, have nothing worth taking. And the valuable little items I carry off are, you will note, not the sort of thing anybody needs in order to keep body and soul together. I don't steal pacemakers or iron lungs. No family is left homeless after a visit of mine. I don't take the furniture or the TV set (although I have been known to roll up a small rug and take it for a walk). In short, I lift the things you can live without, and which you have very likely insured, like as not for more than they're worth.

So what? What I do is still rotten and reprehensible, and I know it. I've tried to give it up, and I can't, and deep down inside I don't want to. Because it's who I am and what I do.

It's not the only thing I am or do. I'm also a bookseller, the sole proprietor of Barnegat Books, an antiquarian bookstore on East Eleventh Street, between Broadway and University Place. On my passport, which you'll find in the back of my sock drawer (which is stupid, because, trust me, that's the first place a burglar would look), my occupation is listed as bookseller. The passport has my name, Bernard Grimes Rhodenbarr, and my address on West End Avenue, and a photo which can be safely described as unflattering.

There's a better photo in the other passport, the one in the hidey-hole at the back of the closet. It says my name is William Lee Thompson, that I'm a businessman, and that I live at 504 Phillips Street, in Yellow Springs, Ohio. It looks authentic, and well it might; the passport office issued it, same as the other one. I got it myself, using a birth certificate that was equally authentic, but, alas, not mine.

I've never used the Thompson passport. I've had it for seven years, and in three more years it will expire, and even if I still haven't used it I'll probably renew it when the time comes. It doesn't bother me that I haven't had occasion to use it, any more than it would bother a fighter pilot that he hasn't had occasion to use his parachute. The passport's there if I need it.

I wasn't likely to need it tonight, so I left it right where it was. I also left my stash of cash, which I didn't expect to need either. The last time I counted it was down to around five thousand dollars, which is lower than I like it. Ideally I ought to maintain an emergency cash reserve of twenty-five thousand dollars, and I periodically boost it to that level, but then I find myself dipping into it for one thing or another, and before I know it I'm scraping bottom.

All the more reason to get to work.

A workman is as good as his tools, and so is a burglar. I picked up my ring of picks and probes and odd-shaped strips of metal and found room for them in a trouser pocket. My flashlight is the size and shape of a fountain pen, and I tucked it accordingly into the blazer's inside breast pocket. I didn't have to keep the flashlight hidden away—they sell them in hardware stores all over town, and it's no crime to carry one. But it is definitely a crime to carry burglar's tools, and the simple possession of a little collection like mine is enough to net its owner an extended vacation upstate, all expenses paid. So I keep them locked up, and stow the flashlight with them so I won't forget it.

Same with the gloves. I used to wear rubber gloves, the kind you put on when washing dishes, and I'd cut the palms out for ventilation. But now they have these terrific disposable gloves of plastic film, light as a feather and cool as a gherkin, and you can buy a whole roll of them for pocket change. I tore off two gloves and put the rest back.

I secured the secret compartment, closed the closet, snatched up the attaché case, let myself out of the apartment, and locked all the locks. All of this takes longer to report than to perform; I was in my apartment by ten-thirty and out of it, dressed and equipped and back on the street, by a quarter to eleven.

There was a cab cruising by as I cleared the threshold, and I could have sprinted and whistled and caught it. But it was hardly the sort of night when cabs were likely to be in short supply. I took my time, walked to the curb at a measured pace, held up a hand, and beckoned to a taxi.

Guess who I got.

"What you shoulda done," Max Fiddler said, "was tell me you had someplace else to go. I coulda waited. How's your leg now? Not too bad, right?"

"Not too bad," I agreed.

"It's good luck, finding you again. I almost didn't recognize you, all dressed up and everything. Whattaya got, if you don't mind my asking? A date? My guess, it's a business appointment."

"Strictly business."

"Well, you look very nice, you make a good appearance. We'll take the Transverse, okay? Go right through the park."

"Sounds good."

"Minute I dropped you off," he said, "I said to myself, Max, what the hell's the matter with you, man's got arthritis and you didn't tell him where to go. Herbs!"

"Herbs?"

"You know about herbs? Chinese herbs, like from a Chinese herb doctor. This woman gets into my cab, using a cane, has me take her down to Chinatown. She's not Chinese herself, but she tells me about this Chinese doctor she goes to. When she started with him she couldn't walk!"

"That's wonderful," I said.

"Wait, I haven't even told you yet!" And, even as we entered Central Park, he launched into a tale of miracle cures. A woman with horrible migraines— cured in a week! A man with high blood pressure— back to normal! Shingles, psoriasis, acne, warts—all of them cleared up! Hemorrhoids—cured without surgery! Chronic back pain—gone!

"For the back he uses the needles. The rest is all herbs. Twenty-eight bucks you pay for a visit and the herbs is free. Seven days a week he's there, nine in the morning till seven at night. . . ."

He himself had been cured of cataracts, he assured me, and now he saw better than he did when he was a boy. At a stoplight he took off his glasses and swung his head around, flashing his clear blue eyes at me. When we got to Seventy-sixth and Lexington he gave me a business card, Chinese on one side, English on the other. "I give out hundreds of these," he said. "I send everybody I can to him. Believe me, I'm glad to do it!" On the bottom, he showed me, he'd added his own name, Max Fiddler, and his telephone number. "You get good results," he said, "call me, tell me how it worked out. You'll do that?"

"I will," I said. "Definitely." And I paid him and tipped him and limped over to the brownstone where Hugo Candlemas lived.

I'd met Hugo Candlemas for the first time the previous afternoon. I was in my usual spot behind the counter, seeing what Will Durant had to say about the Medes and the Persians, of whom I knew little aside from the sexual proclivities alluded to in a limerick of dubious ethnological validity. Candlemas was one of three customers crowding my aisles just then. He was browsing quietly in the poetry section, while a regular customer of mine, a doctor at St. Vincent's, searched the adjacent aisle for the out-of-print mysteries she went through like smallpox through the Plains Indians. My third guest was a superannuated flower child who'd spotted Raffles sunbathing in the window. She'd come in to ooh and ahh over him and ask his name, and now she was looking through a shelf of art books and setting some volumes aside. If she wound up buying all the ones she'd picked, the sale would pay for a whole lot of Meow Mix.

The doctor was the first to settle up, relieving me of a half-dozen Perry Masons. They were book club editions, a couple of them pretty shabby, but she was a reader, not a collector, and she gave me a twenty and got a little change back.

"Just a few years ago," she said, "these were a buck apiece."

"I can remember when you couldn't give them away," I said, "and now I can't keep them in stock."

"What do you figure it is, people with fond memories of the TV show? I came in the back door—I hated the TV show, but I started reading A. A. Fair and decided, gee, the guy can write, let's see what he's like under his own name. And it turns out they're tough and fast-paced and sassy, not like the television crap at all."

We had a nice conversation, the kind I'd had in mind when I bought the store, and then after she left, the flower matron, Maggie Mason by name, brought up her treasure trove and wrote out a check for $228.35, which is what those twelve books came to with tax. "I hope Raffles gets a commission on this," she said. "I must have passed this store a hundred times, but it was seeing him that made me come in. He's a wonderful cat."

He is, but how could the ebullient Ms. Mason possibly know that? "Thank you," I said. "He's a hard worker, too."

He hadn't changed position since she came in, except to preen a little while she'd cooed at him. My irony was unintentional—he *is* a hard worker, maintaining Barnegat Books as a wholly rodent-free ecosystem—but it was lost on her anyway. She had, she assured me, the greatest respect for working cats.

And off she went, bearing two shopping bags and a perfectly radiant smile.

She had barely cleared the threshold when my third customer approached, a faint smile on his face. "Raffles," he said, "is a splendid name for that cat."

"Thank you."

"And appropriate, I'd say."

What exactly did he mean by that? A. J. Raffles was a character in a book, and the cat was in a bookshop, but that fact alone made the name no more appropriate than Queequeg, say, or Arrowsmith. But A. J. Raffles was also a gentleman burglar, an amateur cracksman, while I was a cracksman myself, albeit a professional.

And how did this chap, white-haired, slight of build, thin as a stick, and very nattily if unseasonably turned out in a suit of brown herringbone tweed and a Tattersall vest—how did he happen to know all this?

Admittedly, it's not the most closely held secret in the world. I have, after all, what they call a criminal record, and if it weren't a matter of record they'd call it something else. I haven't been convicted of anything in a long time, but every now and then I get arrested, and a couple of times in recent years I've had my name in the papers, and not as a seller of rare volumes.

I told myself, like Scarlett (another fine name for a cat), that I'd think about it later, and turned my attention to the book he placed on the counter. It was a small volume, bound in blue cloth, containing the selected poems of Winthrop Mackworth Praed

(1802–39). It had been part of the inventory when I bought the store. I had, at one time or another, read most of the poems in it—Praed was a virtuoso at meter and rhyme, if not terribly profound—and it was the sort of book I liked having around. No one had ever expressed any interest in it, and I'd thought I'd own it forever.

It was not without a pang that I rang up $5.41, made change of ten, and slipped my old friend Praed into a brown paper bag. "I'm kind of sorry to see that book go," I admitted. "It was here when I bought the store."

"It must be difficult," he said. "Parting with cherished volumes."

"It's business," I said. "If I'm not willing to sell them, I shouldn't have them on the shelves."

"Even so," he said, and sighed gently. He had a thin face, hollow in the cheeks, and a white mustache so perfect it looked to have been trimmed one hair at a time. "Mr. Rhodenbarr," he said, his guileless blue eyes searching mine, "I just want to say two words to you. Abel Crowe."

If he hadn't commented on the appropriateness of Raffles's name, I might have heard those two words not as a name at all but as an adjective and a noun.

"Abel Crowe," I said. "I haven't heard that name in years."

"He was a friend of mine, Mr. Rhodenbarr."

"And of mine, Mr.—?"

"Candlemas, Hugo Candlemas."

"It's a pleasure to meet a friend of Abel's."

"It's my pleasure, Mr. Rhodenbarr." We shook

hands, and his palm was dry and his grip firm. "I shan't waste words, sir. I have a proposition to put to you, a matter that could be in our mutual interest. The risk is minimal, the potential reward substantial. But time is very much of the essence." He glanced at the open door. "If there were a way we could talk in private without fear of interruption . . ."

Abel Crowe was a fence, the best one I ever knew, a man of unassailable probity in a business where hardly anyone knows the meaning of the word. Abel was also a concentration camp survivor with a sweet tooth the size of a mastodon's and a passion for the writings of Baruch Spinoza. I did business with Abel whenever I had the chance, and never regretted it, until the day he was killed in his own Riverside Drive apartment by a man who—well, never mind. I'd been able to see to it that his killer didn't get away with it, and there was some satisfaction in that, but it didn't bring Abel back.

And now I had a visitor who'd also been a friend of Abel's, and who had a proposition for me.

I closed the door, turned the lock, hung the BACK IN 5 MINUTES sign in the window, and led Hugo Candlemas to my office in back.

TWO

Now, thirty-two hours later, I rang one of four bells in the vestibule of his brownstone. He buzzed me in and I climbed three flights of stairs. He was waiting for me at the top of the stairs and led me into his floor-through apartment. It was very tastefully appointed, with a wall of glassed-in bookshelves, a gem of an Aubusson carpet floating on the wall-to-wall broadloom, and furniture that managed to look both elegant and comfortable.

One deplorable effect of a lifetime of larceny is a tendency of mine to survey every room I walk into, eyes ever alert for something worth stealing. It's a form of window shopping, I guess. I wasn't going to take anything of Candlemas's—I'm a professional burglar, not a kleptomaniac—but I kept my eyes open just the same. I spotted a Chinese snuff bottle, skillfully carved from rose quartz, and a group of ivory netsuke, including a fat beaver whose tail seemed to have gone the way of all flesh.

I admired the carpet, and Candlemas showed me around and pointed out a couple of others, including a Tibetan tiger rug, an old one. I said I was sorry to be late and he said I was right on time, that it was the third member of our party who was late, but that he should be arriving at any moment. I turned down a drink and accepted a cup of coffee, and was not surprised to find it rich and full-bodied and freshly brewed. He talked a little about Winthrop Mackworth Praed, and speculated on what he might have done if tuberculosis hadn't shortened his life. He'd had a seat in the House of Commons; would he have gone further in politics and let poetry take a back seat? Or might he have grown disillusioned with political life, quit writing the topical partisan doggerel he'd turned to toward the end, and gone on to produce mature work to put his early verses in the shade?

We were batting that one around when the doorbell rang, and Candlemas crossed the room to buzz in the new arrival. We waited for him at the top of the stairs, and he turned out to be a thickset older fellow with a pug nose and a broad face. He had a drinker's complexion and a smoker's cough, but you could have been deaf and blind and still known how he got through the days. Unless you had a bad cold, say, and couldn't smell the booze on his breath and the smoke in his hair and clothes. Even so you might have guessed from the way he took the stairs, pausing on the landings to catch his breath, and still having to take his time on the final flight of steps.

"Captain Hoberman," Candlemas greeted him, and shook his hand. "And this is—"

"Mr. Thompson," I said quickly. "Bill Thompson." We shook hands warily. Hoberman was wearing a gray suit, a blue-and-tan striped tie, and brown shoes. The suit looked like what you used to see on third-level Soviet bureaucrats before perestroika. The only man I knew who could look that bad in a suit was a cop named Ray Kirschmann, and Ray's suits were expensive and well-cut; they just looked to have been tailored for somebody else. Hoberman's outfit was a cheap suit. It wouldn't have looked good on anybody.

We went into Candlemas's apartment and reviewed the plan. Captain Hoberman was expected within the hour on the twelfth floor of a high-security apartment building at Seventy-fourth and Park. He was my ticket into the building. Once he got me past the doorman, he'd go keep his appointment while I kept an appointment of my own four floors below.

"You will be alone," he assured me, "and uninterrupted. Captain Hoberman, you will be how long on the twelfth floor? An hour?"

"Less than that."

"And you, Mr. uh Thomas, will be in and out in twenty minutes, although you could take all night if you wished. Should the two of you arrange to meet up and leave the building together? What do you think?"

I thought I should have skipped the whole thing and hopped into the first cab when I had the chance. Instead of riding off with a beautiful woman, I'd wound up learning more than I wanted to know about Chinese herbs. I'd spent the past two weeks watching Humphrey Bogart movies, and it seemed to have done something to my judgment.

"It sounds unnecessarily complicated," I said. "It's not all that hard to get out of a building, unless you've got a TV set under your arm or a dead body over your shoulder."

It's not that hard to get into a building, either, if you know what you're doing. I'd said as much to Candlemas the previous day, suggesting that we could get along without Captain Hoberman. But he wasn't having any. The captain was part of the package. I needed my captain about as much as Tony Tenille needed hers, and had as little chance of dumping him.

Hoberman paused at each landing on the way down the stairs, too, and when we got outside he took hold of the cast-iron railing while he got his bearings. "You tell me," he said. "Where's the best place to get a cab?"

"Let's walk," I said. "It's only three blocks."

"One of 'em's crosstown."

"Even so."

He shrugged, lit a cigarette, and off we went. I counted that a victory, but changed my mind when he steamed on into the Wexford Castle ~~~~ on Lexington Avenue. "Time for ~~~~ nounced, and ordered a do~~~~ bartender, who looke~~~~ thing but reme~~~~ tle with ~~~~

posed to get to our destination by midnight, but before I had the sentence out the captain had downed his drink.

"Something for you?"

I shook my head.

"Then let's get going," he said. "Supposed to get there before midnight. That's when the late shift comes on duty."

We hit the street again, and the drink seemed to loosen him up. "Here's a question for you," he said. "How much wood could a woodchuck chuck if a woodchuck could chuck wood?"

"It's a question, all right."

"Known that fellow a long time, have you?"

Thirty-two hours, getting on for thirty-three. "Not too long," I admitted.

"What do you make of this? When he told me about you, he didn't use your actual name. He called you something else."

"Oh?"

"I want to say Road and Track, but that's not it. Road and Car? Makes no sense. Roadieball?" He shrugged. "Doesn't matter, but it sure wasn't Thompson. Wasn't even close."

"Well, he's getting on in years," I said.

"_____ing of the brain," he said. "That how you

_____ extreme, but—"

"_____" he said, "and I don't

_____ole lot at stake

_____ on this.

"I guess not."

"Talk too much anyway," he said. "Always been my problem." And he didn't say another word until we got to the building.

It was a fortress, all right. The Boccaccio, one of the great Park Avenue apartment buildings, twenty-two stories tall, its sumptuous Art Deco lobby equipped with enough potted plants to start a jungle. There was a doorman out front and a concierge behind the desk, and damned if the elevator didn't have an attendant, too. All three of them wore maroon livery with gold braid, and a pretty sight they were. They wore white gloves, too, which almost spoiled the effect, giving them the look of Walt Disney animals until you got used to it.

"Captain Hoberman," Hoberman told the concierge. "I'm here to see Mr. Weeks."

"Oh, yes, sir. Mr. Weeks is expecting you." He checked his book, made a little note in it, then looked up expectantly at me.

"And this is Mr. Thompson," Hoberman said. "He's with me."

"Very good, sir." Another little note in the book. Maybe it wouldn't have been such a piece of cake getting in here on my own. Still——

The elevator attendant had been watching all this from across the lobby, and probably heard it, too; Hoberman had a booming voice, audible, I suppose, from stem to stern. When we approached he said, "Twelve, gentlemen?"

"Twelve-J," Hoberman said. "Mr. Weeks."

"Very good, sir." And up we went, and out we

popped on twelve. The attendant pointed us toward
the J apartment and watched after us to make sure
we found our way. When we got there Hoberman
shot me a look and cocked a bushy eyebrow. The
stairwell, my immediate goal, was just steps from
where we stood, but the elevator was still within my
view and the attendant was still doing his job. I stuck
out a finger and poked the doorbell.

"But what will I say to Weeks?" Hoberman wondered. Softly, thanks be to God.

"Just introduce me," I said. "I'll take it from there."

The door opened. Weeks turned out to be a short
pudgy fellow with bright blue eyes. He was wearing
a hat in the house, a black homburg, but it was his
hat and his house, so I guess he had the right. The
rest of his outfit was less formal. A pair of suspenders with roosters on them held up the pants of a
Brooks Brothers suit. His shirtsleeves were rolled up
and his tie was off and his expression was under-
standably puzzled.

"Cappy," he said to Hoberman. "Good to see you.
And this is—"

"Bill Thompson," Hoberman said. And off to the
side, and not a moment too soon, I heard the elevator door draw shut.

"I live in the building," I said. "Ran into—"
Cappy? No, better not "—this gentleman in the
lobby, got so caught up in conversation I rode right
on past my stop." I laughed heartily. "Good to meet
you, Mr. Weeks. Good evening, gentlemen."

And I walked on down the hall, opened the fire
door, and scampered down the stairs.

* * *

At least there were no cameras in the stairwells.

The Boccaccio was wired for closed-circuit TV. I'd seen the bank of monitors behind the concierge's desk. One showed the laundry room, and others scanned the street in front, the passenger and service elevators, the service entrance around the corner on Seventy-fourth, and the parking spaces in the subbasement.

The building had stairwells at either end, so to include them in your closed-circuit surveillance you'd need two cameras on each floor, and an equal number of screens for the concierge to go blind staring at. But there's another way to do it: one or more of the screens can be set up to receive multiple channels, and whoever's monitoring the operation can sit back with a remote control and channel-surf the hours away.

I didn't think that was the setup they had here, but I couldn't know until I was actually in the stairwell. I hadn't been all that worried, though. I'd guessed stairwell surveillance was unlikely, and even if they had it I figured I could get around it.

See, when you've got that high a level of protection, you never have an incident. Nobody who doesn't belong ever gets across the threshold in the first place, not even the guys from Chinese restaurants who want nothing more than to slip a menu under every door in Manhattan. With that much security, naturally you feel secure. And, when nothing bad ever happens, you stop paying close attention to your own security devices.

Look what happened at Chernobyl. They had a gauge with a warning device on it, and when the crunch came it didn't fail, it worked the way it was supposed to. And some poor dimwit looked at it and decided it must be broken because it was giving an abnormal reading. So he ignored it.

This notwithstanding, I was just as glad to know I wasn't going to wind up on *America's Funniest Home Videos*.

Four floors below I made sure the hall was clear, then walked the length of it to 8-B. I rang the doorbell. I'd been assured there would be nobody home, but Candlemas could be wrong about that, or he could have steered me accidentally to the wrong apartment. So I rang the doorbell, and when nothing happened I took the time to ring it again. Then I fished out my set of lockpicking tools and let myself in.

Nothing to it. If you're looking for state-of-the-art locks, don't look in a luxury building on Park Avenue. Look in the tenements and brownstones where there's neither doorman nor concierge. That's where you'll find window gates and alarm systems and police locks. 8-B had two locks, a Segal and a Rabson, both of them standard pin-and-tumbler cylinders, solid and reliable and about as challenging as the crossword puzzle in *TV Guide*.

I knocked off one lock, paused for breath, and knocked off the other one—and all in not much more time than it takes to tell about it. In a funny way, I was almost sorry it was so easy.

See, lockpicking is a skill, and on the list of technical accomplishments it ranks several steps below brain surgery. With proper instruction, anyone with minimal manual dexterity can learn the basics. I'd taught Carolyn, for example, and she'd become fairly good at opening simple locks, until she stopped practicing and got rusty.

But for me it's different. I have a gift for it, and it's more than a matter of technique. There's something otherworldly about the whole enterprise, some altered state I slip into when I'm breaking and entering. I can't really describe it, and it would probably bore you if I could, but it's Magic Time for me, it really is. That's why I'm as good as I am at it, and it also helps explain why I can't stay away from it.

When the second lock sighed and surrendered, I felt the way Casanova must have felt when the girl said yes—grateful for the conquest, but sorry he hadn't had to work just a little bit harder for it. I sighed and surrendered my own self, turned the knob, stepped inside, and drew the door quickly shut.

It was dark as a coal mine during a power failure. I gave my eyes a minute to accustom themselves to the darkness, but it didn't get a whole lot brighter. This was good news, actually. It meant the drapes were drawn and the apartment was light-tight, which in turn meant I could flick on all the lights I wanted. I didn't have to skulk around in the darkness, bumping into things and cursing.

I used my flashlight first to make sure that all the drapes were drawn, and indeed they were. Then,

with my gloves on, I flicked the nearest light switch
and blinked at the glare. I put my flashlight back in
my pocket and took a deep breath, giving myself a
moment to relish that little shiver of pure delight
that comes over me when I've let myself into some
place in which I have no business being.

And to think I actually tried to give all this up. . . .

I locked both locks, just to be tidy, and looked
around the large L-shaped room. That was all there
was to the apartment, aside from a tiny kitchen and
a tinier bathroom, and it was furnished in a very tentative fashion, with the kind of Conran's—Door
Store—Crate & Barrel furniture newlyweds buy for
their first apartment. A rug with pastel colors and a
geometric pattern covered about a third of the parquet floor, and a platform bed filled the sleeping
alcove.

I looked in the closet, checked a few of the dresser drawers. The occupant was a male, I decided, but
there were enough female garments on hand to suggest that he had either a girlfriend or a problem of
sexual identity.

"Just take the portfolio," Hugo Candlemas had advised me. "You won't find anything else worth the
taking. The man's some sort of company stooge. He
doesn't collect anything, doesn't go in for jewelry. You
won't find any substantial cash on hand."

And what was in the portfolio?

"Papers. We're bit players in some sort of corpo-
rate takeover, you and I. At the very least, we'll split
a reward for recovering the documents, and your
share of that will be a minimum of five thousand

dollars. If I can entertain offers from the other side, you might net three or four times that amount." He beamed at the prospect. "The portfolio's leather with gold stamping. There's a desk, and if it's not right on top you'll find it in one of the drawers. They may be locked. Will that present a problem?"

I told him it never had in the past.

There was a desk, all right, Scandinavian in design, made of birch and given a natural finish. There was nothing on top of it but a hand-tooled leather box and an 8×10 photo in a silver frame. The box held pencils and paper clips. The photo, in black and white, showed a man in uniform. No GI Joe, this lad; his outfit was fancy enough to get him a place behind the desk at the Boccaccio. He was wearing glasses and a toothy grin, which made him look like Theodore Roosevelt, and he had his hair parted in the middle, which made him look like a drawing by John Held, Jr.

He looked familiar, but I couldn't tell you why.

I pulled up a chair, sat down at the desk and got to work. There were three drawers on each side and one in the middle, and I tried the middle one first, and it was open. And, right smack in the middle of it, there sat a calfskin portfolio, tan in color, stamped in gold with an ornamental border and a network of fleurs-de-lis.

Remarkable.

I sat still for a moment, just looking at the thing and listening to the silence. And then the silence was broken by the unmistakable sound of a key in a lock.

If I'd been doing anything—shuffling through drawers, opening closet doors, picking a lock—I'd have missed it, or reacted too late. But I registered it instantly and sprang from the chair as if I'd been waiting for that very sound all my life.

Years ago, before my time and yours, there was a baseball player in the old Negro Leagues named Cool Papa Bell. I gather he was capable of swift and sudden movement; he was frequently compared favorably to greased lightning, and it was said of him that he could turn off the bedroom light and be in bed before the room got dark. I had always thought of that as colorful hyperbole, but now I'm not so sure. Because I shoved the drawer closed, switched off a lamp, switched off another lamp, raced across the room to kill the overhead light, dove into the hall closet, and yanked the door shut, and it seems to me I was holed up there, flattening myself against the coats, before the lights went out.

If not, I came close.

More to the point, I had the closet door shut before the other door was opened. If my intruder hadn't fumbled a little with the keys, he'd have walked in on me. On the other hand, if he was thin-blooded enough to have worn a topcoat, or anxious enough to have toted an umbrella, he'd be opening the closet door any second now, and then what was I going to do?

Time, I thought. Upstate, with low companions and nothing good to read. But maybe it wouldn't come to that. Maybe I could talk my way out of it, or bribe a cop, or get Wally Hemphill to work a legal miracle. Maybe I could—

There were two of them. I could hear them talking, a man and a woman. I couldn't make out what they were saying—the closet door was thick and fit snugly—but I could hear them well enough to distinguish the pitch of their voices. Two of them, a man and a woman, in the apartment.

Oh, wonderful. Candlemas had assured me I'd have plenty of time, that the portfolio's current owner was out for the evening. But he was quite obviously back, and he had his girlfriend with him, and all I could hope for was that they would go to sleep fairly soon, and without opening the closet door.

They didn't sound sleepy, though. They sounded fervent, even impassioned, and I realized why I couldn't make out what they were saying. They were talking in a language I couldn't understand.

That covered everything but English, actually. But there are other languages I can recognize when I hear them, even if I can't understand what it is I'm hearing. French, German, Spanish, Italian—I know what those all sound like, and can even catch the odd word or phrase. But these folks were flailing away at one another in a tongue I hadn't heard before. It didn't even sound like a language, but more like what you used to hear when you tried to play a Beatles album backward, looking for evidence that Paul was dead.

They went on nattering and I went on stupidly trying to make sense out of it, and struggling mightily not to sneeze. Something in the closet was evidently playing host to a little mold or mildew, and I seemed to be the slightest bit allergic to it. I swallowed and pinched my nose and did all the things you think of, hoping they'll work and knowing they won't. Then I got angry, furious at myself for getting in a pickle like this, and *that* worked. The urge to sneeze went away.

So did the conversation. It died out, with only an occasional phrase uttered and that pitched too low to make out, even if you knew the language. There were other sounds, though. What the hell were they doing?

Oh.

I knew what they were doing. A platform bed doesn't have springs to squeak, so I didn't have that particular auditory clue, but even without it the conclusion was unmistakable. While I languished in the closet, these clowns were making love.

I had only myself to blame. If only I hadn't dawdled, wandering around the apartment, checking the fridge, counting the paper clips in the leather box on the desk. If only I hadn't held the silver-framed photo in my hand, turning it this way and that, trying to figure out why it was familiar. If only I had behaved professionally, for God's sake, I could have been in and out before the two of them turned up, with the portfolio locked away in my attaché case and a fat fee mine for the collecting. I'd have been out the door and out of the building and—

Wait a minute.

Where was the attaché case?

It certainly wasn't in the closet with me. Had I left it alongside the desk, or somewhere else in the apartment? I couldn't remember. Had I even brought it to the apartment? Had I set it down while I picked the locks, or tucked it between my knees?

I was pretty sure I hadn't. Well, had I had it with me when I entered the Boccaccio at Captain Hoberman's side? I tried to visualize the whole process—up in the elevator, saying a few words to Mr. Weeks in 12-J, then hotfooting it down four flights of stairs. It didn't seem to me that I'd been carrying anything, except for five pounds I could have done without, but it was hard to be sure.

Had I left it home? I remembered picking it up, but I could have put it down again. The question was, had I had it when I left my apartment?

The answer, I decided, was yes. Because I could recall having it in my hand when I hailed Max Fiddler's cab for the second time that night, and balanced on my knees when he asked if I was on my way to a business appointment.

Had I left it in his cab? I had his card, or his Chinese herbalist's card, anyway, with Max's phone number on it. There was nothing I needed in the attaché case. There was, in fact, nothing in it at all. It was a good case and I'd owned it long enough to get attached (or even attachéd) to it, but I certainly could live a rich and rewarding life without it if I had to.

But suppose he brought it back of his own accord. He knew where I lived, having dropped me off and picked me up at the same location. I didn't think I'd mentioned my name, or Bill Thompson's name either, but he could describe me to the doorman, or—

What the hell was I working myself up about? I was going stir-crazy in the damned closet. It was an empty attaché case with no identification on it and nothing incriminating about it, and if I got it back that was great, and if I didn't that was fine, and who cared?

Anyway, I'd had it with me when I got out of the cab. Because I could remember switching it from one hand to the other in order to ring Hugo Candlemas's doorbell. Which meant I'd probably left it there when Hoberman and I set out on our fool's errand, unless I'd left it at the Wexford Castle, and I didn't think I had. I had almost certainly left it up in Candlemas's apartment, in which case I could get it back when I went there to drop off the portfolio and collect my money.

Assuming I ever got out of the closet.

Outside, the fires of love were but glowing embers, to judge from the sound track. Maybe, I thought, I could just leave. Maybe they wouldn't notice.

Right.

I wondered what Bogart would do.

In the past fifteen days I had watched thirty movies, all of them either starring or featuring Humphrey Bogart. Some of them were films that everybody knows, like *The Maltese Falcon* and *Casablanca* and *The African Queen,* and others were movies that nobody's ever heard of, like *Invisible Stripes* and *Men Are Such Fools.* My companion at these outings, sitting beside me and sharing my popcorn, seemed to believe that the Bogart on-screen persona would tell you all you needed to know to cope with life. And who was I to say her nay?

But I couldn't think of anything better for Bogart to do than the course I'd chosen for myself, which was an essentially passive one. I was waiting for something to happen. Maybe Bogart would have taken the bit in his teeth and the bull by the horns and made something happen, but it seemed to me that he was most apt to do that when he had a gun in his fist. I didn't even have my fucking attaché case. All I could lay my hands on was a coat hanger.

Outside my door, activity seemed to have resumed, but of a different sort. They were walking about now, and carrying on an audible if incomprehensible conversation.

And then there was a loud sound, and something or someone bumped into the closet door, and then there was silence. Seconds later a door opened—not, thank God, the closet door, but what sounded like the front door. Then it closed. Then more silence.

And then, finally, I heard the sound that had started the whole thing, a key in a lock. Whoever it was must have walked halfway to the elevator before deciding to come back and lock up. Maybe the afterthought was prompted by natural tidiness, or maybe the door-locker figured this way it would take them longer to discover the body.

Because I'd played this scene before. Once before I'd ducked into a closet when somebody came home unexpectedly. That was on Gramercy Park, and the apartment was Crystal Sheldrake's, and when I got out of her closet I found her on the floor with a dental scalpel stuck in her heart. I have stumbled over altogether too many dead bodies in the course of my young life, and maybe you get used to it, but I haven't yet, and don't much want to.

And it had happened again, I just knew it. That was what had bumped into the closet door before—a body, dead as Spam, making the awkward transition from vertical to horizontal. Now it would be in the way when I tried to open the door, and I'd wind up tampering unwittingly with evidence and trying to squeeze through an opening that would have been a snug fit for Raffles.

Or maybe the body wasn't dead. Maybe the person on the other side of the closet door had been merely knocked senseless, and would recover consciousness even as I was emerging from my refuge. A consummation devoutly to be wished, certainly—if one had to have bodies lying about, it was preferable that they be alive—but I didn't really feel up for much in the way of human contact just now. I offered up a quick prayer to St. Dismas, the patron saint of burglars. Let the body be alive but unconscious, I implored him. Better yet, I thought, let it be in Schenectady—but maybe that was too much to ask.

A thought came to me, unbidden, irresistible: Bogart would get the hell out of the closet.

I opened the door, and of course there was no body there. I went all through the place, making sure; while a dead body is not something you want to run into, neither is it the sort of thing you'd care to overlook. No body, anywhere in the apartment. Two people had entered and two people had left, and one of them had stumbled against the closet door on the way out.

The bed, neatly made up before, was a rumpled mess now. I looked at the tangled sheets and felt embarrassed for my own voyeuristic role. It had been involuntary, God knows, and I hadn't seen anything, or made sense of what I'd heard, but I still found it disquieting to look upon the whole thing.

Aside from the bed, you'd never know anyone had been in the place. The guy in the uniform, the Jazz Age Teddy Roosevelt, still grinned dopily from the silver frame. The same clothes still hung in the closet, the same paper clips still huddled together in the leather box.

But the portfolio was gone.

THREE

And so, minutes later, was I. If there was any reason to hang around, I couldn't think of it. I gave the place yet another once-over, just in case one of them had taken the portfolio not to keep but merely to give the other a playful swat. I made sure it wasn't lurking on the floor behind the dresser, or in a pile of books alongside the fireplace, or, indeed, anywhere.

Then I got out of there. I'd had my gloves on all the time I'd been inside the apartment, so I hadn't left any fingerprints, and if the other visitors had done so, that was their problem. I left everything the way they'd left it, unlocked the doors, and was compulsive enough to do with my picks what they'd done with keys—i.e., I locked up after myself.

I walked back up to the twelfth floor and rang for the elevator. It was close to one in the morning, and the shifts change at midnight, but it was clearly a night when nothing could safely be left to chance. It turned out that the elevator attendant was a new face, but I'd rather climb four flights of stairs unnecessarily than have a fellow wonder how the man he'd taken to Twelve had managed to find his way to Eight.

But he didn't say anything to me, or look twice at me, and neither did the concierge. The doorman glanced my way only long enough to assure himself that I didn't want him to call me a cab. I walked over to Lex and headed uptown, and the Wexford Castle was right where I'd left it, looking every bit as dingy and smelling no better than it looked. There were half a dozen old soaks at the bar, and they weren't any more interested in me than the concierge or the elevator man, and who could blame them?

"I was in here an hour or so ago," I told the bartender. "I didn't happen to leave my attaché case here, did I?"

"You mean like a briefcase?"

"Right."

"About so wide and so high? Brass locks here and here?"

"You haven't seen it, have you?"

" 'Fraid not," he said. "I couldn't swear to it, but I don't think you had it with you. I remember you, on account of you were with a guy knocked off a double like he had a train to catch, and you didn't have nothing yourself."

"Well, that was then and this is now," I said.

"What'll you have?"

"What my friend had. Double vodka."

I won't drink anything when I go out housebreaking, not a drop, not so much as a sip of beer. But I'd done my work for the night, if you wanted to call it work. I called it a waste of time, and not a whole lot of fun.

He poured from the same bottle, the one with the guy sporting the astrakhan hat and the savage grin. The brand name was Ludomir, and it was a new one on me. I picked up my glass and tossed off the shot and thought I was going to die.

"Jesus," I said.

"Something the matter?"

"People drink this stuff?"

"What's wrong with it? If you're gonna tell me it's watered, save your breath, okay? Because it's not."

"Watered?" I said. "If it's diluted with anything, my guess would be formaldehyde. Ludomir, huh? I never heard of it."

"We just started pouring it a month or so ago," he said. "I don't do the ordering, but when the boss tells me to make it the house vodka, you know what that tells me?"

"It's cheap."

"Bingo," he said. He hefted the bottle, studied the label. " 'Product of Bulgaria,' " he read. "Imported, no less. Says right here it's a hundred proof."

"At least."

"Guy on the label looks happy, don't he? Like he's about to do one of those dances where they fold their arms and it looks like they're sitting down, but there's no chair under 'em. You or I tried something like that, we'd fall on our ass."

"I might anyway," I said.

"It's cheap shit," he said, "but all the time I been pouring it, you're the first person who didn't like it."

"I didn't say I didn't like it," I said. "All I said was it must have been diluted with nail polish remover."

"You said formaldehyde."

"I did?" I thought for a moment. "You're absolutely right," I said. "I'll tell you what. Why don't you give me another?"

"You sure, buddy?"

"I'm not sure of anything," I said, "but give me another all the same."

The second drink was a little easier to take, and a third might have been easier still, but I had the sense not to find out. I walked out of the Wexford Castle feeling better than I had when I'd walked in, and what more can anybody ask from a bottle of vodka?

I pressed on to Hugo Candlemas's brownstone, and in the vestibule I found his doorbell and tried to decide whether I would have had to switch my attaché case from one hand to the other in order to ring it. After some reflection I decided that it would depend on which hand I was holding the case in to begin with. If I had it in my left hand, it would have been child's play to reach out and poke the button with my right forefinger. But if I'd been holding the case in my right hand, it would have been awkward in the extreme to reach all the way across my body and push the button with my left forefinger. Therefore—

Therefore nothing. The case was either upstairs or it wasn't, and I'd know in a minute. I had both hands free at the moment—no attaché case, alas, and no tan leather portfolio with gold stamping, either. I picked out one of my ten fingers and rang the bell.

To no avail.

I gave him a minute, then rang again. When nothing happened, I found myself looking wistfully at the locked door. I knew the lock would be no problem, and I didn't expect more of a challenge from the one upstairs on the fourth floor. I couldn't think what had become of Candlemas, but suppose he'd tired of waiting for me and ducked around the corner for a plate of scrambled eggs? I could be in and out while he was waiting for the waitress to pour him a second cup of coffee.

The prospect of reclaiming my attaché case without having to endure any human contact was not without appeal. I'd have to talk to Candlemas sooner or later, to tell him what had happened and try to figure out why, but that could wait.

I put my hand in my pocket, let my fingers close around my little collection of burglar's tools.

Wait a minute, I thought. Suppose he's home, relaxing in the bathtub or entertaining a visitor. Or suppose he's out and comes home in time to catch me in the act. *Oh, hi, Hugo. I struck out at the Boccaccio, so I thought I'd take a few minutes to knock off your apartment.*

For that matter, suppose I was overcome by an irresistible impulse to lift something. I'm neither a sociopath nor a kleptomaniac, I don't plunder the digs of my friends, but was Hugo Candlemas a friend? He'd been Abel's friend, or at least had so described himself, and I'd liked him and found him a congenial fellow, but that was before he sent me off to get locked in a closet and come home empty-handed. That might not have been his fault, and indeed it might have been at least partly mine for having taken my time about it, but whoever deserved the blame, it did tend to soften the glue in the bonds of friendship.

From the dispassionate vantage point of the vestibule, the last thing I wanted to do was loot Candlemas's apartment. But how would I feel when I got upstairs and something special caught my eyes and tugged at my heartstrings? Not that gorgeous Aubusson, it was too big to steal, but what about the Tibetan tiger? Or his little display of netsuke, so easy to wrap up and chuck in the attaché case? Or, most appealing of all, some sweet untraceable cash? I could probably hold off, but I was embittered and the job had gone sour and I was not going to pass Go or collect five thousand dollars, and I'd had a couple Ludomirs, and—

Oh.

I couldn't go in, could I? I'd been drinking, and I don't work when I drink or drink when I work.

So that settled that.

I rang his bell one more time, and don't ask me which finger I used. I didn't expect a response and I didn't get one. Out on the street, I walked a block or so to clear my head, and when a cab came along I grabbed it.

It almost figured I'd get Max Fiddler for the third time, but nobody's that lucky. This time my driver was a young fellow who ate pistachio nuts as he drove, spitting the shells all over the front of the cab. He got me home in one piece, but not for lack of trying.

Back in my own apartment, I stowed my tools and flashlight, got out of my clothes and under the shower. I stayed there for a long time, trying to wash the night away, but it was still there when I emerged. I put on a robe and poured myself a nightcap, wondering how Scotch would sit on top of Ludomir.

I drank half of it, then searched my wallet for the slip of paper with Hugo Candlemas's phone number on it. Was it too late to call? Probably, but I picked up the phone and dialed the number anyway, and after two rings someone picked up and said, "Hello?"

It didn't sound like Hugo.

I didn't say anything. There was a silence, and the same voice said the same thing again, sounding a little peevish this time around.

Definitely not Hugo.

I put the receiver in the cradle.

I took another small sip of Scotch and made a mental list. Item: My visit to Apartment 8-B at the Boccaccio had turned out badly. Item: Hugo Candlemas, who was supposed to be home waiting for me to show up with the portfolio, had been absent when I went to see him. Item: An hour later, someone else was answering his phone. Someone who was definitely not Hugo Candlemas, but whose voice was curiously familiar.

Captain Hoberman? No, I decided, after a moment's reflection. Definitely not Captain Hoberman.

But definitely familiar, definitely a voice I'd heard before.

Oh.

I reached for the phone, hesitated, then went ahead and made the call. This time the fellow answered on the first ring, and at first he didn't say anything, which was almost enough in itself to confirm my hunch. Then he said, "Hello," and made assurance doubly sure. It was him, all right.

I broke the connection.

"Hell," I said aloud, and picked up my drink and frowned at it. How had I gotten in this mess? Was this where I deserved to be after fifteen nights in a row of Humphrey Bogart movies?

I should have been watching Laurel and Hardy.

FOUR

Of all the bookstores in all the towns in all the world, she walked into mine.

She did so exactly two weeks earlier, at three o'clock on a Wednesday afternoon. I was behind the counter with my nose in a book. The book was *Our Oriental Heritage*, the first of eleven volumes of Will and Ariel Durant's Story of Civilization. Over the years the Book-of-the-Month Club has been distributing the books as if it were the Gideons and they were the Bible, and it's a rare personal library that doesn't include a complete set, usually in pristine condition, the dust jackets intact, the spines uncracked, and the pages untouched by human eyes.

There had been a set in inventory when I acquired Barnegat Books from old Mr. Litzauer, and over the years I had bought a set every now and then, and occasionally sold one. I hadn't sold quite as many as I'd bought, and so I generally had a few sets on hand, one on the shelves and a couple in cartons in the back. On this particular Wednesday I had four sets in stock, because I'd bought one the previous afternoon, not out of a mad passion to corner the market but because it was part of a lot that included some eminently resalable Steinbeck and Faulkner firsts. By the time I closed the store Tuesday I'd recovered my costs by placing *To a God Unknown* and *In Dubious Battle* with a regular customer, and I was thus feeling well disposed toward the Durants, so much so that I decided I might as well find out what they had to say about the sum total of human history.

So that's what had my attention when she walked into my store, and into my life.

It was a perfect spring day, the kind of magical New York afternoon that makes you wonder why anyone would voluntarily live anywhere else. My door was wide open, so the little bell attached to it did not tinkle at her entrance. My cat, Raffles, often greets customers, rubbing against their ankles in a shameless bid for attention; on this occasion he lay on the windowsill in a patch of sunlight, doing his famous impression of a dishrag.

Even so, I knew I had a visitor. I got the merest glimpse of her out of the corner of my eye, then caught a whiff of her perfume as she crossed in front of the counter and disappeared behind a row of bookshelves.

I didn't look up. I was somewhere in the second or third chapter, reading about cannibalism. Specifically, I was reading about some tribe—I forget who, but you could look it up, I'll give you a good price on the books—some tribe that never held funerals, never had to make the hard choice between burial and cremation. They ate their dead.

I tried to read on, but my mind was awhirl with a

vision of a modern world in which the practice had become universal. Frank Campbell, I realized, would be a society caterer. Walter B. Cooke would own a great chain of fast-food restaurants. In Queens, the Long Island Expressway would be lined not with graveyards but with hotdog stands, and—

"I beg your pardon."

The first thing I noticed about her was her voice, because I heard it before I actually looked up and saw her. Her voice was low in pitch, husky, and her accent was European.

It got my attention. Then I looked across the counter at her. I don't suppose my heart actually stood still, or skipped a beat, or did any of those things that give cardiologists the jimjams, but it certainly took notice.

How do you describe a beautiful woman, short of littering the page with tiresome adjectives? I could tell you her height (five-seven), her hair color (light brown with red highlights), her complexion (light, clear, and flawless). I could inventory her features, striving for clinical detachment (a high, broad forehead, a strong brow line, large well-spaced eyes, a straight and slender nose). Or I could let my inventory reveal that I was smitten (skin like ivory that had learned to blush, brown eyes deep enough to drown in, a mouth made for kissing). Sorry, I can't do it. You'll have to imagine her for yourself.

Of all the bookstores in all the towns in all the world, she walked into mine.

* * *

"I did not want to disturb you," she said. "You seemed so deep in thought."

"I was reading," I said. "Nothing important."

"What are you reading?"

"The history of civilization."

She raised her perfect eyebrows. "Nothing important?"

"Well, nothing that can't wait. The Sumerians have been waiting for thousands of years. They can wait a little longer."

"You are reading about the Sumerians?"

"Not yet," I admitted. "They're the first civilization in the book, but I haven't gotten to them yet. I'm still back there in prehistory."

"Ah."

"Early Man," I said. "His hopes, his fears, his dreams of a better tomorrow. His endearing customs."

"His endearing customs?"

I couldn't seem to help myself. "This one tribe in particular," I said. "Or maybe it was more than one."

"What did they do?"

"They ate their dead." For God's sake, why was I talking like this? She didn't say anything, and my eyes dropped to the page, where a sentence caught my eye. "The Fuegans," I reported, "preferred women to dogs."

"As companions?"

"As dinner. They said that dogs tasted of otter."

"And that is bad, otter?"

"I don't know," I said. "I suppose it tastes of fish."

"Fuegans. I have never heard of them."

"Until now."

"Well, yes. Until now."

"I never heard of them, either," I said. "I gather
Darwin wrote about them. They lived in Tierra del
Fuego, at the southernmost tip of South America."

"Do they live there still?"

"I don't know. I'll tell you, though, if I ever go visit
them I'm taking my own lunch."

"And your own woman?"

"I don't have a woman," I said, "but if I did I don't
think I would take her to Tierra del Fuego."

"Where would you take her instead?"

"It would depend on the woman. I might take her
to Paris."

"How romantic."

"Or I might take her to the movies."

"Also romantic," she said. A smile played on her
lips. "I want to buy a book. Will you sell me a book?"

"Not this one?"

"No."

"Good," I said, and closed *Our Oriental Heritage*,
and set it on the shelf behind me. She'd been holding
a book, and she placed it on the counter where I
could see it. It was Clifford McCarty's *Bogey: The
Films of Humphrey Bogart*, the hardcover edition pub-
lished thirty years ago by Citadel Press. I checked the
penciled price on the flyleaf.

"It's twenty-two dollars," I said. "And, because I'm
honest to a fault, I'll tell you that there's a paperback
edition available. The title's slightly different but it's
the same book."

"I have it."

"It's around fifteen dollars, if memory serves, and sometimes it does." I blinked. "Did you just say you have it?"

"Yes," she said. "It's called *The Complete Films of Humphrey Bogart,* and your memory serves you quite well. The price is fourteen ninety-five."

"And you already own it."

"Yes. I want a hardcover copy."

"I guess you're a fan."

"I love him," she said. "And you? Do you love him?"

"There's never been anybody quite like him," I said, which, when you come right down to it, could be said of just about anyone. "He was one of a kind, wasn't he? He had—"

"A certain something."

"That's just what I was going to say." The tips of my fingers rested on the book, scant inches from the tips of her fingers. Her nails were manicured, and painted a rich scarlet. Mine were not. I fought to keep my fingers from reaching out for hers, and I said, "Uh, I have a copy of the Jordan Manning biography. At least I did the last time I looked."

"I saw it."

"It's out of print, and difficult to find. But I guess you already have a copy."

She shook her head. "I don't want it."

"Oh? It's supposed to be good, but—"

"I don't care," she said. "What do I care about his life? I don't care where he was born, or if he loved his mother. I don't give a damn how many wives he had, or how much he drank, or what he died of."

"You don't?"

"What I love," she said, "is what you see on the screen. *That* Humphrey Bogart. Rick in *Casablanca.* Sam Spade in *The Maltese Falcon.*"

"Dixon Steele in *In a Lonely Place.*"

Her eyes widened. "Everyone remembers Rick Blaine and Sam Spade," she said. "And Fred Dobbs in *The Treasure of the Sierra Madre,* and Philip Marlowe in *The Big Sleep.* But who remembers Dixon Steele?"

"I guess I do," I said. "Don't ask me why. I remember titles and authors a lot, that's natural in this business, and I guess I remember character names, too."

"*In a Lonely Place.* He's a screenwriter, Dixon Steele, do you remember? He has to adapt a novel but he can't bear to read it, and he gets a hat-check girl to come tell him the story. Then she's murdered, and he is a suspect."

"But there's another girl," I said.

"Gloria Grahame. She's a neighbor and gives him an alibi, and then she falls in love with him and types his manuscript and prepares his meals. But she sees the violence in him when his car is in an accident and he beats up the other driver, and again when he beats his agent for taking his script before it was finished. She thinks he must have killed the hat-check girl after all, and she is going to leave him, and he finds out and starts choking her. Do you remember?"

Vaguely, I thought. "Vividly," I said.

"And there is a phone call. The hat-check girl's boyfriend has confessed to the murder. But it's too late for them, and Gloria Grahame can only stand there and watch him walk out of her life forever."

"You don't need the book," I said. "Not in hardcover or in paperback. You've got the whole thing memorized."

"He is very important to me."

"I can see that."

"I learned English from his films. Four of them, I played them over and over on the VCR. I would say the lines along with him and the other actors, trying to pronounce them correctly. But I still have an accent, don't I?"

"It's charming."

"You think so? I think you are charming."

"You're beautiful."

She lowered her eyes, drew a wallet from her purse. "I want to pay for the book," she announced. "It is twenty-two dollars, yes? And then there is the sales tax."

"Forget the tax."

"Oh?"

"And forget the twenty-two dollars. Please, I insist. The book is my gift to you."

"But I cannot accept it."

"Of course you can."

"I want to pay for it," she said. She put a five and a twenty on the counter. "Please," she said.

I slipped the book into a paper bag, handed it to her, and gave her three dollars change. I didn't ring the sale and I didn't collect the tax. Don't tell the governor.

"You are very sweet," she said. "But how can you

make money if you give your books away?" She put
her hand on mine. "I think there is more to you than
shows on the surface. Do you know what I think? I
think you are like him."

"Like—?"

"Humphrey Bogart. Has anyone told you that?"

"No," I said. "Never."

She cocked her head, studying me. "It is not physical," she said. "You do not look like him. And your
voice is nothing like his. But there is something,
yes?"

"Well, uh—"

"Do you have a secret life?"

"Doesn't everybody?"

"Perhaps," she said. "Are you secretly violent, like
Dixon Steele?" She cocked her head, took a long
look at me. "I don't think so. But there is something,
isn't there? It is a very romantic quality, I can tell you
that much."

"It is?"

"Oh, yes. Very romantic." A knowing smile played
on those lips. "Take me out this evening."

"Wherever you say."

"Not to Paris," she said. "That would be romantic,
wouldn't it? If we were to meet like this, and tonight
we flew to Paris. But I don't want you to take me to
Paris, not yet."

"Paris can wait."

"Yes," she said. "We'll always have Paris. Tonight
you may take me to the movies."

* * *

After she left, I went over and touched Raffles to make sure he was alive. He hadn't changed position during her visit, and it was hard to imagine he could have ignored her. I scratched him behind the ear and he swung his head around and gave me a look.

"You missed her," I told him. "Go back to sleep."

He yawned and stretched, then sprang lightly down from the sill and hurried to check his water dish. He is a gray tabby, and Carolyn Kaiser, my best friend in all the world, has assured me that he is a Manx. I've since given the matter some study, and I'm not so sure. As far as I can tell, the only thing Manxlike about him is the tail he doesn't have.

Manx or no, he's a good working cat, and since he took up residence in my store I haven't lost a single volume to mice. It struck me that I owed him a lot. Suppose a mouse had gnawed the spine of *Bogey: The Films of Humphrey Bogart,* so that I'd had to toss it in the trash or consign it to the three-for-a-buck table? Just as she had walked into my store, so would she have walked on out of it, and I'd have gone on reading Will Durant, as unaware of the whole business as Raffles.

I reached for the phone and called the Poodle Factory, where Carolyn spends her days making dogs beautiful. "Hi," I told her. "Listen, I'm not going to be able to join you at the Bum Rap tonight. I've got a date."

"That's funny, Bern. I asked you at lunch if you had anything on for tonight, and you said you didn't."

"That was then," I said.

"And this is now? What happened, Bern?"

"A beautiful woman walked into my store."

"You've got all the luck," she said. "The only person who walked into my store all afternoon was a fat guy with a saluki. Why do people do that?"

"Walk into your store?"

"Buy inappropriate dogs. He's bandy-legged and barrel-chested and he's got an underslung jaw, so what the hell is he doing with a dog built like a fashion model? He ought to have an English bulldog."

"Maybe you can persuade him to switch."

"Too late," she said. "By the time you've had the dog for a few days you get attached and you're stuck with each other. It's not like human relationships where everything falls apart once you really get to know each other. Bern, this beautiful woman. Is it someone you knew?"

"A perfect stranger," I said. "She came in for a book."

"And walked out with your heart. It sounds romantic. Where are you taking her? The theater? The Rainbow Room? Or some intimate little supper club? That's always nice."

"We're going to the movies."

"Oh," she said. "Well, that's always a good choice on a first date. What are you going to see?"

"A double feature. *Chain Lightning* and *Tokyo Joe.*"

"Did they just open?"

"Not exactly."

"Because I never heard of them. *Chain Lightning* and *Tokyo Joe*? Who's in them? Anybody I ever heard of?"

"Humphrey Bogart."

"Humphrey Bogart? *The* Humphrey Bogart?"

"It's a film festival," I explained. "It's at the Musette Theater two blocks from Lincoln Center. Tonight's the first night, and I'm meeting her at the box office at a quarter to seven."

"The program starts at seven?"

"Seven-thirty. But she wants to make sure we get good seats. She's never seen either of these films."

"Have you, Bern?"

"No, but—"

"Because neither have I, and what's the big deal? I never even heard of them."

"She's a major Bogart fan," I said. "She learned English by watching his films over and over again."

"I bet every other word out of her mouth is 'You dirty rat.' "

"That's Jimmy Cagney."

" 'Play it again, Sam.' *That's* Humphrey Bogart, right?"

"It's close."

" 'You played it for her, you can play it for me. I can take it if she can.' Right?"

"Right."

"That's what I thought. What do you mean, she learned to speak English? Where did she grow up?"

"Europe."

"Where in Europe?"

"Just Europe," I said.

"Just Europe? I mean, France or Spain or Czechoslovakia or Sweden or, uh—"

"Of the four you mentioned," I said, "my vote would go to Czechoslovakia. But I can't really narrow

it down because we didn't get into that." I recapped
our conversation, leaving out the dietary excesses of
the Tierra del Fuegans. "There was a lot that went
unspoken," I explained, "a lot of significant glances,
a lot of nuance, a lot of, uh—"

"Heat," she suggested.

"I was going to say romance."

"Even better, Bern. I'm a sucker for romance. So
you're meeting her at the Musette and you're going
to see two old movies back to back. I don't suppose
they'll be colorized, will they?"

"Bite your tongue."

"And then what? Dinner?"

"I suppose so."

"Unless you both pig out on popcorn. So you'll be
getting out of the theater around ten-thirty or eleven
and you'll grab something in the neighborhood. Then
what? Her place or yours?"

"Carolyn—"

"If the Musette's just a couple of blocks from Lincoln Center," she said, "then it's not much more than
a couple of blocks from your place, because your
place is just a couple of blocks from Lincoln Center.
But maybe her place is just as convenient. Where
does she live, Bern?"

"I didn't ask her."

"So you're saying she lives in New York, right? She
comes from Europe and she lives in New York, and
you haven't managed to narrow down either of the
parameters any more than that."

"Carolyn, we only just met."

"You're right, Bern. I'm being silly. I'm probably

just jealous, because God knows I could use a mystery woman in my life. Anyway, if she's a mystery woman, it's more interesting if there are things you don't know about her."

"I guess so."

"And you know the important things. She's beautiful and she likes Humphrey Bogart."

"Right."

"And she comes from Europe, and she lives here now. What's her name, Bern?"

"Uh," I said.

There was a pause. "Hey, what's a name, anyway, Bern? You know what they say about a rose. Hey, maybe that's it."

"Huh?"

"Rose. Lots of European women are named Rose, and they'd smell as sweet even if they weren't. Bernie, have a great time, you hear? And I want a full report at lunch tomorrow. Or call me tonight, if it's not too late. Okay?"

"Okay," I said. "Sure."

FIVE

Two weeks later it was Wednesday again, and it was still May, and a little before one o'clock I hung the clock sign on my door to let the world of book lovers know I'd be back at two. Ten minutes later I was at the Poodle Factory with lunch for two.

I opened containers and dished out the food while Carolyn locked up and hung her own CLOSED sign in the window. She sat down opposite me and studied her plate. "Looks good," she said, and sniffed. "Smells okay, too. What have we got here, Bern?"

"I don't know."

"You don't know?"

"It's the daily special," I said.

"And you didn't even ask what it was?"

"I asked," I said, "and the guy answered, and I have no idea what he said."

"So you ordered it."

I nodded. " 'Give me two of them,' I said, 'with brown rice.' "

"This is white rice, Bern."

"I guess they only had white rice," I said. "Or maybe he didn't understand me. I didn't understand a word he said, so why should I expect him to understand everything I said?"

"Good point." She picked up her plastic fork, then changed her mind and chose the chopsticks instead. "Whatever it is, it tastes okay. Where'd you go, Bern?"

"Two Guys."

"Two Guys From Abidjan? Since when do you get chopsticks with African food? And this doesn't taste African to me." She picked up another morsel of food, then paused with it halfway to her mouth. "Besides," she said, "they closed, didn't they?"

"A couple of weeks ago."

"That's what I thought."

"And just reopened yesterday, under new management. It's not Two Guys From Abidjan anymore. Now it's Two Guys From Phnom Penh."

"Say that again, Bern." I did. "Phnom Penh," she said. "Where's that?"

"Cambodia."

"What did they do, keep the old sign?"

"Uh-huh. Painted out Abidjan, painted in Phnom Penh."

"Must have been a tight fit."

Indeed it was; *Two Guys From PhnomPenh* was what it looked like. "Cheaper than getting a new sign," I said.

"I guess. Remember when it was Two Guys From Yemen? And before that it was Two Guys From Someplace Else, but don't ask me where. It's got to be a hard-luck location, don't you think?"

"Must be."

"I bet there was a restaurant there back when the Dutch owned Manhattan. Two Guys From Rotterdam." She popped a cube of meat into her mouth and chewed it thoughtfully, then chased it with a swig of Dr. Brown's Celery Tonic. "Not bad," she announced. "That was Cambodian food we had up near Columbia, wasn't it?"

"Angkor Wok," I said. "Broadway and a Hundred and twenty-third, a Hundred and twenty-fourth, somewhere around there."

"I think this is better, and God knows it's handier. I hope they stay in business."

"I wouldn't count on it. A few months from now it'll probably be Two Guys From Kabul."

"Be a shame, but at least that would fit on the sign. Did you get the celery tonic at Two Guys?"

"No, I stopped at the deli."

"Because it goes really great with Cambodian food, doesn't it?"

"Like it was made for it."

We ate some more of the daily special, sipped some more celery tonic. Then she said, "Bern? What did you see last night?"

"*The Roaring Twenties*," I said.

"Again? Didn't you see that Monday night?"

"You're absolutely right," I said. "They tend to run together in my mind." I closed my eyes for a moment. "*Conflict*," I said.

"*Conflict?*"

"And *Brother Orchid*."

"I never heard of either of them."

"Actually, I may have seen *Conflict* years ago on

late-night TV. It was vaguely familiar. Bogart's in love with Alexis Smith, who's his wife's younger sister. He hurts his legs in a car crash, but then he hides the fact that he's recovered so that he can kill his wife."

"Bernie—"

"Sidney Greenstreet's the psychiatrist who sets a trap for him. See, the way he does it . . . You don't care, do you?"

"Not hugely."

"*Brother Orchid* was pretty interesting. Edward G. Robinson was the star. He's a gangster, and Bogart takes over the mob while Robinson's in Europe. He comes back and Bogart's men try to rub him out, and he escapes and takes shelter in a monastery, where he takes the name Brother Orchid and spends his time growing flowers."

"What did you do after the movie, Bern? Take shelter in a monastery?"

"What do you mean?"

"You know what I mean. You went out for coffee, right? Espresso for two at the little place down the block from the movie house."

"Right."

"And then you went home to your place, and Ilona went wherever Ilona goes. I've never met anybody named Ilona before. In fact the only Ilona I've ever heard of is Ilona Massey, and I wouldn't know her if it weren't for crossword puzzles. 'Miss Massey, five letters.' She's right up there with Uta Hagen and Una Merkel and Ina Balin."

"Don't forget Ima Hogg."

"I wouldn't dream of it. The two of you went your separate ways after the movie. Right?"

I sighed. "Right."

"What's going on, Bern?"

"For God's sake," I said. "It's the nineties, remember? Dating's a whole new ballgame. People don't jump in bed on the first date the way they used to. They take time, they get to know one another, they—"

"Bern, look at me."

"I wasn't avoiding your eyes."

"Of course you were, and I don't blame you. 'People don't jump in bed on the first date.' How many dates have you had with this woman?"

"A few."

"Try fourteen."

"It can't be that many."

"You've been out with her every night for two weeks. You've seen twenty-eight Humphrey Bogart movies. Twenty-eight! And the closest you've come to physical intimacy is when your hands bump into each other reaching for the popcorn."

"That's not true."

"It's not?"

"Sometimes we hold hands during the picture."

"Be still my heart. Is it some sort of platonic thing, Bern? You're soul mates and there's no real physical attraction?"

"No," I said. "Believe me, that's not it."

"Then what's going on?"

"I'm not sure."

"Have you just been playing it ultracool? Waiting for her to make the first move?"

"No," I said. "The first night I offered to see her home. I didn't really have anything in mind beyond possibly kissing her good night, but she said no, she'd take her own cab, and I didn't press it. I was just as glad. Why ride all the way across town just so I could ride all the way back again?"

"Is that where she lives? On the East Side?"

"I think so."

"You don't know where she lives?"

"Not exactly."

"Not exactly?"

"I mentioned that I lived just a few blocks from the Musette. And she said I was lucky, that she lived a long ways away."

"Didn't you ask where?"

"Of course I did."

"And?"

" 'Oh, a great distance,' she said, and then she changed the subject. What was I going to do, cross-examine her? And what real difference does it make where she lives?"

"Especially since you're never going to wind up there."

I sighed again. "The third or fourth date, I forget when, I suggested she might like to see my apartment. 'Someday,' she said. 'But not tonight, Bear-naaard.' "

" 'Bear-naaard.' "

"That's how she says it. You know something? I hate rejection."

"How unusual."

"I mean I really can't stand it. She was very nice about it, but all the same I felt like an oaf for asking."

"So you never made another move?"

"Of course I did, a few days later, and I got to feel like an oaf a second time. And then Saturday after the movies I said I hated to see the evening end, and we wound up going for a walk."

"And?"

"We walked up Broadway as far as Eighty-sixth Street, and then we walked downtown again on the other side of the street, and we stopped here and there along the way for what you might call a heated embrace."

"Hugs and kisses?"

"Hugs and kisses. And when we got to Columbus Circle we kissed again, and then she leaned back and looked into my eyes and told me to put her in a cab."

"And she didn't want you to get into it with her?"

" 'Zis is not ze right time, Bear-naaard.' "

"I didn't realize her accent was that heavy."

"It is when she's delirious with passion."

"And her passion propelled her—"

"Straight into a cab."

"What do you figure, Bern? Is she a tease?"

"I don't think so."

"Or a freeloader, just stringing you along, taking you for all you're worth."

"Then I can't be worth very much," I said. "She buys her own ticket and pays for her own cab."

"Who buys the coffee afterward?"

"We take turns."

"How about the popcorn?"

"I buy the popcorn."

"Well, there you go. She's only in it for the popcorn. Maybe she's a little bit married. Ever think of that?"

"I thought of it right away," I said. "Then I asked myself how a married woman could possibly sneak out for four hours every night."

"She could tell her husband she's taking a course in Crockpot Macramé at the New School."

"Seven days a week?"

"Who knows? Maybe she doesn't have to tell him anything, maybe he works from seven to midnight hosting a talk show on an FM station. 'All right, callers, the topic tonight is Wives Who Don't Cheat and the Men They Don't Cheat With. Let's see those boards light up now!' " She frowned. "The thing is," she said, "she's doing things sort of ass-backward for a married woman. The ones I've been fool enough to get involved with just wanted to go to bed. The last thing they wanted was to go out in public, let alone do a little smooching on a street corner."

"I don't think she's married."

"Well, what's her story?"

"I don't know. She doesn't seem in any great rush to tell it. We had four or five dates before she got around to telling me where she came from."

"I remember. For a while the best you could do was narrow it down to Europe."

"It's not as though I didn't ask her. It's not an impolite question, is it? 'Where are you from?' I mean, that's not like asking to see her tax return or hear her sexual history, is it?"

"Maybe it's a sensitive subject in Anatruria."

"Maybe."

"You want to know something, Bern? I never heard of Anatruria."

"Well, don't feel bad. Most people never heard of it. See, it never used to be a country, and it still isn't. I heard of it, but that's because I collected stamps when I was a kid."

"It never used to be a country, and it still isn't, but they issued stamps?"

"Around the end of the First World War," I said. "When the Austro-Hungarian and Ottoman empires broke up, a lot of countries declared themselves independent for about fifteen minutes, and some of them issued stamps and provisional currency to increase their credibility. The first Anatrurian stamps were a series of overprints of Turkish stamps, and they're pretty rare, but they're not worth all that much because overprinted stamps have always been easy to counterfeit. Then there was an actual series of Anatrurian stamps printed up during the winter of 1920–21, with the head of Vlados I in a little circle in the upper right corner and a different scene on each stamp in the series. Churches and public buildings and scenic views—you know the kind of things they put on stamps. They were engraved and printed in Budapest."

"Wait a minute. Budapest's in Anatruria?"

"No, it's in Hungary."

"That's what I thought."

"The stamps never got to Anatruria," I explained. "As a matter of fact, the only government independent Anatruria ever had was a government in exile. A little band of patriots scattered all over Eastern Europe proclaimed Anatrurian independence. Then they tried lobbying the League of Nations, but they didn't get anywhere. They even put Woodrow Wilson on one of their stamps, for all the good it did them."

"Why Woodrow Wilson? Did he have relatives in Anatruria?"

"He was big on self-determination of nations. But by the time they got the stamps printed, Warren G. Harding was president. I doubt the Anatrurians ever heard of him, and I'd be willing to bet he never heard of Anatruria."

"Well, neither did I. Where is it, exactly?"

"You know where Bulgaria and Romania and Yugoslavia come together?"

"Sort of. Except there's no more Yugoslavia, Bern. It's five different countries now."

"Well, part of one of them is part of Anatruria, and the same thing goes for Bulgaria and Romania. Anyway, that's where Ilona was born, but she hasn't been home in quite a while. She lived in Budapest for a year or two, or maybe it was Bucharest."

"Maybe it was both of them."

"Maybe. And she was in Prague, which used to be in Czechoslovakia."

"Used to be? Where'd it go?"

"There's no more Czechoslovakia. There's Slovakia and there's the Czech Republic."

"Oh, right. You know what's weird? At the same time that Europe is deciding to be one big country, Yugoslavia's deciding to be five little countries all by itself. Now you've got the former Yugoslavia and the former Soviet Union and the former Czechoslovakia. It's like Formerly Joe's. Remember Formerly Joe's?"

"Vividly."

"Oh, right, we didn't like our meal, did we? I guess lots of people felt the same way, because they didn't last long. There was this restaurant called Joe's at the corner of West Fourth and West Tenth, and it was there for years, and then it was out of business for years. It just sat there vacant."

"I know."

"So then, when a new restaurant finally moved in, they called it Formerly Joe's. And now it's gone, in fact it's been gone for a long time, and when somebody finally takes it over what are they gonna call it? Formerly Formerly Joe's?"

"Or Two Guys From Anatruria."

"I guess anything's possible. You seeing her tonight, Bern?"

"Yes."

"And seeing more Bogart movies?"

"Uh-huh."

"How long's this festival going on, anyway?"

"Another ten or twelve days."

"You're kidding." She looked at me. "You're not kidding. How many movies did the guy make, anyway?"

"Seventy-five, but they didn't manage to get them all."

"What a shame. How long are you gonna stay with it, Bern?"

"I don't know," I said. "I'm kind of enjoying it. The first week there were times when I was wondering what I was doing there, but then it became this magical other world that I would slip into for a few hours every night." I shrugged. "After all," I said, "it is Bogart. He's always interesting to watch even in some dog of a movie you never heard of. And when it's a picture I've seen a dozen times, well, who can get tired of *Casablanca* or *The Maltese Falcon*? They get better every time you see them."

"What's the program for tonight?"

"*The Caine Mutiny*," I said, "and *Swing Your Lady*."

"I remember *The Caine Mutiny*. He was great in that, playing with those marbles."

"Ball bearings, I think they were."

"I'll take your word for it. What's the other one? *Swing Your Partner*?"

"*Swing Your Lady*."

"I never heard of it."

"Nobody did. Bogart's a wrestling promoter in the Ozarks."

"You're making this up."

"I am not. According to the program, Reagan has a small part."

"Reagan? Ronald Reagan?"

"That's the one."

"Well, at least it's only a small part. Wrestling in the Ozarks. And square dancing, I'll bet. Why else would they call it *Swing Your Lady*?"

"You're probably right."

"Wrestling and square dancing and Ronald Reagan. You know what, Bern? I bet you get lucky tonight. Any woman who'd make a man go through all that has got to reward him for it."

"I don't know, Carolyn."

"I do," she said. "Better pack your toothbrush, Bern. Tonight's your lucky night."

And, after Bogart had followed his electrifying portrayal of Captain Queeg with a stint as barnstorming wrestling promoter Ed Hatch, and after his wrestler had quit the business to marry a lady blacksmith and spend the rest of his life shoeing horses, we'd gone across the street for a quick espresso and a little holding of hands and trading of long looks. Then we went outside and I hailed her a cab, and when I held the door for her she came into my arms for a kiss.

"Bear-naaard," she murmured. "Come with me."

"Come with you?"

"Come home with me. Now."

"Oh," I said, and was ready to stammer out some lame excuse when fifteen nights at the movies came along and rescued me. "Not tonight, sweetheart," I drawled. "I'm afraid I'll have to take a rain check." And I kissed her lightly on the lips and tucked her into the cab and watched her ride away from me.

Some lucky night.

SIX

I woke up surprisingly clear-headed, if not entirely thrilled about it, and was downtown in time to open my store at ten. I fed Raffles and refilled his water dish, dragged my three-for-a-buck table outside, and settled myself behind the counter with Will Durant. The world, he reassured me, had always been a pretty nasty place. I found this curiously comforting.

I had the front door closed against the chill of the morning, and so I got to hear the tinkling of little bells each time it opened. I had a couple of early browsers, rang up two sales for a few dollars each, and looked through the sack of books that Mowgli brought me. He's a curious creature who looks as though he might indeed have been raised by wolves—gaunt, hollow-eyed, with a mop of hair and a scraggle of beard. Speed and acid have burned some substantial holes in his brain, and he'd dropped out of a doctoral program in English at Columbia to take up a nomadic existence, shifting his residence from one abandoned building to another as circumstances dictated.

He'd collected books during his student days, and on the way down he sold them off piecemeal. His stock was pretty much gone by the time he found his way to Barnegat Books, but I'd bought a few things from him then, including a nice clean set of Kipling. He'd disappeared for the better part of a year, and I gather he started sucking on a crack pipe and pretty much lost touch with the planet for a while there, but when he turned up again he had his act together, in a marginal sort of way. He nowadays limited his chemical adventures to a little righteous herb and the odd hit of organic mescaline, and supported himself by buying books at street fairs and thrift shops and flea markets and reselling them to people like me.

I picked out a few things, passed on the rest. He had some nice fifties paperback noir, David Goodis and Peter Rabe, but my customers wouldn't pay collector prices for that kind of material. "Figured as much," he said. "I'll run these by Jon at Partners and Crime. Thought you might like to see them, though. Don't you love the covers?"

I agreed they were great. I picked out a biography of Thomas Wolfe and Mark Schorer's life of Sinclair Lewis and a couple of other books I thought I could sell, and we hemmed and hawed until we found a price we could both live with. Toward the end I asked him a question I ask most of my regular suppliers.

"These aren't stolen," I said. "Are they, Mowgli?"

"How could they be otherwise? 'Property is theft.' You know who said that, Bernie?"

"Proudhon."

"Give the man a cigar. Proudhon indeed. Matter of fact, St. John Chrysostom said something much along the same line. You wouldn't expect it of him, would you?" We kicked that around, and then he said, "What can I tell you, Bernie? None of this stuff was stolen by me, unless it's stealing to buy a David Goodis first from the Sally Ann for two bits when I know I can get a finif for it. Is that stealing?"

"If it is," I said, "then we're all in trouble."

The next time the bell rang it was a couple of Jehovah's Witnesses who wanted to talk with me, and we had a nice conversation. Proudhon's name didn't come up once, or St. John Chrysostom's, either. I had to cut the conversation short—they'd still be talking if I hadn't—but they went away happy and I went back to Will Durant. And a few minutes later the bells sounded again, but this time I didn't look up until I heard a familiar voice.

"Well, well, well," said the best policeman money can buy. "If it ain't Mrs. Rhodenbarr's boy Bernard. Every time I see you you got your nose in a book, Bernie. Which more or less figures, seein' as you got your ass in a bookstore."

"Hello, Ray."

" 'Hello, Ray.' You want to put more energy into it, Bernie. Otherwise it don't sound like you're glad to see me."

"Hello, Ray."

"That's a little better." He leaned forward, propped an elbow on my counter. "But you always seem nervous when I drop in for a visit, like you're waitin' for the third shoe to drop. Why do you figure that is, Bernie?"

"I don't know, Ray."

"I mean, whattaya got to be nervous about? Respectable businessman, never strays on the wrong side of the law, it oughta be a load off your mind when a sworn police officer comes into your place of business."

"Sworn," I said.

"How's that, Bernie?"

"I like the phrase," I said. "A sworn police officer. I like it."

"Well, be my guest, Bernie. Use it anytime the urge comes over you. Say, tell me something, will you?"

"If I can."

"Ever seen this before?"

He'd been holding it out of sight below the counter.

"Indeed I have," I said. "Many times. It's my attaché case. How do you know Hugo, and why has he got you running errands for him?"

"What the hell are you talkin' about, errands?"

"Well, what else would you call it? I told him he didn't have to be in any rush to return it." I reached for the case, and Ray snatched it away from me. I looked at him, puzzled. "What's going on?" I demanded. "Are you giving me the damn thing or aren't you?"

"I don't know," he said. He set it down flat on the counter, settled his thumbs on the little buttons. "What do you figure's inside?"

"The Empire State Building."

"Huh?"

"The Lindbergh baby. How many more guesses do I get? I don't know what's inside it, Ray. When Hugo Candlemas left here the other day there were some hand-colored engravings he didn't want to risk creasing, along with a couple of other packages he'd picked up along the way."

"I didn't know you sold pictures, Bernie."

"I don't," I said. "Don't ask me where he bought them. All I sold him was a book of poems for five bucks plus tax."

"And you threw in this here? Very generous of you."

"I lent it to him, Ray. He's a decent old gent and a good customer. I can't pay the rent on guys like him, but he's pleasant company and he usually buys something before he leaves. Why? What's this all about, anyway?"

He popped the locks, opened the case.

"Why, it seems to be empty," I said. "Nice showmanship, Ray, but a little bit anticlimactic, don't you think?"

"It looks empty," he said. "Don't it? But it ain't."

"Because it contains air? What is this, physics class?"

"I got no need for physics," he said, "bein' as I'm regular as clockwork. What's in here's your prints, Bernie."

"The engravings?" I leaned forward, squinted. "They seem to have grown transparent. I don't see them."

"Not that kind of prints. Your fingerprints."

"My fingerprints?"

"A full set."

"Well, that's nice," I said, "but not terribly surprising. It's my case. I already told you that."

"So you did, Bernie, and what's surprisin' is for you to admit it."

"Why shouldn't I admit it? What have I got to be ashamed of? It's not Louis Vuitton, but it's a perfectly respectable piece of luggage. And if you're going to tell me it's stolen, the statute of limitations ran out a long time ago. I must have owned the thing for eight or ten years."

He struck a pose not unlike Rodin's *Thinker* and took a long searching look at me. "You're slicker than ice on the sidewalk," he said. "I thought you'd twitch a little when I showed you the case, but no, it was like you expected it. That was you on the phone, right?"

"What are you talking about?"

"Let it go. I'll tell you, soon as we ran the prints on this thing and they turned out to be yours, I couldn't wait to hear you explain how your prints wound up all over this guy Candlemas's case. I figured it'd be a good story. But you went one better and got the nerve to claim it's your case. I like that, Bernie. It's real imaginary."

"It happens to be the truth."

"Truth," he said sourly. "What the hell's truth?"

"You're not the first officer of the law to ask that question," I told him. "What happened to Candlemas?"

"Who said anything happened to him?"

"Oh, please," I said. "Why would you dust an empty attaché case for prints? You found it in his apartment, and he could have told you how it got there, so I can only conclude he wasn't doing any talking. Either the place was empty or he was in no shape to talk. Which was it?"

He measured me with a long look. "I guess there's no reason not to tell you," he said. "Anyway, another couple of hours an' you'll be readin' about it in the papers."

"He's dead?"

"If he's not," he said, "then it's a hell of an act he's puttin' on."

"Who killed him?"

"I don't know, Bern. I was kind of hopin' it'd turn out to be you."

"Get a grip, Ray. It never turns out to be me, remember? I'm not a killer. It's not my style."

"I know that," he said. "All the years I known you, you never been a violent fellow. But who's to say what might happen one of these days if somebody surprises you while you're burglarizin' their premises? And don't give me any of that crap about how you're spendin' all your time sellin' books these days. You're a burglar through an' through, Bernie. You'll still be breakin' an' enterin' when you're six feet under."

There was a cheering thought. "Tell me about Candlemas," I said. "How was he killed?"

"What's the difference? Dead is dead."

"How do you even know it was murder? He wasn't a kid. Maybe he died of natural causes."

"Naw, it was suicide, Bernie. He stabbed himself a couple of times in the chest and then ate the knife to throw us off."

"That's what killed him? Stab wounds?"

"That's what the doc tells us. A lot of internal bleedin', he said. Plenty of external bleedin', too. Made a mess of the rug."

I winced, feeling sorry at once for Hugo Candlemas and his Aubusson. I told Ray I hoped he hadn't suffered much.

"He must of," he said, "unless he was some kind of a massy-kissed. Somebody sticks a knife into you two or three times, naturally you're gonna suffer." He frowned, considering. "They say you go into shock the first time you get stabbed and don't feel the others, an' I guess I'll have to take their word for it. I wouldn't want to test it out for myself."

"Neither would I. The murder weapon didn't turn up?"

He shook his head. "Killer took it away with him. Time the lab's done, they'll be able to tell you the size an' shape of the blade, along with the name an' home phone number of the guy who made it. Right now all I can say for sure is it was some kind of a knife. Long an' thin'd be my guess, but all I'd be is guessin'."

"How did you get the case, Ray?"

"Somebody called it in around one in the morning. Couple of blues responded, found the door locked, went next door an' got the super to open up for 'em. Except there were three locks on the door an' the super only had keys for two of 'em. That's your fault, Bernie."

"How is it my fault?"

"Wasn't for guys like you, people wouldn't hang three locks on a goddam door. The whole city's walkin' around with more keys in their pockets than a person oughta have to carry, and it's the burglars of New York who are the cause of it. I ran into this woman one time, she had six locks on her front door. Six of 'em! Time she got out of her house in the morning, it was pretty near time for her to go back in again." He shook his head at the very idea.

I said, "So what did they do? Kick the door in?"

"No reason to. All they got is an anonymous tip, sounds of a struggle up on the fourth floor. This was on the Lower East Side you'd maybe think about kicking it in, but not in a good neighborhood. They called a locksmith."

"You're kidding."

"What's wrong with that? There's plenty of 'em of-fer twenty-four-hour service, an' they're not like doc-tors. They still make house calls."

"It's a good thing. It'd be tough to bring the door to them."

"Or squirt aspirin in the lock and call 'em in the mornin'. Guy they called, though, either he wasn't so good or the lock was a pip. It took him half an hour to open it."

"Half an hour? You should have called me, Ray."

"Been up to me, I mighta done just that. But I wasn't in the picture until they got inside and found the body. Then I got called an' went over, an' I was takin' a good look at the late laminated when the phone rang. That was you, wasn't it?"

"I don't know what you're talking about."

"Yeah, tell me another. Two calls, maybe five minutes apart. Both times I answered an' both times the other party didn't say a word. Don't tell me it wasn't you, Bern. Be a waste of time. I recognized your voice."

"How? You just said the caller didn't say anything."

"Yeah, an' there's plenty ways of not sayin' nothin', an' this was you. Don't try an' tell me different."

"Whatever you say, Ray."

"I knew it was you right away. Of course, I got to admit I had you on my mind. You know where the body was layin'?"

"Of course not. I wasn't there."

"Well, you know the little round table, has a lamp on it looks like a bowl of flowers?"

It was a Tiffany lily lamp, almost certainly a reproduction, resting atop a drumhead table with cabriolet legs. "I don't know it at all," I said. "I've never been to his apartment. I know he was on the Upper East Side, and I've probably got his address written down somewhere, but I can't recall it offhand. And I've certainly never been there."

"Right," he said. "You were never there but your case here"—he gave the surface a tap—"was. I don't buy that for a minute, Bernie. I think you were there, and probably last night. Time you called, I didn't know this was your case. But I already seen a receipt for five bucks an' change sittin' on top of that little round table. Barnegat Books, it said, an' the date on it was the day before yesterday."

"I told you about that, Ray. He bought a book of poems."

"It said"—he consulted a pocket notebook—"Praed."

"That's the name of the poet. Winthrop Mackworth Praed."

He waved a hand dismissively to show what he thought of anybody with a name like that. "This Praed's dead, right?"

"Long dead."

"Like most poets. So the hell with him. He didn't do it, an' much as I like yankin' on your chain, I know you didn't do it either. Why would you want to kill him?"

"I wouldn't," I said. "He was a customer, and I can use all the ones I've got. And he was a nice man. At least I think he was."

"What do you know about him, Bernie?"

"Not much. He was a snappy dresser. Does that help?"

"It didn't help him. He shoulda been wearing a Kevlar vest under his shirt. Maybe that woulda helped. Snappy dresser? Yeah, I guess so, but what kind of man wears a suit around the house? You get home, you want to rip off your tie, hang your jacket over the back of a chair. That's what I always do."

"I can believe it."

"Yeah? I didn't know better, I'd think that was a crack. I'll tell you this much, Bernie. It's a good thing for you your name ain't Kay Fobb."

"Well, it's not," I said, "and it never has been. What are you talking about?"

"Kay Fobb. Ring a bell?"

"Not even a tinkle. Who is she?"

"You figure it's a woman? I don't even know if I'm sayin' it right, Bernie. Here—whyn'tcha take a squint at it yourself an' tell me what you make of it."

He flipped the case over and showed it to me. There, in block capitals of a rusty brown that stood out sharply against the beige Ultrasuede attaché case, someone had printed CAPHOB.

SEVEN

In *Dead End*, Bogart plays Baby Face Martin, a gangster making a sentimental visit to his boyhood home on the Lower East Side. By the time it's over, he's been slapped by his mother, Marjorie Main, and shot dead on a fire escape by Joel McCrea. There were a lot of other good people in the movie, including Claire Trevor and Sylvia Sidney and Ward Bond, along with Huntz Hall and Leo Gorcey, who had evidently wandered over from the Bowery. Lillian Hellman wrote the screenplay and William Wyler directed, but my favorite credit was costumes, by someone named Omar Kiam.

During Bogie's death scene, Ilona reached over and took my hand.

She held it through to the end of the picture, and when she came back from the ladies' room at intermission she reached to take my hand in both of hers. "Bear-naaard," she said.

"Ilona."

"I was afraid you would not be here tonight. All day I was afraid."

"What made you think that?"

"I don't know. When I rode off in the taxi last night fear clutched at my heart. I thought, 'I will never see him again.' "

"Well, here I am."

"I am so glad, Bear-naard."

I gave her hand a squeeze.

The second feature was *The Left Hand of God,* one of Bogart's last films. He plays an American pilot in China during the war, working for Lee J. Cobb, who's a Chinese warlord. Cobb's men kill a priest, and Bogart winds up escaping in the dead priest's clothing and holing up at a mission, where he poses as the priest's replacement, reminding me a little of Edward G. Robinson in *Brother Orchid.*

It all works out in the end.

Across the street, we sipped cappuccino and split an eclair. After a long silence she said, "I was so worried, Bear-naard."

"Were you? I knew he and the nurse were going to wind up together. I thought he might have to kill Lee J. Cobb, but that was a nice touch, having them throw dice."

"I am not talking about the film."

"Oh."

"I thought I had lost you. I thought you were on your way to another woman."

"Didn't I tell you it was a business appointment?"

"But you would say that, no? Even if it were not so." She looked down at her hands. "I would understand if you were with another woman. I have been . . . distant. But I have had so much on my mind

these past weeks. The only time I feel alive is when
we are in the movies together. The rest of the time
I can barely breathe."

"What's the matter, Ilona?"

She shook her head. "I can't talk about it."

"Sure you can."

"Not now. Another time." She sipped her cappuccino. "Tell me about your business appointment. Or
is it a confidential matter?"

"Someone had a library for me to look at," I said.
"I usually do that sort of thing in the early evening,
but we've been at the movies every night. I thought
I would be safe scheduling it for late last night."

"Because I have been hard to get, yes?"

"Well . . ."

"You have another library to look at tonight, Bear-
naard?"

"No."

"I have a few books. I do not think they are valuable, but maybe you can come and see them." She
extended her forefinger, ran it along my jawline, then
touched it to my lips. "But perhaps you have another
business appointment, and I will have to go home all
by myself."

It turned out she lived on Twenty-fifth Street between Second and Third avenues, in a fifth-floor
walk-up over a shop called Simple Pleasures. They
sold crystals and incense and tarot cards, and signs
in the window advertised classes in witchcraft and
bondage.

The stairs were steep, and there were lots of them.

I could imagine what Captain Hoberman would have made of them.

She lived in one of the two rear apartments, just one room with a single window that looked across an airshaft to the blank wall of a much taller building on Twenty-sixth Street. She turned on the bare-bulb ceiling fixture, then switched it off as soon as she'd turned on a green-shaded brass student lamp on the little one-drawer desk, then turned that off after she'd lit the three candles that stood on top of an old-fashioned brass-bound footlocker in the far corner. The flames of the candles illuminated the artifacts of a little homemade shrine. There were photos, framed and unframed, an icon of a Madonna and child, another of a bearded sunken-eyed saint, and a collection of other small objects, including a quartz crystal that could have come from the shop downstairs.

Otherwise the apartment didn't have much to make it hers. A pair of plastic milk cartons housed her books, and a bound broadloom remnant, stained and worn, covered about half of a floor that badly needed refinishing. The bed and dresser looked to have come with the apartment, or from a thrift shop. The walls were bare except for a Birds of the World calendar hanging from a nail and, Scotch-taped to the wall above the desk, a *National Geographic* map of Eastern Europe. It was impossible to make out much in the candlelight, but it would have been hard to miss the small jagged area outlined in red Magic Marker.

"This must be Anatruria," I said.

She moved to stand beside me. "My country," she said, her voice heavy with irony. "The center of the universe."

"You're wrong," I said. "This is the center of the universe."

"New York?"

"This room."

"You are so romantic."

"You are so beautiful."

"Oh, Bear-naard . . ."

And there, if you don't mind, I'm going to be old-fashioned enough to draw a curtain. We embraced and disrobed and went to bed, but you'll have to imagine the details for yourself. We didn't do anything you couldn't see on television, anyway, if you've got cable and stay up late enough.

"Bear-naard? Sometimes I smoke after I make love."

"I can believe it," I said. "Oh. You mean a cigarette."

"Yes. Would it bother you?"

"No, of course not."

"My cigarettes are in the drawer of the night table. Could you reach them for me?"

I passed her a half-full pack of short unfiltered Camels. She put one in her mouth and let me scratch a match and light it for her. She sucked in the smoke as if it were life-sustaining, then pursed her lips and blew it out like Bacall showing Bogart how to whistle.

"Of course a cigarette," she said suddenly. "What else would I smoke? A herring?"

"Hardly that," I agreed.

"It is to lessen the sadness," she said. "Shall I tell you something? I wanted to make love with you the first night, Bear-naard. But I knew it would make me sad."

"I guess I must not be very good at it."

"But how can you say that? You are a wonderful lover. That is why you break my heart."

"I don't understand."

"Look at me, Bear-naard."

"You're crying."

I reached to wipe a tear from the corner of her eye. A fresh one promptly took its place.

"It is no use to wipe them away," she said. "There are always more." She took another deep drag on her cigarette. When she smoked, she really smoked. "It is the way I am," she explained. "Lovemaking saddens me. The better it is, the worse I feel."

"That's a hell of a thing," I said. "I'm almost ashamed to admit it, but I feel terrific."

"I have a good feeling, too."

"Well, then—"

"But underneath it is this sadness. And so I smoke a cigarette. I don't like to smoke cigarettes, but I do it to hold back the sadness."

"Does it work?"

"No." She handed me the cigarette. "Would you put it out? You can use that little dish for an ashtray. Thank you. And now would you stay with me for a little while? And hold me, Bear-naard."

* * *

After a while she started to talk. The apartment was awful, she said, but it was all she could afford. New York was so expensive, especially for someone without a steady salary. And the location was good because she often got work in the area of the United Nations, translating or proofreading documents. She could take a bus right up First Avenue, or even walk if the weather was good and she had the time.

She knew there were things she could do to make the place nicer. She could paint the walls, she could replace the horrible rug, she could buy a TV set. Maybe she would get around to it someday. If she was still here. If she didn't move. . . .

Her breathing changed and I decided she was sleeping. My own eyes had closed by that time, and I could feel myself drifting. But "Would you stay with me for a little while?" wasn't exactly an invitation to bed down for the night, nor was her bed wide enough for two people to sleep in. It was okay for presleep activity, as long as you didn't get overly athletic, but when it came time to make a long string of zzzz's, it was a tad crowded.

I slipped out of bed, careful not to wake her, picked out and put on the pieces of hastily discarded clothing that were mine. Before extinguishing the candles I went to the door and unlocked the locks so I wouldn't have to fumble with them in the dark.

Then I went to put out the candles and found myself drawn to her little shrine. There was a family portrait in a drugstore frame, a stiffly posed snapshot of a father, a mother, and a daughter that must have been Ilona at age six or seven. Her hair was lighter and her features undefined, but it seemed to me that her eyes already held their characteristic expression of ironic self-amusement.

You're falling in love, I thought, with a little ironic self-amusement all my own.

I picked up the crystal, felt its weight in my palm, put it back. I looked at the icons and decided they were authentic old ones, although probably not of great value. I fingered a military or ecclesiastical decoration, a bronze medallion with a portrait of a mitered bishop and an inscription in Cyrillic lettering, hanging from a ribbon of gold and scarlet. There was a Maria Theresa thaler, and a white-metal medallion with the bust of some king I couldn't recognize, reposing in the bottom half of its original velvet-lined presentation box.

Family treasures, no doubt. And there was a tiny menagerie, including a cast-iron dog and cat (hand-painted, the paint gone in spots), another dog of hand-painted china, a trio of china penguins (one missing the tip of one wing), and a very well carved if stolid wooden camel. Childhood souvenirs, as no doubt were the miniature cup and saucer, the probable sole survivors of a dollhouse tea set.

Another photo caught my eye as I set about snuffing the candles. It stood in an easel-backed frame and showed a man and woman about my age. She had really big hair; it was piled high on her head, and reminded me of the fur hat on the Ludomir vodka label. She was wearing a tailored jacket, and around her shoulders she'd draped a silver fox stole. He wore a belted Norfolk jacket and a flowing silk scarf, and he had one arm around the woman's waist and was raising the other hand in greeting, and aiming a blinding smile at the camera.

He reminded me of somebody I knew, but I couldn't think who.

I was still working on it when I pinched out the third and final candle, at which time I could no longer see his smiling face. So I found other things to think about, like where the door could have been the last time I'd seen it. Very little light came in through Ilona's window; it was almost as dark as the apartment at the Boccaccio had been, and this time I didn't have my flashlight along. There was a narrow band of light from the hallway showing at the bottom of the door, and I managed to walk to it without bumping into anything along the way.

I stepped out into the hallway and drew the door shut, then tried it to make sure the snaplock had engaged. I hated to leave her with only a snaplock between her and the big bad world, but I hadn't brought my tools with me. If I had I could have locked up properly, but maybe it was just as well. It would have been hard to explain.

It had threatened to rain late that afternoon, but the evening turned out clear and mild and it was nice out now. I was a fifteen-minute walk from the bookstore, but if I went there now I'd be nine hours early for work.

The lovemaking that had saddened Ilona had left me edgy, which made the two of us a hell of an advertisement for great sex. I felt as though I could walk clear to St. Louis and punch somebody in the mouth when I got there. I walked eight or ten blocks and flagged a cab. As I scrunched up my legs to get them into the backseat, the first thought that came to me was to take a run up to the Wexford Castle and see if Ludomir was as bad as I remembered. The second thought was to recognize the first thought for the idiocy it was, and I told the driver to take me home.

EIGHT

Around ten-thirty the next morning I was reading *Hop To It*, a slender volume on how to train your pet rabbit. I'd rescued it from my own bargain table, and was taking a break from Will Durant before reshelving it under Pets & Natural History. The photos of the bunnies were endearing, but the text made it clear they were much given to chewing things, like books and electrical wiring. "Don't worry," I told Raffles. "We're not getting one. Your job is safe."

He gave me a look that suggested the issue had never been in doubt, and I crumpled up a piece of paper and threw it for him to chase. He was in mid-pounce when Carolyn came in. "Hi, Raffles," she said. "How's the training coming?"

"He's doing fine," I said. "This is just a tune-up session, to keep his mousing skills from getting rusty. You're two hours early, incidentally."

"I'm not early," she said. "I'm instead of. I can't do lunch today, I've got a dentist appointment."

"You didn't mention it."

"I didn't have it to mention," she said, "until about an hour ago. I lost a filling during dinner last night.

I think I must have swallowed it. The worst part is I can't keep from checking it out, poking my tongue into the hole to make sure it's still there. Would you look at it for me, Bern?"

"What for?"

"Tell me it's not as huge as I think it is. I swear the hole's bigger than most teeth. You could park cars in there, Bern. You could house the homeless."

She came over and stuck her face into mine, gaping and pointing at a molar. "Erg-awrghghm," she said.

"Come on," I said. "How am I going to see anything in there? You need the right kind of lighting, and one of those little mirrors on the end of a stick. Anyway, I'm sure it's fine."

"It's a lunar crater," she said. "It's the Grand Canyon. Fortunately, two hours from now it'll be history. My dentist's gonna fit me in during lunch hour."

"That's good."

"Uh-huh." She leaned a hip against the counter, sent an appraising glance my way. "So?"

"So what?"

"So how'd it go last night?"

"Well, the movies were pretty good," I said. "The first one was made in 1937, and—"

"I'm not talking about the movies, Bern. How'd it go with Ilona?"

"Oh," I said. "It went all right."

"All right?"

"It went fine."

She went on studying me, then broke into a smile that lit up her whole face.

"Cut it out," I said.

"Cut what out? I didn't say a word."

"Well, neither did I, so what the hell are you grinning about?"

"Beats me. Where'd you wind up, Bern? Your place or hers?"

I stared at her, stubbornly silent, and she stared right back at me. "Hers," I said finally.

"And?"

"And what? I had a good time, okay? You happy now?"

"I'm happy for you. She's beautiful, Bern."

"I know."

"And obviously crazy about you."

"I don't know about that part," I said. "And what makes you so sure of it? For that matter, how come you're telling me she's beautiful? Are you just feeding my own words back to me?"

She pursed her lips and whistled soundlessly, like Ilona blowing out cigarette smoke. "It was just the sheerest coincidence," she said.

"What was? I don't even know what you're talking about, and already I don't believe you."

"I just happened to be in front of the Musette," she said, "when the show let out last night."

"You just happened to be there."

"Everybody's gotta be someplace, Bern." Raffles had long since abandoned the paper I'd tossed him, and was now rubbing himself against Carolyn's ankle, in the manner of his tribe. "Hey, look what he's doing. Did you forget to feed him this morning, Bern?"

"He ate enough to glut a python," I said. "Quit changing the subject. How did you happen to be there last night?"

"I was in the neighborhood," she said. "Sue Grafton's got a new book out, and I went up to Murder Ink to pick it up."

"You went all the way up there for it?"

"Partners and Crime was sold out, and Three Lives didn't have it in yet. So I hopped on the subway."

"Murder Ink's at Broadway and Ninety-second."

"I know, Bern. I was just there last night."

"That's twenty-some blocks from the theater."

"Well, I hadn't had dinner."

"So?"

"So I was headed downtown, looking for a restaurant, and nothing appealed to me. I finally settled for a coffee shop around Seventy-ninth Street. You know, I think we may have been overdoing it with ethnic foods lately. I sat in a booth and had a bacon cheeseburger and french fries and cole slaw and a piece of apple pie for dessert, and I drank two cups of ordinary American coffee with cream and sugar, and the whole meal struck me as wildly exotic."

"And after your meal—"

"I felt stuffed, so I figured I'd walk a few blocks."

"And the next thing you knew you were in front of the Musette Theater."

"All right, so I planned it. Is that a crime?"

"No."

"I got there a few minutes before the show let out and stood where I could keep an eye on the entrance. For a minute there I thought I'd missed you. The two of you were just about the last people out."

"We like to stay and watch the credits."

"She's a real beauty, Bern. And the way she was holding your arm, and the looks she was giving you. Forget Humphrey Bogart. I figured you were in like Flynn."

"How long were you spying on us, anyway?"

"I don't see why you have to call it spying," she said. "I was just acting on some perfectly justifiable friendly concern. You'd do the same for me, wouldn't you?"

"I wouldn't dare," I said. "If I lurked around a dyke bar like that I'd get arrested."

"Not true, Bern. Beat up, maybe, but not arrested. Anyway, I didn't lurk for very long. As soon as the two of you went across the street for coffee I went home."

"And read the new Sue Grafton."

She shook her head. "I'm saving it until my tooth is filled. I lost the filling toward the end of the cheeseburger. I think I must have swallowed it. It won't poison me, will it?"

"It's probably better for you than the cheese-burger."

"That's what I figured. I read the blurbs on the new book, and I think it's going to be great, but I'll wait and read it over the weekend. In the meantime I'm rereading one of her early books. I'm about half-way through it. It's the one with the horticultural background."

"I don't think I read it."

"Really? I thought you read them all. This one's about the Chinese landscape architect who gets strangled with his own pigtail."

"I'd remember that. I must have missed it. What's the title?"

" *'Q' Is for Gardens*. I'll lend it to you when I'm done with it. I gotta run, I got a springer spaniel coming any minute for a wash and set. Did she cook you breakfast or did you take her out?"

"I didn't stay over."

"Probably a good move. You know me, one flop in the feathers and I want us to go pick out drapes together. You called her, though, right?"

"No answer. I don't think she spends much time around the apartment. If you were ever there you'd know why."

"What's on the program for tonight? More Bogart?"

"What else?"

"So afterward you'll take her to your place."

"Maybe."

"Bernie? Look at me, Bern. Are you in love?"

"I don't know," I said.

"Does that mean yes?"

"Yeah," I said. "I think it does."

The rest of the morning passed without incident. With Carolyn off getting a tooth filled, I didn't want to make a big deal out of lunch. I ducked around the corner and ate a slice of pizza standing up (I was standing up, the pizza was essentially horizontal). I wasn't away from the store for more than ten minutes, but that was long enough for Ray Kirschmann to make his appearance. I found him leaning against my bargain table, thumbing a Fodor guide to West Africa.

"Some security system you got here," he said. "I wasn't as honest as the day is warm, I coulda walked off with all of these here."

"You'd get yourself a hernia before you hurt me much financially," I pointed out. "The books on that table are three for a dollar."

"Even this here?"

"It's four years old."

"You got books a lot older than that an' charge ten, twenty bucks for 'em. Sometimes more'n that."

"What you've got is a guidebook for travelers," I explained, "and they don't improve with age. They actually depreciate pretty rapidly, because people planning trips generally want up-to-date information. How would you like to fly all the way to Gabon and find out your hotel went out of business a year ago?"

"You'd never get me there in the first place," he said. "You gotta be crazy to go someplace like that. You're layin' on the beach there, drinkin' somethin' with fruit in it, and the next thing you know they're havin' theirselves a cootie tah."

"A what?"

"You know, where they overthrow the government. Before you know it you're the main course at a cannibal banquet." He tossed Fodor back on my table, where it glanced off Vol. II of *The Life and Letters of Hippolyte Taine*—God alone could tell you what had become of Vols. I and III—and skidded the length of the table before dropping to the pavement.

"Don't know my own strength," he said. "Sorry about that."

I had the door unlocked and stood there holding it open, gazing pointedly at the book on the sidewalk. After a moment he went over, bent down, grunted, straightened up, and placed the book on the table.

Inside, I asked him how the Candlemas investigation was coming.

"Movin' right along," he said. "There's a team of investigators workin' right now, tryin' to find out what Cap Hob means." That's how he pronounced it. "They got a computer that's like havin' every phone book in America lined up, only it can go through 'em in seconds. If Caphob's somebody's name, they'll know it in nothin' flat."

"If Mr. Caphob's got a phone."

"Just so he's got a pulse. There's city directories in the computer, too, an' everything else you can think of. You wouldn't believe all the things they can do with their computers."

"Science is wonderful," I said.

"Ain't it the truth." He made a show of consulting his watch, then leaned forward confidentially and planted an elbow on my counter. "Might need a little help from you, though, Bernie."

"Don't tell me you locked yourself out of your car again."

"Might ask you to come down to the morgue and make a formal ID of the guy."

I'd been waiting for him to ask me a favor. I knew it was coming the minute he took the trouble to pick up the book.

"I don't know," I said. "I barely knew the man."

"I thought he was such a good customer."

"I wouldn't call him a regular. I saw him once in a while."

"You knew him well enough to loan him your sashay case."

"Attaché case."

"You know what I meant. You gave it to him to carry home a book he paid five bucks for, or at least that's your story." He straightened up. "Speakin' of which, we could go over that story a few more times if you don't want to cooperate and ID the poor dead son of a bitch. Put in a couple of hours down at the station house, takin' a statement from you, lettin' you tell your story to a few different cops so's we can all get the whole picture."

"It's nice to know I have a choice in the matter."

"Damn right you got a choice," he said. "You can do the right thing, or you can suffer the consequences. Up to you."

"Naturally I want to cooperate with the police," I said, with all the sincerity of a game show host. "But what do you need me for, Ray? The man had neighbors. They must have known him better than I did."

He shook his head. "Way it's shapin' up," he said, "they didn't know him at all. I'll take that back, the woman on the ground floor knew him, said he was a very nice man. Trouble is she's blind, spends most of her time listening to books on tape. One flight up you got a couple named Lehrman on the second floor, except you don't at the moment because they left ten days ago to spend the next four months in the south of France. They're college professors and they swapped their apartment in some kind of triangular deal. The Frenchman's in Singapore for the spring an' summer, an' there's a businessman with a Chinese name in the Lehrmans' apartment, so I guess he's from Singapore. Wherever he's from, he's only been here a little over a week an' he says he never met Candlemas. We showed him a photo the lab boys took an' it didn't refresh his memory none.

"Who else we got? A couple of gays in the basement apartment, also new in the building, an' they got a separate entrance all their own. They never met Candlemas. The super lives next door, he takes care of three or four buildings, an' he's only had the job for a couple of months. Candlemas never asked him to do anything for him, so they never met. The guy says he went lookin' to introduce hisself once or twice, just in the interest of makin' contact, an' if you ask me in the interest of settin' Candlemas up for a decent tip come Christmas. But Candlemas wasn't around the time or two he went lookin' for him. No way in the world he could ID him."

"What about the third floor?"

"The third floor?"

"The gay couple's in the basement," I said, "and the blind woman's on the ground floor, with the Lehrmans directly above her."

"Except they're not there," he said, "seein' as they're in France. Go on."

"Candlemas was on the fourth floor," I said. "So who's on three?"

"Now that's a real interestin' question," he said. "You know, if I was what's-his-name, the guinea with the raincoat, I'd save this for when I got one foot out the door. 'Oh, by the way . . .' But who's got the fuckin' patience?"

"What are you talking about, Ray?"

"What I'm talkin' about is how you happen to know there's four floors and Candlemas lived up on four. That ain't a detail I ever mentioned."

"Sure you did."

"Uh-uh."

"Then he must have."

"Who, Candlemas?"

"Who else?"

"What I think," he said, "is you're full of crap, but I thought that all along. What did I say yesterday? I knew you were up there at one time or another. Bernie, tell me the truth. You got any idea at all who killed this guy?"

"No."

"You want to cooperate and make the formal identification? And the hell with who lives on the third floor. They're like everybody else, they don't know shit. Be a pal, Bernie. Do us both a favor."

I frowned. "I hate looking at dead bodies," I said.

"Be glad you're not a mortician. How about it? All I care, you can keep your eyes closed when they bring the body up. Just so you swear it's him."

"No, I'll look," I said. "If I'm going to do it the least I can do is keep my eyes open. When do you want to go over there?"

"How about right now?"

"What, during business hours?"

"Yeah, an' I can see how much business you're doin'. It won't take but a few minutes an' then it'll be out of the way." He shrugged. "Or, if you'd rather, I'll pick you up at closing time. You close around six, right?"

"That's no good," I said. "I'm meeting somebody at a quarter to seven. But if I go now I have to close up and reopen and . . . I'll tell you what. Come by for me around a quarter to five and I'll close an hour early. How's that?"

As the afternoon wore on, I began wishing I'd locked up then and there and gone straight to the morgue. It was Friday and the weather was great, and as a result everybody who could manage it was leaving town early and getting a jump on the weekend. And they weren't stopping to buy books on their way, either.

The morgue would have been livelier than where I was. At times like that I'm glad I have a cat for company, but on this particular occasion he was no company at all. He slept on the windowsill for a while, and then when the sun got too strong for him he found a perch he liked on a high shelf in Philosophy & Religion. I couldn't even see him from where I sat.

I called Ilona a couple of times. No answer. I sat down with that week's copy of *AB Bookman's Weekly* and looked through the listings to see if anybody was hunting for something I happened to have in stock. I check now and then, and sometimes I've actually got something that some dealer somewhere is searching for, but I rarely follow through and do anything about it. It just seems like too much trouble to write out a postcard with a price quote and put it in the mail and then hold the book in reserve until the person does or doesn't order it. And then you have to wrap the damn thing, and stand in line at the post office.

And all for what, two dollars profit? Or five, or even ten?

Not worth it.

Of course, if you do it regularly, and develop a system for quoting and packing and shipping, it can be a profitable element of the business. At least that's what various articles have assured me, and I have to assume that they're right.

But it still seems like more trouble than it's worth.

See, that's how thieving spoils a man.

There was a time a while back when the store began to turn a small but steady profit. What I'd begun as a combination of a respectable front and a cultured pastime was supporting itself, and looked as though it might even support me in the bargain. Before I knew it I had stopped burgling.

Well, I got over that. Prompted by a rapacious landlord, I'd saved the business by stealing myself solvent. Flush with ill-gotten gains, I'd gone and bought the building. Barnegat Books was secure, and I could run it for good or ill as long as I wanted.

And I didn't have to pinch pennies, either, or send postcards full of price quotations to dealers in Pratt, Kansas, and Oakley, California. I could leave the bargain table where it was while I trotted around the corner, and I didn't have to have an apoplectic fit if someone walked off with a water-damaged second printing of a Vardis Fisher novel. And when I cover expenses that's fine, and when I don't, well I can always flimflam my way into a building and pick my way past a lock and pick up a quick five grand for my troubles.

Of course I hadn't received anything for my recent night's efforts.

And who said my troubles were over?

That happy thought sent me to the telephone, to try Ilona's number again. No answer. I put the phone down and thought about the question Carolyn had asked me, and the answer I had given. I didn't know if it was true, but it was close enough to be disturbing.

Reverie carried me back to that grotty little top-floor room on East Twenty-fifth Street. I found myself thinking about the man in the photograph. Where the hell had I seen him before?

He wasn't the same man as the fellow in the stiff family portrait. I was pretty sure of that. For one thing, the guy with his arm around the huge-haired lady would never be that rigid, not even after rigor mortis had set in. He was used to having his picture taken. The way he was beaming, he looked as though he thrived on it.

I frowned, as if that would bring the photograph into sharper focus. The woman, I remembered, had shoulders like a halfback. But she didn't get them on a football field, or in a gym, either. She was wearing shoulder pads, even more exaggerated than the ones that had blossomed anew in the recent shoulder-pad renaissance.

You weren't seeing shoulder pads as much lately. And you weren't seeing silver fox stoles either, the kind she was wearing with little heads and feet still attached. They hadn't experienced a revival, as far as I knew, and I could understand why.

Probably an old photo. Notes from the world of fashion notwithstanding, it had looked like an old photograph to me. Was it because cameras were different then? Had the print faded with time? Or was it just that people composed their faces differently in different eras, so that their faces were indelibly marked as if with a date stamp?

He was a crowd pleaser, this Smilin' Jack. A credit to his dentist, too. Damn, where had I seen his beaming countenance before? And what would he look like if he covered those big teeth with his lips and took a serious picture?

He had a face that would look good on a coin, I decided. Not an old Roman coin, his wasn't that sort of face. Something more recent. . . .

Bingo.

I don't think I said anything, but maybe my ears perked up, because Raffles leaped from his perch over in Philosophy & Religion and came out to see what was going on. "Not a coin," I told him. "A stamp."

That seemed to satisfy him; he did a set of stretching exercises and trotted off to the john. I found my way to Games & Hobbies, where there was a Scott's world postage stamps catalog on the very bottom shelf, right where I'd last seen it. It was four years out of date but too useful a store reference to consign to the bargain table.

I carried it to the counter and flipped pages until I found the one I was looking for. I squinted at an illustration, then closed my eyes entirely and compared it to the picture in my memory.

Was it the same guy?

I thought it was, but it was hard to be sure. Postage stamps are illustrated in black and white in the catalog, and at less than half their actual size. Years ago there was a federal regulation in the United States requiring that an illustration of a postage stamp be broken by a horizontal white line, so that unscrupulous persons couldn't cut them out of the book, paste them on envelopes, and defraud the government. Nowadays, when a ten year old can run off color Xeroxes of twenty-dollar bills that will make it past your average bank teller, that old rule has been discarded as obsolete, and it's now legal to illustrate postage stamps as realistically as you wish, and to print actual-size photographs of U.S. currency.

The more recent stamp illustrations don't have the white lines, but the catalog people haven't troubled to rephotograph all the earlier issues, and the stamps I was looking at were of that sort, having been issued over seventy years ago. I tilted the book to get all I could from the light, and I squinted like the first runner-up in a gurning competition, and finally I went to my office in the back and looked through drawers until I found the magnifying glass.

Even with the glass, the results were not anything you'd want to go to court with. Of the series of fifteen stamps, the folks at Scott had chosen to illustrate only four. Three showed local scenes, including a church, a mountain, and a gypsy leading a dancing bear on a leash. In each of these, an unsmiling version of the man in Ilona's photograph gazed at you from a circular inset in the upper right corner.

The fourth stamp shown was the 100-tschirin stamp. (The nation's currency was based on the tschiro, and each tschiro was worth a hundred dikin. The cheapest stamp was a single dik. It's remarkable how much you can learn from a postage stamp catalog, even an outdated one, and of how little value the information is.) The 100-tschirin stamp was the high value of the series, and it differed from its fellows in two respects. It was larger, about one and a half times their size, and it was vertical in format, taller than it was wide. And the portrait of Ilona's buddy, instead of being confined to a little porthole up in one corner, filled the entire stamp.

Hard to be sure. The reproduction, as I've said, left a lot to be desired. And I didn't have the photograph with me, just my memory of the photo, glimpsed briefly in the dim and flickering light of a single candle. So I couldn't swear to it, but it certainly looked to me as though this was the man.

Vlados I, the first—and so far the only—king of Anatruria.

* * *

For a minute there it looked like I was on to something.

My God, I thought, it all tied together. Ilona wasn't just someone who wandered in to buy a book. It wasn't sheer coincidence that, of all the bookstores in all the towns in all the world, she walked into mine. It was all part of—

Part of what?

Not part of the abortive burglary, and not part of the death of Hugo Candlemas. Because what did Anatruria have to do with all that, or that with Anatruria? Nothing. Ilona had a photo of the erstwhile king of Anatruria in her room, just as she had a map on her wall with the country's purported borders outlined thickly in red. And why not? She was an Anatrurian, and she might well be a patriotic one, though not without an ironic sense of the comic-opera aspect of it all.

Was there a coincidence? It seemed to me there had to be a coincidence, but I couldn't spot it. What gave it all a touch of the dramatic, at least at first glance, was that it had taken me something like sixteen hours to figure out why the guy with the big smile looked faintly familiar. If I'd recognized him on the spot, I wouldn't have given it a second thought. "Oh, there's King Vlados, I'd know him anywhere, even in the apartment of one of his loyal subjects."

On the other hand, if I'd passed his photograph without the barest twinge of recognition, I would never have known who he was. Or, come to think of it, cared.

So if anything was remarkable (and it certainly-seemed as though something ought to be) it was that I had subconsciously retained the image of Vlados in my mind from an earlier glance through the Scott catalog. But that, damn it to hell, wasn't remarkable either, because I'd looked up Anatruria in that very volume a week or so ago, after Ilona had acknowledged it as her birthplace. That was why I'd been able to rattle off all that historical data so glibly, impressing the daylights out of Carolyn.

I used the magnifying glass and had another look at His Highness. He was better, I decided, at flashing smiles than at looking solemn. The smile might not have been appropriate for a serious philatelic occasion like this, but it gave him a leg up on the legion of royal twits who've left their faces on the stamps and coins of Europe. I wondered what might have been the source of his claim to the Anatrurian throne, and if he was related to the other kings and princelings. Most of them are descended one way or another from Queen Victoria, and are almost as much fun at parties as she was.

What about Vlados's consort, she of the high-piled hair and the pathetic little foxes? The Scott people hadn't provided a picture of her, but they were nice enough to tell me her name. According to the descriptive listing, she appeared twice in the series— alone on the 35-tschirin stamp, and with her husband on the 50-tschirin denomination. And her name was Queen Liliana.

Scott's hadn't priced the Anatrurian issues, noting at once that they were very rare and of dubious philatelic legitimacy; they had been printed to carry not the mail but a message, and, while postally used copies did in fact exist, these seemed to represent contrived cancellations affixed by postmasters sympathetic to the cause of Anatrurian independence.

So Scott knew they were valuable, but didn't want to go on record with a price. There weren't many specimens up for grabs, and then again there weren't all that many hands out there grabbing. If the stamp collection I knocked over happened to contain a set of these gummed portraits of good King Vladdy, I could figure out how to unload them. It would take a little research—specialized catalogs, auction records, some library time spent closeted with back issues of *Linn's*. I might not net as high a percentage of retail value as I would with more popular material, but I wouldn't have any real trouble getting a decent price.

But that wasn't my problem, because I didn't have the stamps. I had an Anatrurian girlfriend, but Anatruria was out of business as a stamp-issuing enterprise half a century before she was born, and she might not even know her country had a postal history.

Might that not be something for us to talk about? I could lift the photo from its hallowed place on her footlocker and say, "Ah, King Vlados, and his lovely Queen Liliana! I'd recognize them anywhere." Would that impress her? Would she be dazzled by my familiarity with her nation's history, touched by my interest in her heritage?

Maybe. Or maybe she'd just raise her eyebrows

the slightest bit and give me that look of skeptical amusement.

I reached for the phone and dialed her number again, with no more success than the other times I'd tried.

Then the little guy came in and stuck a gun in my face.

NINE

When I first saw him on his way through the door I thought he was a kid wearing his father's clothes. He couldn't have been more than five-three, and judging by the way he walked he already had lifts in his shoes. He had a very narrow face, as if it had gotten in the way when Mother Nature clapped her hands. His nose was long and narrow, his lips thin. His hair and eyebrows were black and his skin was very pale, almost translucent. There were patches of color on his cheeks, but they were more suggestive of consumption than radiant good health.

He was wearing a lime-green sport shirt with flowing collar points and he'd buttoned it all the way up to the neck. His pants were of high-gloss blue gabardine, and his shoes were wing-tip slip-ons of woven brown leather. He was wearing a hat, too, a straw panama with a feather in its band, and I think it must have been the hat that made him look like an overdressed child. It was the crowning touch, all right.

"Name your price," he said.

I didn't hesitate. "I'm sorry," I said, "but I'm afraid it's not for sale."

The first thing I thought—the *only* thing I thought—was that he was looking to buy my store. I didn't delude myself that he'd made a study of Barnegat Books and concluded that it was a gold mine. On the contrary, I figured he saw it as the commercial real estate equivalent of a teardown; he'd buy me out so that he could take over my lease, sell my whole stock *en bloc* to Argosy or the Strand, and establish in Barnegat's stead a Thai restaurant or a Korean nail shop, something that would be a great cultural asset to the neighborhood. I get offers like that all the time, strange as it may seem, and I don't bother explaining that I own the building, and that consequently I'm the landlord as well as the tenant. For one thing, that part's a secret; for another, it would simply invite further inquiry. I just tell them all the business is not for sale, and sooner or later they believe me and go away.

But not this fellow. Damned if he didn't reach into his pocket and come out with a gun.

It was a very small gun, a flat nickel-plated automatic with pearl grips, small enough to carry in his pants pocket, small enough to fit in his very small hand. I don't know what caliber bullet it held—.22 or .25, I suppose—but either one will kill you if it hits you in the right place, and he was right across the counter from me, close enough to put a bullet wherever he wanted it.

If I'd thought it over I'd have been terrified. He was just the right size to be one of those sawed-off psychopaths you used to see on the screen all the time, those little reptilian hit men who seem to kill without hesitation, and certainly without any change of expression. And here he was in my store and pointing a gun at me.

"You idiot!" I snapped. "What the hell's the matter with you? Put that away this minute."

Well, see, it looked like a toy. Like a cap gun, say, or like a cunningly disguised cigarette lighter. I'm not saying that's what I thought it was, I knew it was a real gun, but I can't think of anything else that would explain my reaction. Instead of reacting sensibly in fear and trembling, I was pissed off. Where did this, this *kid*, get off coming into my store and waving a gun around? And didn't the little punk need a stern talking-to?

"Right this minute!" I said when he hesitated. "Don't you realize you could get in trouble with that thing? Do you know what time it is?"

"Time?"

"It's four-thirty," I said. "And there's a policeman who's due here any minute, and how would you feel standing there with that thing in your hand and having a cop walk in on you? How'd you like to try explaining that?"

"But—"

"God damn it, put it away!"

And damned if he didn't do just that. "I . . . I am sorry," he said, the spots of color on his cheeks darkening even as the rest of him seemed to grow paler still. He glanced at the gun as if it were something shameful, hiding it in his hand as he lowered it and tucked it back where it had come from. "I did not mean . . . I would not wish . . . I deeply regret . . ."

"That's better," I said graciously. "Much better. Now tell me what I can do for you. Is there a book you're looking for?"

"A book?" He looked at me, his eyes as wide as they could get. "You know what I am looking for. And please, I regret the gun. I only meant to impress you."

"There are better ways to make an impression," I said.

"Yes, of course, of course. You are of course correct."

He had a foreign inflection to his speech, and he hissed his S's. I hadn't noticed this earlier; it was the sort of subtlety that slides right past me when I'm looking down the barrel of a gun.

"I will pay," he said.

"Oh?"

"I will pay an excellent price."

"How much?" And for what, I wondered.

"How much do you want?"

"As much as I can get."

"You must understand that I am not a rich man."

"Then perhaps you cannot afford it." Whatever it was.

"But I must have it!"

"Then I'm sure you'll find a way."

He thrust his narrow face forward, aimed his sharp chin at me. "You must assure me," he said, "that he does not have it."

"Who are we talking about?"

He grimaced. "Must I say his name?"

"It would help," I said.

"The fat man," he said. "Tsarnoff."

"Sarnoff?"

"Tsarnoff!"

"Tsorry," I said.

"He is dangerous. And you cannot trust him. Whatever he tells you, it is a lie."

"Really."

"Yes, really. And I will tell you something else. Whatever he will pay, I will pay more. Tell me he does not already have it!"

"Well," I said honestly, "I can tell you he didn't get it from me."

"Thank God."

"Just to clear the air," I said carefully, "and to make sure we're not at cross-purposes here, suppose you tell me what it is."

"What it is?"

"That you're seeking from me. You want it and Tsarnoff wants it. Well, why don't you come right out and say what it is."

"You know what it is."

"Ah, but how do I know that *you* know what it is?"

"No!" he cried, and doubled up his fists and pounded my counter. I hate it when people do that. "Please, I beg of you," he said. "I am very high-strung. You must not tease me."

"It'll never happen again."

"I need the documents. You may retain the rest, I want only the documents, and I will pay well, whatever you ask if only it is within reason. I am a reasonable man, and I believe you are a reasonable man yourself, yes?"

"Reason," I said, "is my middle name."

He frowned. "I thought 'Grimes.' Is it not so?"

"Well, yes. You're quite right. It was my mother's maiden name."

"And Rhodenbarr? This is your name also?"

"That too," I agreed. "It was my father's maiden name. But what I just said, about Reason being my middle name, that's an idiom, an expression, a figure of speech. It's a way of saying that I'm a reasonable man."

"But I am just saying this myself, yes?" He shrugged. "It confuses me, this language."

"It confuses everybody. Right now I'm confused, because I don't know your name. I like to know a man's name if I'm going to do business with him."

"Forgive me," he said, and reached into his pocket. I braced myself, but when his hand came out the only thing in it was a leather card case. He extracted a card, glanced dubiously at it, and presented it to me.

"Tiglath Rasmoulian," I read aloud. In response he drew himself up to his full height, if you want to call it that, and clicked his heels.

"At your service," he said.

"Well," I said brightly, "I'll just hang on to this, and if I ever come across these mysterious documents, I'll certainly keep you in mind. In the meanwhile—"

The red patches blazed on his cheeks. "You are treating me like a child," he said. There's not a single S in that sentence, so I don't see how he could have hissed it, but I swear that's what he did. "That is not a wise thing to do."

And his hand went into his pocket.

It stayed there while his eyes swung toward the door, which had just opened. "Ah," I said, "just the man I've been waiting for. Ray, I'd like you to meet Tiglath Rasmoulian. Mr. Rasmoulian, this is Officer Raymond Kirschmann of the New York Police Department."

I didn't get the impression that this was what Rasmoulian had been hoping to hear. He took his hand out of his pocket but did not offer it to Ray. He nodded formally to Ray, then to me. "I will go now," he said. "You will keep it in mind, what we discussed?"

"Definitely," I said. "Have a good weekend. Oh, don't forget your book."

"My book?"

I turned around and grabbed a book off the shelf behind me. It was the Modern Library edition of *Nostromo,* by Joseph Conrad, with slight foxing and the binding shaky. I checked the flyleaf, where I'd priced it reasonably enough at $4.50. I picked up a pencil, casually added a two to the left of the 4, and smiled at him. "It's twenty-four fifty," I said, "but your discount brings it down to twenty dollars even. And of course there's no sales tax, since you're in the trade."

He went into his pocket again, but it was the other pocket this time, and he came out with a money clip instead of a gun, which struck me as a vast improvement. He peeled off a twenty while I wrote out a receipt, carefully copying his name from his card. I took his money, slipped his receipt inside the book's loose front cover, and slid the book into a paper bag. He took it, gave me a look, gave Ray a look, started to say something, changed his mind, and scuttled past Ray and out the door.

"Odd-lookin' bird," Ray said, reaching for the card. " 'Tiglath Rasmoulian.' What kind of name is Tiglath?"

"An unusual one," I said. "At least in my experience."

"No address, no phone number. Just his name."

"It's what they call a calling card, Ray."

"Now why in the hell would they call it that? You want to try callin' him, I'd say you're shit out of luck, bein' as there's no number to call. He in the book business?"

"So he says."

"An' that's his business card? No phone, no address? An' on the strength of that you gave him a discount and didn't charge him the tax?"

"I guess I'm a soft touch, Ray."

"It's good you're closin' early," he said, "before you give away the store."

Twenty minutes later I was standing in a gray-green corridor looking through a pane of glass at someone who couldn't look back. "I hate this," I said to Ray. "Remember? I told you I hated this."

"You're not gonna puke, are you, Bernie?"

"No," I said firmly. "I'm not. Can we leave now?"

"You seen enough?"

"More than enough, thank you."

"Well?"

"Well what? Oh, you mean—"

"Yeah. It's him, right?"

I hesitated. "You know," I said, "how many times did I actually set eyes on the man? Two, three times?"

"He was a customer of yours, Bernie."

"Not a very frequent one. And you don't really look at a person in a bookstore, at least I don't."

"You don't?"

"Not really. What usually happens is we both wind up looking at the book we're discussing. And if he's paying by check I'll look at the check, and at his ID, if I ask him for ID. Of course Candlemas paid me in cash, so I never had any reason to ask to see his driver's license."

"So instead you looked at his face, like you just did a minute ago, and that's how you're able to tell it's him."

"But did I really look at his face?" I frowned. "Sometimes we look without seeing, Ray. I looked at his clothes. I could swear he was a sharp dresser. But now all he's wearing is a sheet, and I never saw him on his way to a toga party."

"Bernie . . ."

"Think about the man you just met in my store. That was no more than half an hour ago, Ray, and you looked right at him, but did you really see him? If you had to do it, could you furnish a description of him?"

"Sure," he said. "Name, Tignatz Rasmoolihan.

Height, five foot two. Weight, a hundred an' five. Color of hair, black. Color of eyes, green."

"Really? He had green eyes?"

"Sure, matched his shirt. Probably why he picked it, the vain little bastard. Complexion, pale. Spots of rouge here an' here, only it ain't rouge, it's natural. Shape of face, narrow."

He went on, describing the clothes Rasmoulian was wearing down to an alligator belt with a silver buckle, which I certainly hadn't noticed. I must have seen it but it didn't register. "That's amazing," I said. "You barely looked at him and you got all that. You fluffed the name a little, but everything else was picture-perfect."

"Well, I'm what you call a trained observer," he said, clearly pleased. "I'll screw up a name now an' then, but I get the rest of it right most of the time."

"Now that just shows you," I said. "I'm the other way around. I guess I'm just more verbal than visual. I'll get the names right every time, but the faces are another story."

"I guess it comes from hangin' around books all the time."

"I wouldn't be surprised."

"Instead of gettin' out and mixin' with people."

"That must be it."

"So?"

"How's that, Ray?"

"So are you gonna ID this poor dead son of a bitch or what?"

"Just hypothetically," I said. "Suppose I wasn't a hundred percent certain."

"Aw, Jesus, why'd you have to go an' say a thing like that?"

"No, let me finish. I get the impression that my identifying the body is really nothing more than a formality."

"That's exactly what it is, Bernie."

"You've probably already identified him from fingerprints and dental records. You just need somebody to eyeball the deceased and confirm what you already know."

"So far we didn't get any kind of a bounce from the prints or the dental records. But we sure as hell know who he is."

"So it's just a formality."

"Didn't I just say that, Bernie?"

I made up my mind. "All right," I said. "It's Candlemas."

"Way to go, Bern. For the record, you're formally identifying the man you just saw as Hugo Candlemas, right?"

If this had been a movie there'd have been an ominous chord right about now, so that you'd know the hero was about to put his foot in it. No, you'd want to cry. No, you fool, don't do it!

But would he listen?

"Ray," I said, "there's no question in my mind."

TEN

Ray dropped me at the subway and I was in my own apartment with time for a shower and shave before I headed for the Musette. I was there first so I bought two tickets and waited in the lobby.

I was still waiting when they opened the doors and started letting people take seats. I followed the crowd inside and threw my jacket over a pair of seats halfway down the aisle on the left, then went back to the guy taking tickets. He knew me by now, and why wouldn't he? He'd been seeing me every night for the past two and a half weeks.

He said he hadn't recognized me at first, that he wasn't used to seeing me without my lady friend. That, I told him, was the problem. I gave him Ilona's ticket and said she'd evidently been delayed en route. He assured me there would be no problem; he'd let her in and steer her toward where I was sitting.

I went and bought popcorn. What the hell, I hadn't had anything to eat since that slice of pizza around noon. It felt strange, though, sitting there with no one next to me, dipping into the popcorn without risk of encountering another hand.

I glanced around the theater, surprised at what a large proportion of the audience looked familiar to me. I don't know that there were many diehards like us who never missed a night, but a lot of people came more than once. I guess if you saw one Bogart picture you saw them all, or as many as you could.

If we ran to type, I couldn't tell you what the type was. There were quite a few college kids, some with the serious look of film students, others just out for a good time. There were older West Siders, the intellectual-political-artsy crowd you see at the free afternoon concerts at Juilliard, and some of them had probably seen many of these films during their initial run. There were singles, gay and straight, and young marrieds, gay and straight, and people who looked rich enough to buy the theater, and people who looked as though they must have raised the price of admission by begging on the subway. It was a wonderfully varied crowd, drawn together by the enduring appeal of an actor who'd died more than thirty-five years ago, and I was happy to be a part of it.

But not as happy as I would have been if Ilona were sharing my popcorn.

The thought made the popcorn stick in my throat, but sometimes it tends to do that anyway. I told myself it was a little early to start wallowing in self-pity, that she'd be slipping into the seat beside me any minute now.

The seat was still empty when they brought the

house lights down. I wasn't surprised, not really. I fed myself another handful of popcorn and let myself get lost in the movie.

That's what it was there for.

The first feature, *Passage to Marseille,* was made in 1944, not long after *Casablanca* and obviously inspired by it, although the credits said it was based on a book by Nordhoff and Hall. (You remember them, they wrote *Mutiny on the Bounty.*) Bogart plays a French journalist named Matrac who's on Devil's Island when the movie opens, framed for murder and serving a life sentence. He and four others escape, only to be picked up on the high seas by a French cargo ship. Of course the convicts want to go fight for France—has there ever been anyone as fiercely patriotic as a criminal in a Hollywood movie?—but France has just surrendered, and Sydney Greenstreet wants to turn the ship over to the Vichy government. His attempted mutiny is thwarted, and Bogart and his buddies join a Free French bomber squadron in England. His plane is the last to return from a mission, and after it lands his crewmates bring him off, dead.

Well, hell, he died for a good cause, and until then he got to spend time with Claude Rains and Peter Lorre and Helmut Dantine and, well, all the usual suspects. It wasn't the best film he ever made, but it was a quintessential Bogart role, the hard-bitten cynicism shielding the pure idealist, the beautiful loser coolly victorious in defeat.

A shame she had to miss it.

* * *

When the lights came up I checked with the usher and he shrugged and shook his head. I inquired at the box office, tried her number from a pay phone in the lobby. Nothing. On my way back into the theater the usher asked me if I wanted to cash in my unused ticket. I told him to hang on to it, that she might still turn up.

At the refreshment stand a tall guy with a goatee but no mustache said, "All by yourself tonight."

I'd seen him and his dumpling of a girlfriend just about every night, but this was the first time either of us had spoken. "All alone," I agreed. "She said she might have to work late. She might still turn up."

We talked about the film we'd just seen, and about the one coming up. Then I went back to my seat and watched *Black Legion*.

It's an early one, released in 1937, with Bogart playing a member of the Ku Klux Klan, only they called it the Black Legion and the members wore black hoods sporting white skulls and crossbones. I'd seen it sometime within the past year on AMC, and it wasn't that great then, and by the time the picture got underway I knew Ilona wasn't going to show up. It seemed to me that I'd known all along.

I felt like walking out, but I stayed where I was and got caught up in the film in spite of myself. The film had a neat twist. At the end, with Bogart arrested for murder, it turns out that the Legion was set up by the crime syndicate for commercial purposes. Maybe they had a stranglehold on the hood-

and-sheet business. They want Bogart to plead self-defense, but for the sake of his wife's reputation he turns state's evidence instead, bringing down the whole Black Legion and saving the day for truth and justice.

Even so, he winds up with a life sentence. The poor son of a bitch, he must have had the worst lawyer since Patty Hearst.

Don't ask me why, but I went across the street to make sure she wasn't waiting for me over a cup of coffee. And of course she wasn't. I scanned the room from the doorway, then left and went back to my place.

I called her number and wasn't surprised when no one answered. I picked up what I'd come home for and went out again, taking the same combination of subways I take to work every morning but getting off a stop sooner than usual, at Broadway and Twenty-third. I just missed my crosstown bus and was all set to hail a cab, but what was my hurry?

I walked across Twenty-third Street and tried her number one last time from a pay phone two blocks from her apartment. When my quarter came back I walked the rest of the way and stood on the sidewalk across the street from her building. Simple Pleasures, the ground-floor shop, was closed and dark. There were no lights in the fourth-floor windows, but that didn't tell me anything. Her apartment was in the back of the building.

I put my hand in my pocket, felt the burglar's tools I'd gone home for. It seemed to me that I had no

moral right to enter Ilona's apartment. I evidently
didn't have much in the way of moral fiber, either,
but I'd known that for years.

I looked both ways and crossed the street—it's a
one-way street, but try telling that to the guys on bi-
cycles delivering Chinese food—and then I looked
both ways a second time and mounted the half-flight
of steps to the vestibule of her building. I checked
the buzzers for one marked MARKOVA and couldn't
find it, but there was only one top-floor buzzer with
no name on it, and I decided that had to be hers.
(This, incidentally, was faulty reasoning; Carolyn's
buzzer on Arbor Court is still marked ARNOW, the
long-vanished tenant of record. I don't know about
the rest of the country, but in New York more people
have learned anonymity from Rent Control than ever
discovered it in a 12-Step program.)

I leaned on the unmarked buzzer, and either it was
hers or it rang in some other empty apartment, because it went unanswered.

The trouble with front doors is that they're right
out there in public view. A tenant, coming or going,
can catch you in the act. A passerby can spot you
from the street. The longer you spend mucking
about with the lock, the more likely it is that this will
happen.

On the flip side, the nice thing about front doors
is they're rarely very hard to open. They're just spring
locks—if they used deadbolts an upstairs tenant
couldn't buzz anyone in—and the locks see so much
action that they become as loose and as yielding as,
well, a very old practitioner of an ancient profession,

let us say. This one at least had a protective lip so you couldn't loid your way in with a credit card or strip of spring steel, but aside from that it had precious little going for it. About the only person it could be expected to keep out was a tenant who had lost his key.

Actually, I told myself, the threshold was not the Rubicon; I could cross it without committing myself. Even if I ran smack into Ilona herself in the hallway, I could explain I'd found the door ajar, or that another tenant had held it for me. The door to her apartment, now that was a different matter.

A few minutes later, I was standing in front of the door to her apartment.

No one responded to my knock, and no light showed under her door. The previous night I'd noticed that she only locked two of the three locks, and which way she'd turned the key in each of them. (I can't help it, I notice things like that. To each his own, I say; Ray Kirschmann had noticed the silver buckle on Tiglath Rasmoulian's alligator belt.) I took out my picks and had at it. I worked rapidly—one doesn't want to dawdle—but there was no need to rush. I opened one lock, I opened the other lock, and I was inside.

I hadn't brought my gloves and wouldn't have put them on if I had. I wasn't worried about fingerprints, for God's sake, but about making a fool of myself and destroying a relationship almost before it had begun. If I got away clean, no forensic evidence of my visit would harm me; if she caught me in the act, all the gloves in Gloversville wouldn't help me.

I drew the door shut right away and stood unmoving in the pitch-dark room, not even troubling to breathe until I'd taken a moment to listen for any breathing other than my own. Then I took a breath, and then I reached for the light switch—I remembered where it was, too—and switched it on. The bare bulb overhead came on and I blinked at its glare, then looked around.

I felt like an archaeologist who'd just broken into an empty tomb.

ELEVEN

The furniture was still there. The narrow bed nestled against the far wall, unmade, with the rickety night table at its head and the squat thrift-shop dresser nearby. I counted the same three chairs—two unmatched wooden card chairs, one at the little one-drawer desk and one at the foot of the bed, and one armchair with a broken spring, clumsily reupholstered some time back in metallic green velvet. And the rug was there, too, as ugly as ever.

Nothing besides remained, as Shelley said of Ozymandias. Gone were the plastic milk cartons and the books they'd housed. Gone was the brassbound footlocker and the shrine that had perched on top of it, candles and crystal and icons and animals and all. Gone was the stiff family snapshot of Ilona and her parents, gone too the framed photo of Vlados and Liliana. Gone from the wall was the map of Eastern Europe, gone from its nail the bird calendar.

Gone whatever the desk and dresser had contained; I checked their drawers and found them empty. Gone, except for three wire coat hangers and a grocery bag collection, whatever the closet might have held. Gone, lock, stock, and barrel. Gone, kit and caboodle. Gone.

The bed linen remained on the bed, the twisted sheets still holding her scent.

I walked over to the desk and picked up the phone. I got a dial tone, and if the phone had been equipped with a redial button I could have determined the last call she made before she disappeared. Instead I dialed my own number, which didn't answer, and then dialed the store and wondered what Raffles would make of the ringing. I dialed Candlemas's apartment on East Seventy-sixth and let it ring a few times, but there were no cops there this time around and no one answered.

I cradled the receiver and sat down in the hideous green chair, taking care to avoid the broken spring. It wasn't terribly comfortable, but it would serve. I had some thinking to do, and this seemed like the time and place to do it.

Ordinarily I don't like to hang around after I break into somebody's home. It's an unnecessary risk, and one I prefer to avoid. But I couldn't think of a safer spot than where I was right now. I was like Mowgli, holed up in an abandoned building. No one lived here, and it took some imagination to believe that anyone ever had.

I could take my time. No one would be coming back.

I didn't note the time when I let myself into Ilona's place, but it was just past midnight when I left it. I walked over to Third Avenue to catch a cab headed uptown, and sprinted the last twenty yards to snag one cruising across the intersection.

"Running yet," Max Fiddler said. "Can't be the herbs. How could they work so fast? He makes miracles, this Chinaman, but even miracles take a little time to work. When did I see you, three, four nights ago?"

"Something like that."

"No, it was two nights ago. I know it for a fact, because right after I dropped you off the second time I picked up the woman with the monkey. Where to?"

"Seventy-first and West End."

"Right where I dropped you and then picked you up again. And then we took the Transverse and I dropped you at—gimme a minute—"

"Take all the time you want," I said.

"—Seventy-sixth and Lexington," he said triumphantly. "Am I right or am I right?"

"You're right."

"Some memory, eh?"

"I'm impressed."

"Ginkgo."

"I beg your pardon?"

"Ginkgo biloba," he said. "An herb! Comes from the ginkgo trees, you see 'em around town, got a funny little leaf shaped like a fan. I take these pills, my Chinaman told me about them, you get 'em in any health food store. I used to have a memory like Swiss cheese, now I got a memory like a hawk."

"That's wonderful."

"You want to test me on state capitals, names of the presidents, be my guest."

"No, that's all right."

"Or New York streets, anywhere in the five boroughs. Or something else. Go ahead, try and stump
me."

"Well, here's an easy one. Did I happen to leave
my attaché case in your cab the other night?"

"No," he said without hesitation. "You want to
know how I remember? I got this picture in my
mind, you're limping away from the cab, the case is
knocking against your leg with each step you take."

"That's amazing," I said. And even more amazing,
I thought, was that I had managed to forget for a
moment there that I already knew where the attaché
case was. Ray Kirschmann had shown it to me yesterday, with an incomprehensible six-letter word
printed on its side in blood.

"Ginkgo," he said. "I recommend it."

"Maybe I'll get some. Except it's not my memory
that bothers me so much as the feeling I get sometimes that I'm not thinking too clearly."

"It's good for that, too. Mental clarity!"

"That's what I could use."

"Also a ringing in the ears."

"It gives it to you or gets rid of it?"

"Gets rid of it!"

"Well, that's good to know," I said, "although that's
not something I've had to worry about."

"Yet."

"Yet," I agreed. "Tell me about the woman and the
monkey."

* * *

He told me about the woman and the monkey in considerable detail, but I don't know that it consti- tuted much of a testament to his memory, or to the efficacy of ginkgo biloba. I've never touched the stuff myself, and I expect to remember the whole episode long into my dotage. All I'll say is this—the woman had a well-developed figure ("Cantaloupes!" Max Fiddler said), while the monkey was a scrawny spec- imen with a mean little sour apple of a face. And they both should have been ashamed of themselves.

The story of their courtship carried us all the way to my corner. He was reaching to throw the flag when I told him to wait a minute.

"You said New York streets," I said. "Anywhere in the five boroughs, you said."

"So?"

"How about Arbor Court?"

"Arbor Court," he said. "There's only one Arbor Court and it's in Manhattan. Is that the one you mean?"

"That's the one."

"In the Village, right?"

"Right."

"Child's play," he said. "I thought you'd give me something hard, like Broadway Alley or Pomander Walk, but the best you can do is Arbor Court. Do I know Arbor Court? Of course I know Arbor Court, and you could take away my ginkgo and I'd still know it."

"You know how to get there from here?"

"Why wouldn't I know? Over to Broadway, then down Columbus and Ninth Avenue and Hudson

Street, and then you pick up Bleecker and take it until you swing right on Charles, and—"

"Fine," I said. "Let's go."

He put a hand on the back of his seat, turned around, and looked at me. "You want to go there?"

"Why not?"

"You want me to wait, and you'll go inside and get whatever you came here to get?"

"No," I said, sinking back into my seat. "Let's just go straight downtown."

"To the Village. To Arbor Court."

"Right."

"You're the boss," he said, and pulled away from the curb. "Arbor Court, coming up. You know what I think? I think there's a pattern developing here. Night before last I picked you up on Broadway and Sixty-seventh and brought you here, and ten minutes later I picked you up here and took you somewhere else. Tonight I pick you up and bring you here, and this time you don't even get out of the cab before we're off to someplace else. Next time you know what? You're going to be able to skip this intersection altogether."

"You may be right." It was going to be a long ride. "Say," I said, "I was wondering. Have you ever had anything else happen in your cab like what happened with the woman and the monkey?"

It took three anecdotes to get us all the way to Carolyn's place, and I'm not sure I believe the one with the two sailors and the little old lady. I suppose it's possible, but it certainly strikes me as highly unlikely. Still, it passed the time.

The ARNOW bell went unanswered, and I didn't let myself in. I could have, and wouldn't have needed my tools, as Carolyn and I have keys to each other's stores and apartments. But I figured it would be quicker to go looking for her, and I found her in the second place I tried, a bar called Henrietta Hudson's. When I went in I got a whole batch of looks ranging from wary to hostile, and then Carolyn spotted me and called me by name and the other women relaxed, knowing it was safe to ignore me.

Carolyn was at the bar drinking Scotch and listening to a willowy woman with improbable red hair. Her name was Tracey and I'd met her before, along with her lover, Djinn, who could have posed as her twin except that her equally unconvincing hair color was ash blond. You rarely saw one without the other, but they had evidently had a falling-out, which was why Tracey was knocking back shots of Jaegermeister and telling Carolyn her troubles, which seemed to be legion.

Carolyn introduced me, and Tracey was polite enough, but when it was clear that I wasn't just passing through she turned gracefully away from Carolyn and joined a conversation on her other side. "Move down a little ways, Bern," Carolyn suggested. "That'll give us more room."

"I'm sorry," I said. "Am I interrupting something?"

"You are," she said, "which means I owe you a big one. It's all over between her and Djinn, and she's about one drink away from inviting me to go home with her, and I'm about two drinks away from agreeing. Where are you going?"

"Home," I said, "so you can have a chance to get on with your life."

"Get back on your stool, Bern. The last thing I want is to go home with her."

"Why? I think she's gorgeous."

"No argument there, Bern. She's a beauty. So's Djinn, and when they broke up forever a year ago last November it was Djinn who told me her troubles and went home with me, and within a week the two of them were back together again and it was months before Tracey would speak to me. They break up three times a year and they always get back together again. Who needs it? That's not what I'm looking for these days, a quick little tumble in the feathers. I want something meaningful, something that might lead somewhere. Like you and Ilona might have, from the way you were talking this morning." My face must have shown something, because hers darkened. "Uh-oh," she said. "I stepped in it, didn't I? If I stopped to think, I would have wondered what you were doing in a dyke bar at one in the morning. What happened to the course of true love? It's not running smooth?"

"It's not running," I said. "Can we go somewhere and have a drink?"

"We're in a bar, Bern. We can have a drink right here."

"Someplace a little quieter."

"The tables are quieter. You want to take a table?"

"Someplace really quiet," I said, "and where I

won't be the only person in the room with a Y chromosome."

"Let's see. There's Omphalos on Christopher Street. Everyone there's got a Y chromosome."

"I don't think so."

"Not Slumgullion's, that's all college kids and noise. Oh, I know. There's that place around the corner on Leroy Street. They don't get a gay crowd or a straight crowd. Nobody goes there. It's always dead."

"It sounds perfect," I said. "I hope we can get in."

It was just us and the bartender. He gave us our drinks and left us alone, and I brought Carolyn up to date.

"That's just so strange about Ilona," she said. "The last you saw of her . . ."

"She was sleeping like a lamb."

"And you never spoke to her afterward? No, you called and there was nobody home. And then you went there, and there was really nobody home. It's hard to believe she moved out, Bern. Are you sure she wasn't downstairs doing her laundry?"

"She took everything, Carolyn."

"Well, maybe everything was dirty. You know how a person'll put off doing the laundry, and the first thing you know there's nothing to wear, so you do it all at once."

"And she took the dry cleaning the same day," I said. "And all her shoes to the shoemaker."

"I guess it's pretty farfetched, huh?"

"And her books to be rebound, and her pictures to be framed, and—"

"I get the point, Bern. It was a dumb idea."

"All she left," I said, "is a little Scotch tape residue on the wall, where the map was hanging. And her fingerprints, maybe, but for all I know she wiped the place down before she took off."

"Why would she do that?"

"I don't know. I'll ask you one. Why would she disappear like that?"

"I don't know, Bern. Was it something you said?"

"Very funny."

"You know what I mean. What was she like afterward?"

"Sad. But she said lovemaking always makes her sad."

"Right away? I don't get sad until the next morning, when I wake up and find out who I went home with." She shuddered at a memory and chased it with a sip of Scotch. "If it always makes her sad," she said, "maybe that explains why it took her two weeks to get around to it. But I still don't get the disappearing act."

"Neither do I."

"Do you think she could have been abducted?"

"I thought of that. But if you were going to kidnap her, why pack up all her things?"

"That way she disappears without a trace."

"What do you mean?"

"When's the last day of the month, Tuesday? Wednesday whoever took her calls her landlord and tells him he can rent the place, because she's not coming back. So he looks and everything's gone but the furniture, and you said you thought that came with the place?"

"It didn't look like anything she would have picked out for herself."

"So she's gone, bag and baggage, and he gets a new tenant in there and that's it. Gone without a trace."

"Why not just leave her stuff? Then no one would even know she was missing. I wouldn't even have a clue she'd moved out if there'd been clothes in the closet and all the other stuff where it had been last night."

"So that means she must have left voluntarily."

"I would think so," I said. "And she packed everything because she wanted to keep it. Maybe she was behind in her rent or skipping out on a lease, maybe that's why she left so abruptly, but there has to be more to it than that. Why didn't she call me? Even if she wasn't going to meet me at the movies, why stand me up? Why not spend a quarter and clue me in?"

"Maybe she didn't know how to break it to you."

"Break *what* to me?"

"If she'd broken it," she said, "then we'd know. Bern, she must have done her own packing. Anybody else would have packed up the sheets and blankets along with everything else."

"Whereas she'd leave them behind because she regarded them as contaminated?"

"She would know if they came with the apartment, and sometimes they do in furnished rooms or sublets. What about the kitchen stuff?"

"There was a two-burner hot plate and tabletop refrigerator. I didn't notice any pots or pans."

"She probably ate out all the time."

"As far as I know, all she ever ate was popcorn. And half of an eclair." I shrugged. "I didn't check to see if there was anything in the fridge. Maybe I should have. I had a slice of pizza for lunch and popcorn for dinner."

"That's terrible, Bern."

"Well, I had a real breakfast," I said. "At least I think I did. It's hard to remember."

"We should get you something to eat."

"We should get me something to drink," I said, and carried our glasses back to the bar.

A little later she said, "Bernie, I keep thinking that I ought to tell you to go easy on the booze. And then another voice tells me to let you drink all you want."

"That second voice," I said, "is the voice of truth and reason."

"I don't know about that, Bern. You're putting a lot of alcohol into an empty stomach."

"That's a good place for it," I said. "Anyway, I wouldn't call it empty." I patted the organ in question. "Popcorn takes up a lot of space," I said. "If you want to fill a stomach, you can't beat popcorn."

"It's all air, Bern."

"It's heavier than air. If it were all air, it wouldn't stay in the barrel. It would float away."

"Bern . . ."

"I ate a whole barrel of it all by myself," I said.

"That's what they call them, barrels. Or sometimes they call them tubs."

"I know."

"Usually I only have half a barrel, because Ilona has the other half. You want to know something? When she wasn't there at a quarter to seven, I knew she wasn't coming. Before I bought the tickets, I knew."

"How did you know, Bern?"

"I just knew," I said. "The way you know a thing." I thought about what I'd just said. "Well, the way you know certain things," I amended. "That's not the way I know Pierre is the capital of South Dakota, for example. I know that because Mrs. Goldfus made us learn all the state capitals."

"Who was Mrs. Goldfus and why would she do a thing like that?"

"She was my fifth-grade teacher, and she did it because it was her job."

"All the state capitals. And you never forgot them?"

"I never forgot Pierre. I may have forgotten some of the others. If I take enough ginkgo biloba I'll be able to tell you which ones I forgot. Except once I remember them, how will I know they were forgotten for a while there?"

"It's confusing."

"You said it."

I picked up my drink and looked at it. It was vodka on the rocks, and it wasn't Ludomir, because they didn't carry the brand. This, I decided, was probably just as well.

"I knew she wouldn't be there tonight," I said, "and it doesn't matter how I knew. I just knew."

"Got it, Bern."

"I bought two tickets anyway. I probably could have gotten a refund on one of them, but I didn't even try." I snapped my fingers. "Easy come, easy go."

"You said it."

"And I could have bought a small barrel of popcorn instead of a large one, because by then I definitely knew she wasn't going to show. But what did I do? I went right ahead and bought a large one."

"Easy come, easy go?"

"You took the words right out of my mouth. I told you how I got twenty dollars out of Tiglath Rasmoulian, didn't I?"

"You did, Bern."

"It was like taking candy from a baby. So why not blow it on popcorn?"

"They get twenty dollars for a barrel of popcorn?"

"No, of course not."

"I'm glad to hear it. Bern, no matter how much popcorn you've got in your stomach, I think you're starting to feel your drinks."

"Was I talking loud, Carolyn?"

"Kind of."

"Damn," I said, and dropped to a whisper. "I don't know why that happens."

"It's nothing to worry about, Bern. Especially since there's nobody around to hear us."

"Good point."

"And it's probably not a bad idea for you to get a little bit drunk. Maybe it'll help you forget her."

"Forget who?"

"Gee," she said. "I never thought it would work that fast."

"Oh, Ilona? I can't forget her, Carolyn."

"That's what you think now," she said earnestly, "but we've been friends a long time, and think of all the women we've both had to forget over the years. And where are they now? Forgotten, every last one of them. Time heals all wounds, Bern, especially when it's got a little Scotch to back it up."

"I'm drinking vodka tonight."

"I know, and it's not like you. How come?"

"For Captain Hoberman." I picked up the glass again and gazed down into it, then raised it a little higher and looked through it at the ceiling light fixture. "The trouble with vodka," I said, "is it's not as good to stare at. You hold a glass full of amber whiskey to the light, it's as though you're looking through it and seeing the secrets of the universe. You do the same thing with vodka and it might as well be a glass of water."

"That's true, Bern. I never thought of it that way, but it's true."

"And yet," I said, "as soon as you swallow it, it doesn't make a bit of difference what color it is. It works just fine." I tilted my glass and proved the point. "Carolyn? Is it okay if I stay over at your place tonight?"

"Sure," she said, "and it's a good idea, too. This is no night for you to be alone."

"That's not it."

"And I wouldn't want you going uptown on the subway in your condition, or even in a cab."

"Neither would I," I said, "but that's not it, either. I want to get an early start tomorrow."

"An early start on what?"

"The case."

"What case?"

"What case?" I stared at her. "Have I been talking to myself? Haven't you been paying any attention? A man's dead, a portfolio is missing, a beautiful woman has disappeared—"

"Bern," she said, "all those things are true, and at least one of them is a shame, but what does it have to do with you?"

"I have to do something about it," I said.

"That's the booze talking, Bern."

"No," I said, "it's me."

"It sounds like you," she said, "but I think it's the booze. Ilona packed up and moved out. If she wants to be found, she knows how to get in touch with you. If she doesn't want to be found, what do you want with her? I know it was wonderful, what the two of you had, but evidently she's profoundly neurotic or leading some kind of a double life, and as soon as you begin to get close to her she runs away. I've known women like that, Bern. None of them ever disappeared quite so abruptly, but some of them pulled things that weren't all that different."

"I have to find Ilona," I said, "but that's not the main thing I have to do. I have to solve the case."

"How?"

"By recovering the portfolio that was stolen out from under me, and finding out more about those documents that Tsarnoff and Rasmoulian are so hot to get hold of. And by figuring out what CAPHOB means and what it's doing on the side of my attaché case. But most of all by catching the person who committed murder in that fourth-floor flat on East Seventy-sixth Street."

"Bern," she said gently, "don't you think that's a job for the police?"

"No, it's not. It's my job."

"How do you figure that?"

"When your partner is killed," I said, "you have to do something about it. Maybe he wasn't much good and maybe you didn't like him much, but that doesn't matter. He was your partner, and you're supposed to do something about it."

"Gee," she said. "I never thought of it that way. I have to admit, Bern, when you put it like that it sounds so forceful and clear-cut that it's hard to argue with you."

"Why, thank you, Carolyn."

"You're welcome. 'He was your partner, and you're supposed to do something about it.' I'll have to remember that." She looked sharply at me. "Wait a minute. Who said that?"

"I did," I said. "Just a minute ago."

"Yeah, but Sam Spade said it first. In *The Maltese Falcon*, when Miles Archer is murdered. Maybe it's not word for word, but that's exactly what he said."

I thought about it. "You know," I said, "I think you're right."

She reached out a hand, laid it on top of mine. "Bern," she said, "do you want to know what I think? I think you've been going to too many movies."

"Maybe."

"You're starting to get yourself mixed up with Humphrey Bogart," she said, "and that can be dangerous. The line's a great one, but it doesn't fit the situation."

"It doesn't?"

"Hugo Candlemas wasn't your partner. If he was anything, he was an employer. He hired you to steal that portfolio, and he never even paid you."

"That's true. On the other hand, I never stole the portfolio."

"And it's not as though the two of you got to be best friends. I know you identified his body this afternoon, but look at all the trouble you had doing it."

"I didn't have any trouble."

"That's not the way it sounded when you told me about it. You hemmed and hawed and told Ray a lot of crap about how you've got a better memory for names than faces. Isn't that what you said?"

"Something like that."

"So if his features were that faintly etched on your memory—"

"His features were etched upon my memory," I said, "as if by a diamond on glass."

"But you said—"

"I know what I said. Don't tell me what I said."

"I'm sorry, Bern."

"I'm sorry, too. I didn't mean to snap at you. That was Bogart talking just then, not me." I picked up my glass. The vodka was gone but some of the ice had melted, so I took a swallow of that. "All I needed at the morgue was one quick look," I said. "I hemmed and hawed because I didn't want to make the identification."

"Why not?"

"Because it wasn't Candlemas."

"It wasn't?"

"No, it wasn't. You're right, Candlemas wasn't my partner, but that's not who I was talking about. I mean the man who helped me get past the doorman and elevator operator at the Boccaccio."

"Not Captain Hoberman?"

"That's who it was, all right, and he was my partner, or as close as I had to a partner in that little caper. He didn't have the world's hardest task to perform, but he did what he was supposed to, and he deserved more for his troubles than a drawer in the morgue." I drew a breath. "It doesn't matter if I got the line from a movie or thought it up myself. It's just as true either way. He was my partner, and he's dead, and it's up to me to do something about it."

TWELVE

Over breakfast she said, "I don't know if you re-member this, Bern, but just before you fell asleep you were saying something about Ilona's dis-appearance being tied in with Captain Hoberman's murder. But you wouldn't say how, and then you passed out."

"I remember."

"You do?"

"Except for the part about passing out."

"I'm surprised you remember any of it. I figured you were delirious. I was mad at you because I was sure I'd be up all night looking for a connection, but the next thing I knew it was morning and Ubi and Archie were yowling for their breakfast."

Ubi's a Russian Blue, Archie an extremely vocal Burmese. "I never even heard them," I said.

"Well, you're a sound sleeper, Bern. Plus they weren't walking on you at the time. Anyway, the last thing you said was you'd tell me in the morning. It's morning, so let's hear it. Unless you weren't serious."

"I was serious."

"So?"

"I can't remember how much I already told you. Do you know about the photograph? The one Ilona lights candles to?"

"King Whatsis."

"Vlados."

"Whatever. You recognized him from the stamps, because your parents let you have a stamp collection when you were a kid."

"You mean yours didn't?"

She shook her head. "Too butch. I think they had an inkling, and they tried to steer me in the other direction. Instead of stamps, I got Story Book Dolls. You know, in the little boxes, and wearing their national costumes?"

"What did you do, break their heads off?"

"Are you kidding? I loved those dolls."

"You did?"

"I thought they were adorable. I'd still have 'em if I had the space. I gave them to my cousin's kids on the Island. 'This is just a loan,' I told them. 'They still belong to Aunt Carolyn.' In case I ever move to a larger apartment, but I never will, and if I did I'd have trouble getting the dolls back from those kids. They're crazy about them, especially Jason."

"Jason?"

"Yeah, and his father's getting a little nervous about it. 'Look how I turned out,' I told him. As soon as I could I moved to the Village and tried to get a girlfriend from every country."

"Wearing their national costumes."

"I don't think I ever had an Anatrurian doll," she said, "or an Anatrurian girlfriend, either, since I

never even heard of the country until you started going to the movies with Ilona. I had a couple of dolls
from that part of the world, though, with peasant
blouses and lots of embroidery on their skirts. Beautiful faces, too."

"Don't remind me."

"I'm sorry, Bern. Look, Ilona's from Anatruria and
she had a picture of the king and queen. How does
that tie her in with Candlemas and Hoberman and
Tiglath Whatchamacallit—"

"Rasmoulian."

"If you say so. And Sarnoff."

"Tsarnoff."

"Tso? I still don't see the connection."

"Neither did I. It wasn't until last night that it hit
me. I was in the cab, and Max Fiddler was telling
me this incredible story about a woman and her dis-
gusting pet monkey. I didn't tell you, did I?"

"No."

"Well, I'm not going to. Before that he went on
and on about his memory and how great it was, and
maybe that planted a seed and got me thinking about
memory, I don't know. But just as we got to my
apartment building, I remembered. That's why I had
him bring me back downtown again."

"I thought you wanted to see me."

"I did," I said, "but I probably would have waited
until morning. Or I would have gone upstairs first
and put my things away and then come downtown
on the subway." I patted my pockets. "I've still got
my picks and my flashlight," I said. "Well, that's just
as well. I may need them."

"Bern, what was it you remembered?"

"The photograph."

"The one of King—"

"Vlados," I supplied. "Right. I thought I recognized it from the stamps. But I didn't."

"You didn't? But you checked in the Scott catalog, and there he was, big as life and twice as ugly."

"Not ugly at all," I said. "He's a good-looking man. Or was, because he'd have to be a hundred and ten by now. But one thing he certainly wasn't in the stamp catalog was big. The pictures are tiny. I had to use a magnifying glass to make sure it was the same person I saw in the photograph."

"So?"

"So the point is I recognized him from another photograph, and *that* was what triggered the memory."

"What other photo? The one of Ilona with her mother and her father?" Her mouth dropped open. "Bern, is it the Anatrurian version of Anastasia? Is Ilona a long-lost princess? Bern!"

"What is it?"

"Don't you see? That explains why she packed up and disappeared. She's in love with you, Bern."

"That would explain it, all right."

"No," she said, impatient. "Don't you get it? She can't marry you because you're a commoner!" She got a faraway look in her eye. "Maybe she'll abdicate, like the Duke of Windsor, giving up the Anatrurian throne for the man she loves. Why are you looking at me like that, Bern? It's possible, isn't it?"

"No."

"It's not?"

"I don't think so. I don't think she's a princess, either, any more than that apartment was Buckingham Palace. Ilona's father didn't look anything like Vlados the First. They're two different guys."

"Oh."

"The photo I'm talking about," I said, "was the one at the Boccaccio."

"At the Boccaccio?" Light dawned. "In the apartment you burgled!"

"Tried to burgle."

"There was a photo of a guy in a uniform. And it was him? Vlad the Unveiler?"

"I didn't spend a lot of time looking at the photograph," I admitted. "At the time I didn't notice much besides his teeth and the way he combed his hair. It was parted in the middle and slicked down."

"He sounds like a dreamboat."

"And his uniform," I said. "I noticed his uniform. He looked like a member of the palace guard in a Sigmund Romberg operetta. That was before I went to Ilona's apartment, and there was something faintly familiar about the guy, but I just thought he looked like Teddy Roosevelt would have looked if he was going on a date with a flapper. Then the next night I saw Ilona's photo and I knew I'd seen the guy somewhere before. But I wasn't thinking of the photo from the Boccaccio, not consciously. I don't know, maybe Max Fiddler's right. Maybe I ought to start taking ginkgo biloba."

"If you can remember to buy it," she said, "you don't need it."

"Good point. Anyway, when I saw Ilona's photo Thursday night it rang a bell, and I didn't know why. Last night it finally came to me."

"And you couldn't wait to get downtown with the news. Except you forgot to tell me."

"I had other things to tell you. And the reason I was in a rush to come downtown, well, I didn't want to go into my own building."

"Why not?"

"I had a feeling somebody might be waiting there for me."

"Who?"

"I don't know."

"You don't mean Ilona. You mean somebody dangerous."

I nodded. "I already had a gun pulled on me. I snapped at Rasmoulian to behave himself and put it away, and damned if he didn't. But how many times can you get away with that? The next time around he might shoot me. How did he know to come to the bookstore? He even knew my middle name, for God's sake."

"Is he Anatrurian, too, Bern?"

"I don't know what he is. Rasmoulian sounds as though it could be Armenian. And Tiglath might be Assyrian."

"Assyrian? You mean like from Assyria? Is that a country?"

"Not recently," I said. "Remember 'The Assyrian came down like a wolf on the fold'? It's a poem, but that's the only line I remember. I think the king of ancient Assyria was Tiglath-Pileser. But I might have him confused with somebody else."

"How do you know all this, Bern? Did Tiggy happen to have his picture on a stamp?"

I shook my head. "Will Durant wrote about him, but I forget what he said. You read that stuff and it's all very interesting, but then you put the book down and it all runs together. I think Tiglath-Pileser kicked a lot of ass back in ancient times, but then most of them did."

"And you think Tiglath Rasmoulian is named after him?"

"Jesus, I don't know. Maybe he changed his name from Caphob. Maybe he's planning on opening a restaurant called Two Guys From Nineveh."

"Nineveh?"

"That was the big city in Assyria. I think." I stood up. "You know what the trouble is? I know all this crap, or half know it, everything from scraps of poetry to the capital of South Dakota, but I don't know any of the important stuff, like what the hell's going on. One man's been stabbed to death and another man stuck a gun in my face and I went and fell in love with a beautiful woman just hours before she disappeared without a trace, and all I know is the name of a city in Assyria, and I'm not even sure if I'm right. What are you doing?"

"I'm looking in the dictionary," she said. "How do you spell it, anyway? Never mind, I found it. 'Nineveh, a capital of Assyria, the ruins of which are located on the Tigris River, opposite Mosul.' Do you want me to look up Mosul?"

"What for?"

"I don't know. Mosul, Mosul, Mosul. Where are you, Mosul? Ah. 'Mosul, a city in northern Iraq, on the Tigris opposite Nineveh.' Maybe Tiglath got his name from the Tigris."

"That's the whole problem in a nutshell," I said. "We've got a million questions and we're looking for the answers in stamp catalogs and dictionaries. I'm not going to find out what's in that portfolio by looking in a book, and I'm not going to catch Hoberman's killer by browsing in a library."

"I know," she said, "but you have to start somewhere, Bern. Don't you?"

"I have to start with a person," I said, "but I don't know how to find any of them. Ilona disappeared. So did Hugo Candlemas. Hoberman's dead. Who does that leave?"

"How about Tiggy?"

"Rasmoulian? He gave me a card, but there was nothing on it but his name."

"Maybe he's in the book."

"Which book? The stamp catalog or the dictionary?"

"The phone book."

"Fat chance," I said, but I went and looked anyway, and he wasn't listed.

"Speaking of fat . . ."

"Tsarnoff," I said. "The fat man. But I don't know his first name."

"How many Tsarnoffs can there be, Bern?"

"Good point," I said, and checked. There weren't

any, which saved having to call them all and try to guess their weight over the phone.

"I bet there are plenty of Sarnoffs," Carolyn said.

"Rasmoulian was very adamant about the *Tsss* sound. But maybe the fat man spells it with a Z." I looked, and there weren't any Tzarnoffs, either.

Carolyn said, "Who else is there? The two burglars? We don't know their names. You said a man and a woman, huh?"

"They made love."

"It could still be a man and woman. Maybe it was the guy who lived there and his girlfriend. Did you think of that?"

"Yes."

"You did?"

"Sure. It would explain how they happened to have a key. Maybe they weren't burglars at all, maybe the guy suddenly got the urge to check his portfolio in the middle of the night. Maybe that's the kind of guy he is."

"Who is he, anyway, Bern?"

"Good question."

"Candlemas didn't tell you?"

"Candlemas didn't tell me anything. He told me what a good friend he was of Abel Crowe's, and he told me how I'd pick up five thousand dollars, or maybe a lot more, for an hour's work, and that's pretty much all he told me. Can you believe I risked a felony arrest on the basis of that little information?"

"Frankly," she said, "no. Bernie, we just went through the list and drew nothing but blanks. I know you want to do something about Hoberman's death—"

"He was my partner," I said. "I'm supposed to do something about it."

"Whatever you say. The thing is, there's no place to start."

"Weeks," I said suddenly.

"Weeks?"

"Hoberman knew him," I said. "That's why I needed Hoberman, because he knew Weeks, who lived in the building. Weeks doesn't have anything to do with it, but maybe he can tell me something about Hoberman."

I reached for the phone book again. I didn't know his first name, but I knew his address on Park Avenue, and there weren't that many Weekses listed to start with. His first name turned out to be Charles.

I dialed his number, and when he answered I said, "Mr. Weeks? Sir, my name is Bill Thompson, and I met you very briefly several nights ago in the company of a Captain Hoberman." It took him a minute to place me, but then he remembered. "I need to talk to you," I said. "I wonder if you could give me perhaps fifteen minutes of your time." He hesitated, and said he hoped I wasn't selling anything, or soliciting for some fund-raising effort, however worthwhile it might be. "I'm not," I assured him. "I'm in a pickle, Mr. Weeks, and you may be able to help me. I'll come to your apartment, if that's all right. Good. In half an hour, say, or forty-five minutes at the outside? Very good. And it's Bill Thompson."

I hung up. Carolyn said, "Bill Thompson?"

"I'll explain later. I've got to get going. Do I look all right to go over there?"

"You look fine."

I brushed a hand across my cheek. "It wouldn't hurt me to shave," I said.

"It will if you use my razor. You look fine, Bern, and you're not going to ask the guy for a job, are you? Anyway, you haven't got time to shave. Let's go."

"You're not coming, are you?"

"I'm not staying home," she said. "Remember what you said? When your partner gets killed, you're supposed to do something about it. Well, when your best friend's up a creek, you're supposed to help."

"I guess it won't hurt anything," I said. "I told Weeks I was coming. I didn't mention that anybody would be with me."

We were in the hallway, and she turned to lock up. "Relax, Bern," she said. "I'm not coming to the Boccaccio with you. That wouldn't be any help. I'd just get in the way."

"Then where are you going?"

"To your store," she said. "Remember Raffles? Somebody's got to feed him."

THIRTEEN

"Mr. Thompson," Charles Weeks said. "I remember you now. I didn't get more than a glimpse of you the other night, and I couldn't picture you in my mind. I wasn't sure I'd recognize you, but of course I do. Come right in, won't you? And tell me how you know Cap Hoberman, and why you think I can be of help to you."

I'd had a clear picture of him in my mind, but I don't know if I'd have recognized him if I'd passed him in the street. The other night he'd been in shirtsleeves and suspenders and wearing a homburg, and this morning he'd left the hat on the shelf and was wearing a Hawaiian shirt over white cotton trousers and espadrilles. He was bald now except for a gray fringe. I suppose he'd been every bit as bald the other night, but the hat had concealed it.

"If you'd called five minutes earlier," he said, "you would have missed me. I have a cup of coffee upon rising, and then I walk for an hour, or close to it. On the way home I pick up my newspaper, and I read it with my breakfast. I used to have it delivered and read it with my coffee, but I found I'd never get out

the door for my walk. This morning I was just breaking an egg when you called."

His eyes were on me as he nattered away, and I
sensed he was watching me carefully. "So your timing was excellent," he went on, "but for all I know
you called more than once, because I don't have an
answering machine. I'm retired, you see, and I don't
get that many calls, and few of them are terribly urgent. A disheartening percentage of the ones I do get
are to advise me that someone of my acquaintance
has died, and you can't leave that sort of news on an
answering machine, can you?" He smiled gently. "At
least I couldn't, although I'm sure there are people
who can. There's coffee, but I'm afraid it's the sort
with the caffeine left in it, and I must warn you it's
rather strong."

"That's the way I like it."

"I'll just be a moment."

He went off to the kitchen and left me in a room
comfortably outfitted with traditional furniture, everything showing wear but nothing shabby. It could
have been a room in the house I grew up in. There
were books in a revolving oak bookcase, the titles
running to history and biography. The only art on the
walls was an impressionistic landscape in oils in a
simple gallery frame.

The coffee was as advertised, almost strong
enough to walk on. I expressed approval and he nodded with satisfaction.

"My doctor told me he doesn't want me to drink
strong coffee," he said, "and I told him he could go
to hell. I'm a widower, I've no children, and my life's

work is done. Drinking strong coffee is as close as I come to having a bad habit, and I'll be damned if I'll change it just so I can outlive a few more of my old friends. You're William Thompson, or do you prefer Bill?"

"Bill is fine."

"And if I remember correctly you said you lived here in the building, although I can't recall seeing you before. Of course it's a large building."

"Yes."

"And you had the chap on the desk call up and announce you, although you could have dropped by unannounced, since I was already expecting you. That was courteous of you. Was that Ramón on the desk, or Sandy?"

Something in his eyes warned me. "I couldn't say," I said. "I don't live here at the Boccaccio, Mr. Weeks."

"But you did thus introduce yourself the other night, did you not? Or is my memory at fault?"

His memory was as good as ginkgo. "I'm afraid I told an untruth," I said.

"I don't suppose that's anything like a lie, is it?"

I felt as though I ought to have my mouth washed out with soap. "It is," I said, "and I'm afraid it's not the only one I told."

"Oh?"

"I'm not an old friend of Captain Hoberman's. We met for the first time less than an hour before I introduced myself to you."

"And this was a stratagem to make my acquaintance?"

"No, sir. I wouldn't have met you at all if things had gone according to plan. When Hoberman and I got off the elevator, it was my intention to get to the staircase before he rang your bell."

"What went wrong?"

"The elevator operator was watching."

"So you had to appear to be visiting me. But you had business elsewhere in the building."

"Yes."

"What sort of business, if you don't mind my asking?"

"I'm a security specialist," I said. "I'd been enlisted to pay a visit to an unoccupied apartment."

"In the Boccaccio? I didn't realize that there were any unoccupied apartments here."

"Unoccupied that evening."

He considered this. "In other words, the tenants were not at home. And you had been provided with a key?"

"Not exactly."

"Then you must be a man who doesn't require one. Don't hang your head. There's no shame in being in possession of a skill, even one that's so often put to a bad use. By God, is that the only reason Cappy Hoberman came over here? So that he could get you into the building?"

"I'm sure he was delighted to visit you," I said, "but—"

"I wondered what all that was about," he said. "Cappy's not made for deception, never was. Very much a meat-and-potatoes fellow."

"Tobacco and vodka, too."

"Indeed. I had a call from him just a day or two before you both came over. I was astonished to hear from him, hadn't had any word of or from him in years. Didn't actually know if he was alive or dead." He paused, his eyes probing. "Wanted to see me, he said. Well, I've nothing but time these days. I looked forward to an hour or so of talk about the old days. Wednesday night, he proposed. Late, around midnight. He hadn't much time to spend in New York, he said, and that was the only time he could fit in a visit. I suggested we might meet somewhere for a drink but he wouldn't hear of it, said he might be late, didn't want to leave me stranded. Besides, he had something for me, wanted to bring it to my home." He cocked his head. "I suppose that was all in aid of getting you into the building."

"It must have been."

"A lot of trouble to go through. He had a gift for me, a little mouse. On the table to your left."

It was a little over an inch long and skillfully carved. "It's beautiful," I said. "Ivory?"

"Bone." His gaze was less probing now, and his eyes had a faraway look in them. "I'd seen it before, shortly after it was carved. It was pure white then. It's yellowed with age. 'I saw it in a shop window,' Cappy said, 'and I thought of you. Almost a match for the one the old fellow carved.' Well, it's more than a match for old Letchkov's work, it's the very specimen. I knew that much at a glance, and I didn't believe for a moment that Cappy found it in a shop. When was he ever the sort to go looking in shop windows? But he could hardly have kept it all those years. How on earth had he managed to lay hands on it?" His eyes sought mine. "You don't know what I'm talking about, do you?"

"No."

"How could you? We knew each other many years ago, Cappy Hoberman and I. Along with Wood, of course, and Rennick and Bateman. The five of us were known back Stateside as the Bob and Charlie Show. Rennick and Bateman were both named Robert, you see, and the rest of us were all Charles. Working together, we had to modify our names. Alliteration suggested Rob for Rennick and Bob for Bateman. I remained Charles, but Wood became Chuck, which was what he'd been called as a boy. And we called Hoberman Cappy."

"Because he was a captain?"

"Ha! All he ever captained was his college football team. He had the air of a leader, that's all. And we didn't have ranks. We weren't military. Officially, we didn't exist." He took a sip of coffee. "These are ancient cats I'm letting out of the bag. I can't think anyone would care at this late date. The Cold War's over, isn't it? I don't know that we've won it, but the other side does seem to have lost. Or at least to have wandered off the playing field."

"When was this?"

"Oh, ages ago. When was Masaryk killed in Czechoslovakia? You wouldn't remember, but I ought to. 1948? Our little adventure began the year after that. My God, I was only a boy. I thought I was a grown man, I thought I was mature beyond my years, but I must have been callow beyond sufferance."

"And you were in Czechoslovakia?"

"Why would you think that? Oh, because I mentioned Masaryk. No, we were south and east of Czechoslovakia. We were in the Balkans, mostly. Slipping across borders, exchanging code words in cafés and back alleys. We thought it was a game, and we believed what we were doing was very much in the national interest. And I daresay we were wrong on both counts."

"What did you do?"

"Raised people's hopes and risked their lives, and risked our own as well." He was silent for a moment, thinking about it. "None of it matters now," he said, "and it can't have much to do with your recent visit, can it?"

"I think it does."

"How, for God's sake? It was almost half a century ago. Most of those people are dead."

"Let me ask you this," I said. "Were you ever in a country called Anatruria?"

"Sweet Christ," he said. "That's no country. Before Garibaldi and the Risorgimento, they used to say that Italy was just a geographical expression. Anatruria wasn't even that."

"They had a king, didn't they?"

"Old Vlados? I'm not sure if he ever set foot inside his own purported realm. They proclaimed independence around the time of the Treaty of Versailles, you know, but it seems to me they did so from a distance. By the time I heard mention of Anatruria it was three decades later and Vlados was an old man living where you'd expect him to be, in Franco's

Spain or Salazar's Portugal, I can't remember which. Anatrurian independence was an idea whose time had come and gone. No one gave it a thought, no one outside of a handful of ethnocentric lunatics who'd been marrying their cousins for a few generations too many."

"And the five of you?"

"And the five of us, the Bob and Charlie Show. We were supposed to foment a rebellion. Now who could have thought that was a good idea? Or a feasible one?" He shook his head. "A few years later I was back in the States, out of the game. And there was an uprising in Hungary, students hurling Molotov cocktails, trying to take out Russian tanks with bottles of gasoline. The rabbit died there."

"The rabbit?"

"Bob Bateman. We all had animal code names. I was the mouse, of course. That's why Cappy brought me the little carving, though how he laid hands on it is something else again. Bateman was the rabbit. Well, he looked a little like a rabbit, didn't he? A rabbity face, a rabbity nose, a rabbit's timid manner, although there was nothing timid about him when the chips were down. *I* didn't look much like a mouse, but it was somebody's contention that I was shy in a presumably mouselike fashion. I don't think I was shy, but I may have been."

"What about Hoberman?"

"He was the ram, putting his head down and charging straight ahead. Playing college football, I imagine he ran every play right into the middle of the line. Rob Rennick had a sly feline quality, so he was the cat. And you ought to be able to guess Charles Wood's code name."

"The elephant," I said.

"The elephant? Why an elephant, for heaven's sake?"

"Never forgets," I said. "Keeps his trunk packed. I never met the man, so why would you think I'd be able to guess his code name?"

"Ah, well. It will become instantly obvious when I say it. His was the only code name with purely verbal origins. His name was Chuck Wood and his code name was the woodchuck. I can't say he bore any physical resemblance to the animal, but there was a patient but obdurate quality to his work. He would just gnaw away at something forever until he carried the day."

"And the carvings?"

"A man named Letchkov made them. That's a Bulgarian name. He was Bulgarian, like most of them in that crowd, although to call him that was tantamount to challenging him to a duel. He would insist he was Anatrurian. Letchkov was an old man then, so he'd be long since dead. An animal for each of the five of us, and there were others in the series, too. A pig, a goat, some I can't recall. Some of the Anatrurian activists, you see, had animal code names of their own."

"What became of the carvings?"

"They stayed behind in Anatruria, if you want to call it that. Or at least I assumed they did. My little mouse seems to have found a way to cross the water. A long way for a little mouse to swim."

"If it's the same mouse."

"It would surprise me greatly," he said, "to learn that it was not. But I've talked far too long about a closed chapter of my life, Mr. Thompson, and while I don't suppose I've compromised national security at this late date, I think I'll give you a chance to tell me how our actions in Anatruria could possibly have linked you with Cappy Hoberman, and brought you into this building."

"There's a young woman I've been seeing," I said. "She's Anatrurian, and—"

"What's her name?"

"Ilona Markova."

"That sounds Bulgarian, and could be Anatrurian."

"She told me she was Anatrurian," I said, "and she had a map of Eastern Europe on her wall with the borders of Anatruria outlined in red. And a photograph of Vlados and Liliana in a place of honor in her apartment."

"Liliana," he said. "That was the queen, all right. I'd forgotten her name. Did your friend tell you how Liliana died?"

"She didn't even tell me who the two people were. How did Liliana die?"

"In a car crash in the south of France a year or so before the outbreak of the Second World War. Vlados was badly injured but survived. It was an article of faith among Anatrurian separatists that the car was ambushed by agents of IMRO."

"IMRO?"

"The Internal Macedonian Revolutionary Organization, and God knows that sort of thing was their

style, but would they waste time assassinating the
pretender to the mythical throne of a nonexistent nation? My guess is that Vlados was drunk. Or his
chauffeur was, if he had one." He'd been looking
across the room at the landscape on the far wall.
Now he swung his eyes around to me. "How'd you
know it was them? Vlados and Liliana?"

"From the stamps."

"The stamps? Oh, of course! The Anatrurians we
worked with talked about the stamp issue, as if a
printing press in Budapest could somehow have established the legitimacy of their cause. I don't know
that any of them had actually seen any of the elusive
stamps. You don't own a set, do you? I understand
they're quite scarce."

I explained about the illustrations in the Scott catalog.

"All right," he said. "A friend of yours is Anatrurian, and would seem to regard herself as a loyal
subject of Vlados the One and Only. There must be
more to explain your interest."

"She's disappeared."

"I see. Utterly?"

"Without a trace."

"What ties her to the Boccaccio? Was it her idea
you break into an apartment here?"

"No."

"Which apartment? Who lives there?"

"Apartment Eight-B, and I don't know who lives
there. But he's another Anatrurian."

"And how do you know that?"

"He had a photo of Vlados."

"You're serious? Yes, I can see you are. The same photo? The same pose, I mean to say, not the same physical object."

"A different photo. He's alone in this one, and he's wearing a uniform."

"The royals love military dress," he said, "especially when they haven't got a country to go with the uniform. You did enter the apartment, then. You must have, in order to have seen the photo."

"Yes."

"And left with what you'd gone to get?"

"No. I was interrupted," I said, and explained how I'd hid in the closet, emerging to find the portfolio gone.

"You must still have been trapped there when Cappy left. He didn't stay any time at all. I'd expected a longish visit, but I'd guess he was in and out of here in ten minutes. For my part, I can't say I pressed him to stay. His presence brought up memories, not all of them welcome. His gift had much the same effect. The mouse. I always thought it the best of Letchkov's carvings, but that may have been because it was mine. My code name, I mean. Now the actual carving's mine, isn't it, and I'm glad to have it, but I find I care less and less about possessions with each passing year. What's happened to Cappy?"

The question caught me off-balance, but I didn't have to hesitate. I'd known it was coming sooner or later and had made up my mind how I was going to answer it.

"He's dead," I said. "Somebody killed him."

FOURTEEN

"This man Candlemas," Charles Weeks said. "It would seem obvious that he killed Cappy, wouldn't it? But why leave the body in his own apartment?"

We were in his kitchen, sitting at an oval pine table and drinking more of his coffee. Once I'd told him about Hoberman there didn't seem to be any reason not to tell him the rest of it.

"Unless," he went on, "he didn't expect it to be found."

"It would have been hard to overlook," I said. "The way I heard it, it was right in the middle of the room."

"Bleeding into the carpet."

"Right."

"And writing a truncated form of his own name on an attaché case."

"Yes."

"Specifically, your attaché case, though I don't imagine there was any significance in his choice of a writing surface. It was very likely the only thing at hand. I wonder if the murder was just as impulsive a choice."

"What do you mean?"

"If I were Candlemas," he said, "and you were Cappy Hoberman, and I wanted to kill you, I wouldn't snatch up a knife and have at you right in the middle of my own living room. But suppose I wasn't planning to kill you. Suppose I was suddenly presented with a strong motive for wishing you dead and a means for achieving it. Suppose time was very much of the essence. Awkward or not, inconvenient or not, I couldn't afford to wait."

"Hoberman was here," I said.

"For ten minutes, fifteen at the outside."

"When he left here, he probably went straight back to Seventy-sixth Street. I was going to be bringing the portfolio there directly, so he must have wanted to be there when I arrived."

"But well before you could arrive, Candlemas struck him down. To avoid splitting the take, even before there was any take on hand to split?" He waved a hand, dismissing the question. "We don't need to know the reason. It was a sudden and urgent one, so that Candlemas felt obliged to do what he would have greatly preferred to do at another time and in another place. In his own residence, and with you likely to appear at any moment, he plunged a knife into his fellow."

"And left him there."

"Left him to write his last words, quite as mysterious as the only trace of the original colonial settlement at Roanoke Island. They'd all utterly disappeared, you know, and they'd left the word CROATOAN carved in a tree trunk, and no one's ever been able to make head or tail out of it. What could they possibly have meant? And what could Cappy have meant by CAPHOB, and why did Candlemas let him write it?"

"If somebody other than Candlemas killed him, it still doesn't figure that he'd go away and leave the dying message behind."

"No," he agreed, "it doesn't. But if it was Candlemas, he'd have a problem."

"I'll say. The problem would be lying right in the middle of his living room."

"Exactly. What would he do about it?"

"He'd have to get rid of it."

"How? Cappy was still a big man. Was Candlemas a huge brute, capable of slinging Cappy over his shoulder and carrying him downstairs?"

"Hardly. He was no more than medium height, and slightly built."

"Not a weight lifter, certainly."

"No."

"Well, what was he going to do? What would you do in his position?"

"Me?"

"Yes, you. Suppose you found yourself with a dead body on your hands. It's not like a stain on the wall, you can't hide it by throwing a coat of paint over it. How are you going to get rid of it?"

"Actually," I said, "I had that happen once."

"Oh?"

"In my store," I said quickly, "and I had nothing to

do with it, but all the same I had to get the body out of there. I rented a wheelchair."

"That was damned clever," Weeks said admiringly. "Hard to manage in the middle of the night, however, and not terribly useful anyway on the fourth floor of a walk-up."

"No."

"Nothing for it, then. You'd have to make several trips."

"How's that?"

"Unpleasant subject," he said, "but there's no way around it, is there? You'd cut the corpse into manageable segments and carry them out one at a time, disposing of them wherever your ingenuity might suggest."

"An arm here, a leg there. But Captain Hoberman wasn't missing any pieces when the cops got there. Otherwise I'm sure they would have mentioned it."

"Your Mr. Candlemas wouldn't have begun the operation yet," he said gently. "He'd need tools, wouldn't he? And wouldn't have them lying around unless he made a habit of this sort of thing. He'd need a saw or an ax or both. The average suburban householder might have such tools close at hand, but not the average New York apartment dweller."

"So he goes out in the middle of the night looking for a meat saw?"

"That's a point. He can't have expected to find a restaurant supply outlet open at that hour. But a restaurant would be another matter. Perhaps he knows a friendly chef who will lend him the necessary items with no questions asked. Or perhaps he does own a heavy-duty knife equal to the task, and goes out to buy some stout plastic bags and tape to seal them up. He's out of his apartment, poor Cappy's stretched out on the floor, and you're still stuck in a closet on the eighth floor."

"And the cops turn up, roust the super, and wind up waiting around for a locksmith to open the door for them."

"What brought the police in the first place? An anonymous call?"

"That's what Ray Kirschmann said. Somebody heard a noise."

"Hmmm. Candlemas comes home, I suppose, and sees that there are people in his apartment, or on the landing waiting for the locksmith. So what does he do?"

"Gets all the money he can out of his bank's ATM," I said, "and jumps ship for Australia, determined to make a new life for himself. Because he's never been heard from since."

"That's true, he hasn't. Why hasn't he contacted you, do you suppose? As far as he knows, you got out of Eight-B with the portfolio. Wouldn't he want to collect it?"

"Maybe he tried. Maybe he sent somebody."

"The fellow with the unusual name?"

"They've all got unusual names," I said. "I never ran in to this many people with unusual names outside of a Ross Thomas novel. But if you mean Tiglath Rasmoulian, yes, Candlemas could have sent him. He wouldn't want to show himself because the cops think they've got him neatly filed away at the morgue. In fact, when Rasmoulian came to my store, I hadn't gone yet to identify the body."

"So if Candlemas had walked into your store on his own—"

"I'd have thought I was seeing a ghost. Maybe Candlemas did send him. Who else knows I'm involved?"

"If there's one thing I learned over there," he said, waving a hand in what I suppose must have been the general direction of Europe, "it's that more people know something than you would suspect. Information leaks out, you see. People play multiple roles. Very little remains a secret."

"Candlemas walked into my store Tuesday, and the following night I committed illegal entry at about the same time that he was committing homicide. By Friday afternoon, Tiglath Rasmoulian knew enough about me to come into my shop and point a gun at me. For God's sake, he even knew my middle name."

"Grimes."

"Right. Now what time was there for word to get around? The only two people who knew I was involved were Candlemas and Hoberman, and Hoberman was dead."

"Aren't you forgetting the girl?"

"Ilona."

"Of course."

After a moment I said, "I thought of that myself. That she didn't walk into my shop by accident. It's too much of a coincidence otherwise. But all we ever did was go to the movies, and all we ever talked about was what we'd just seen on the screen. If she was setting me up, she was taking her time about it. And then, when she had me ready to slay dragons, or at least jump through hoops for her, she disappeared. I don't get it."

"It's puzzling. But then the Anatrurians are a puzzling people."

"Evidently."

"Candlemas is puzzling enough to be Anatrurian. Did he have an accent?"

I shook my head. "He spoke educated American English. I'd guess he was born here, though not necessarily in New York. His name certainly doesn't sound Anatrurian."

"He sounds like the sort of fellow who could have had many names over the course of a lifetime. Candlemas would be English. It's a church holiday, you know. In the winter, if I'm not mistaken, after Twelfth Night but well before Lent. It celebrates the purification of the Virgin Mary and the presentation of the infant Christ in the temple. Early in the year, probably so many days before or after a new moon. Hugo Candlemas—perhaps it is indeed the name he was born with. It would be an odd one to invent."

"Names," I said. "Candlemas, Tsarnoff, Rasmoulian. All I've got is a batch of names and nothing to go with them. Maybe I should drop the whole thing."

"Why don't you?" he said. "You don't have a great investment. A night's work went for nothing, but I suspect that must happen now and then in your line of work."

"More than now and then," I said.

"I can understand your infatuation with the woman. But she would seem to have disappeared voluntarily. Have you any reason to suspect she's in danger? Or in need of your assistance?"

"No. And if she wants to see me again I'm not that hard to find."

"Exactly." He leaned forward, eyes bright. "It can't be hope of profit, can it? Since you don't know who has the portfolio or even what's in it, you can't be counting on it to make you rich. The police aren't after you, so you don't need to solve the crime in order to clear yourself. So why don't you go back to selling books and breaking into people's houses?"

"I feel committed," I said.

"Just that, then. You feel committed, irrespective of the illogic of it all, and without regard to the consequences. You're in all the way, and devil take the hindmost."

"I guess it sounds pretty stupid."

"Stupid? By God, my boy, if we'd had a few more like you in Anatruria it might have been a different story." He sat up straight, rubbed his hands together. "I have some ideas," he said. "It's been a while, but I'm not entirely without experience in these matters."

He drew lines and circles on his note pad as he talked, suggesting avenues of approach, clarifying what we did and didn't know so far. I didn't see the point of the lines and circles, but his thinking was right on target.

"This is great," I said at length, "but I'm taking up far too much of your time, and—"

"My time? You'll be taking up far more of it before

we've seen this through to the end. If you're committed, so am I."

"But why? I mean, you're not remotely involved, so—"

"I don't know if this will make any sense to you," he said evenly. "But there was a time when Cappy Hoberman and I worked together as if our lives depended upon it, as indeed they did. I hadn't seen him in years, I'd lost all contact with him, and when he turned up with that mouse like a Greek bearing gifts it turned out that we didn't have a great deal to say to each other. Whatever we'd once been to another, a vast stretch of years had passed. There was all that water under the bridge, or over the dam, or wherever it goes.

"Water." He snorted. "If we'd been kin, I'd say that blood was thicker than water. But we were something else. We were partners in an enterprise, and that slender fact puts me under an obligation. I don't expect you to understand this. I'm sure it's hopelessly old-fashioned." He sat up straighter, raised his voice a notch. "But when your partner is killed, you're supposed to do something about it. It doesn't matter how you felt about him, or what sort of man he was. He was your partner, and you're supposed to do something about it."

I looked at him. "Mr. Weeks," I said, "this could be the start of a beautiful friendship."

"Indeed it could," he said, and reached to pump my hand. "Indeed it could. But let's forget Mr. Weeks and Mr. Thompson, shall we? I'll call you Bill, and I'd like you to call me Charlie."

"Uh," I said.

"Is something the matter?"

"Charlie," I said, "there's one more thing I forgot to tell you."

FIFTEEN

"I feel good about this," Charlie Weeks said. "A man needs a purpose in life. He needs a reason to get out of bed in the morning. I think we'll make a good team."

"I think you're right, Charlie."

"I don't understand what's taking so long," he said, and extended a hand toward the elevator call button. I beat him to it. "Give it a good poke this time," he urged. "Maybe the connection's worn."

"He's probably stuck on another floor," I said, "helping someone with luggage or a key that's stuck in a lock. Listen, there's no reason for you to stand out here in the hall. I'm sure he'll be along in a few minutes."

"Oh, I don't mind," he assured me. But when a few more minutes passed without the elevator's appearing, he shifted his weight from one foot to the other, clearly impatient. "I suppose I could get to work on our project," he said. "If you're sure you won't feel I've abandoned you."

"Please," I said. "I feel guilty wasting your time like this."

The elevator still hadn't come by the time he disappeared into his own apartment and drew the door
shut. I wasn't greatly surprised; the attendant would
have had to be psychic to stop on our floor, as I'd
faked pressing the button. I gave Charlie Weeks another minute, just in case he might remember one
last thing that would send him darting into the hallway again. When he failed to reappear, I took the
stairs down to the eighth floor.

Well, why not? I had my picks with me, never having returned home to unload them the previous evening. When I arranged to drop in on Weeks, I'd had
it in the back of my mind to pay a call downstairs after I'd ended my visit. I hadn't really expected much
from my conversation with Weeks, and was counting
on him as much for entrée to the Boccaccio as for
what he could tell me about Hoberman.

It turned out he'd been able to tell me a lot, and
had wound up enlisting as my partner. And it did
seem like the start of a beautiful friendship, and I
suppose I could have told him I wanted to pay another visit to the fellow four flights below, but I decided to keep it to myself. Otherwise the beautiful
friendship might turn out to be stillborn. Because I
was in Charlie's building, after all, and people with a
very cavalier attitude toward burglary are apt to turn
into law-and-order hard-liners as soon as a burglar
starts operating close to home. After all, I'd met
Charlie the first time under false pretenses, in order
to knock off 8-B, and I'd turned up today flying the
same false colors and with the same goal in mind. I'd
been almost out the door before I'd gotten around to

telling him that I was Bernie Rhodenbarr and not Bill Thompson.

So I'd keep this little venture to myself for the time being. If I came up with some important information, I could pick a convenient moment to tell him when and where I got it. And if I left 8-B as clueless as I entered it, nobody ever had to know I'd been there.

I moved quickly but quietly down the stairs, eased the door open at the eighth-floor landing, assured myself with a glance that the hallway was happily deserted, and walked along it to 8-B.

I didn't have gloves, and I wasn't much concerned about that. I wasn't likely to leave prints, nor was anyone likely to go looking for them. I had my flashlight, although I couldn't see what need I'd have of it in the middle of a bright sunshiny day. I had my picks, too, and I knew they'd open 8-B's locks because they'd done so almost effortlessly the other night.

I didn't need them, either, as it turned out.

But I didn't know that, and I had them in hand as I stood before the door of the apartment in question. I remembered how I'd had the portfolio in hand, only to lose it, and I remembered the time I'd spent in the closet, and the musty smell of the coats. I didn't figure I was going to get another crack at the portfolio, but maybe I could at least find out who lived there, and maybe get another look at the photo while I was there and make sure it was really King Vlados.

I had my hand on the doorknob and the tip of one

of my picks a quarter-inch into the top lock when it
occurred to me to ring the bell. I was sure no one
was home, I just took that for granted, but I reminded myself that this was one of those little professional procedures I never neglected to perform,
and I might as well play this one by the book.

So I rang, and I waited for a moment because that
too is part of the way you do it, and you can just
imagine my surprise when I heard the footsteps approaching the door.

I just had time to get the incriminating evidence
out of the lock and back in my pocket when the door
opened to reveal a young man standing about six-
two, with broad shoulders and a narrow waist and a
handsome, square-jawed, open countenance. He had
a big smile on his face; he may not have had the
faintest idea who I was, but that didn't mean he
wasn't glad to see me.

"Hello," he said heartily. "A beautiful day, yes?"

"Gorgeous," I agreed.

"And how may I help you?"

Good question. "Ah," I said. "I'm Bill Thompson,
and I'm the building's representative for the American Hip Dysplasia Association."

"You are from the building?"

"I live in the building," I explained. "On another
floor. I work on Wall Street, but I volunteered to collect for this charity. Very good cause, as I'm sure you
know."

"Yes," he said, one hand dipping into a pocket of
his jeans. He was wearing black Levi's and a polo
shirt that I'd call blue-green, but that the Lands' End

catalog probably calls teal. "Well, of course I would like to make a donation."

Jesus, maybe I was in the wrong business. "I don't even have my receipt book with me," I said. "That's not what I came to see you about. Let's see now, you'd be James Driscoll, have I got that right?"

He smiled and shook his head.

"No? How can that be?" I dug out my wallet, consulted a slip of paper—one I'd be well advised to hang on to, if I ever wanted to get my shirts back from the Chinese laundry—and looked up at him again. "O'Driscoll," I said. "You're either James O'Driscoll or Elliott Bookspan. Or else I've got the wrong apartment."

"It would seem you have the wrong apartment."

"Well, I'll be. This is Eight-B?"

"It is."

"And your name is—?"

"Not O'Driscoll, I assure you. Or the other either. What was the second name you said?"

What indeed? I had to think a moment myself. "Bookspan," I said.

"Bookspan," he agreed. "No, not that either."

"Well, hell," I said, and shook my head and clucked my tongue. "I guess you'd be a better judge of that than I. Man's a good bet to know his own name. Obviously I copied down the apartment number wrong, and I'm sorry to bother you."

"It's no trouble."

What did I have to do to get a name out of him? Or a look around his apartment? Tentatively I said, "I don't suppose I could use your phone?"

Another smile, another shake of the head. "I'm so sorry," he said, "but that would be awkward. I have company."

"Oh, I see."

"Ordinarily it would be my pleasure, but—"

"I understand. Say no more."

"Well," he said.

"Well," I said. "Again, my name's Bill Thompson"— and what's yours, you idiot?—"and I'm very sorry to have disturbed you."

"Please. There is no need for apology."

"That's damned decent of you," I said, "and I hope you'll be just as gracious a couple of days from now when I come around again to ask you for a donation."

"Ah," he said, and went for his pocket again, this time coming up with a black morocco billfold. He reached in and drew out a twenty.

"That's damned generous of you," I said, "but I wasn't planning on collection today. I don't have my receipts with me."

"I won't need a receipt. And this will save you a visit next week." And would save him an interruption, but that he left unsaid.

"Well . . ."

"Please," he said.

I reached for the bill but did not let my fingers close around it. "I'm supposed to give you a receipt," I said. "I suppose I could put it in the mail. At any rate, I need your name for the records."

"Of course," he said. "It's Todd."

"Good to meet you, Todd. And your last name?"

"No, no. Todd is the last name."

"Well, it's certainly not O'Driscoll or Bookspan, is it?" We chuckled at that one, and I asked him his first name.

"Michael," he said.

"Michael Todd. The same name as—"

"As the filmmaker, yes."

"I bet you get that all the time, jokers asking you what it was like being married to Elizabeth Taylor."

"Not so much," he said. "After all, it is not an uncommon name."

"Hell, neither's mine. When I think of the number of Bill Thompsons in the world—"

"Yes," he said, "and now I really must not keep you any longer, Mr. Thompson."

"Michael," a woman called from deep within the apartment. "What is taking so long? Is anything the matter?"

"One moment," he called to her. He gave me a smile that was not so much sheepish as goaty. "You see?" he said. "I really must say good day now. Thank you again."

For what? But I nodded and smiled while he closed the door, and then stood there for another few seconds, taking it all in, thinking it all over. Then I walked to the nearest stairwell and headed up to the twelfth floor again. It struck me that it would be just my luck to run into Charlie Weeks in the hallway, and I tried to figure out what to tell him. I couldn't pretend I'd spent all that time waiting for the elevator, or he'd be on the phone in a flash, wanting to

know what the hell had gone wrong with the
Boccaccio's vaunted white-glove service.

I'd tell him the truth, I decided, but I'd amend it
a little. I'd say that I did spend a long time waiting
for the elevator, and at length decided to have a look-
see on Eight. And should I tell him the fellow had
been home? No, I'd say nobody was home, and that
I'd decided against letting myself in. Or maybe I
should say—

But I didn't have to say anything. The elevator
came, the doors opened, the attendant and I beamed
at each other, and I went down and out.

It was a beautiful day, by God, just as Michael
Todd—not the film producer—had said it was. I
walked two blocks west to the park, bought a hot dog
and a kasha knish from a vendor, and found a bench
to sit on. It seemed like a good enough venue for
thought, and I had some things to think about.

First of all, the woman hadn't called him Michael.
She'd said something that sounded more like
Mikhail.

Second, I'd recognized her voice.

I walked across Central Park, pausing at the zoo to
watch the polar bear. He'd had a lot of press recently
because someone had noticed that he was swimming
an endless series of figure eights in his pool. This
made a lot of people anxious, and there was specu-
lation that his behavior was neurotic at best, and
possibly cause for considerable concern. Various
experts blamed various elements—his close confine-
ment, his diet, his yearning for female companion-

ship, his irritation at being observed so closely, his sense of alienation at not being observed closely enough, his lack of engaging reading material. The immediate result of all of this media attention was that the bear got visitors like never before, and pleased everybody by continuing to put four and four together. "He's doing it," they would announce, and he'd keep on doing it, and finally they'd go away and others would take their place. "He's doing it!" the new ones would cry, whereupon he'd do it some more.

I watched, and sure enough, he was doing it. I felt he was making a hell of a good job of it, too. If you were going to swim a number, it seemed to me that eight was definitely the one to go with. Two and four and five were altogether too tricky, and even seven was getting complicated these days, with so many people crossing it in the European fashion. For day-in-day-out swimming, the only real alternative to eight was zero, and then you'd just be going around in circles.

So I didn't know what the hell they wanted from the poor bear. In an easier town—Decatur, say—people would be proud of a bear that could swim any number at all. But New Yorkers are a demanding lot. If our bear started churning out 314159, people would wonder what kind of a moron he was, unable to work out π beyond five decimal places.

Across the park, I stopped at a phone booth and tried Carolyn twice, first at her apartment, then at the Poodle Factory. No answer. I walked on across to

West End and Seventy-first, and I got the same prickly feeling on the nape of my neck that I'd had the night before. Then it had kept me from getting out of Max Fiddler's taxi. Now it led me to stand under an awning on the far corner, doing what I could to observe without being observed.

After ten minutes I was fairly certain my place was staked out, although I couldn't absolutely swear to it. There was a car parked some fifty feet from the front entrance with two men in it, and inside the lobby, where I couldn't see too clearly, there was what might be a man sitting in a chair reading a newspaper. But it could also have been a shadow, and if it was a man that didn't mean he was waiting for me.

Still, why take chances? I circled the block and wound up at the service entrance, which was locked and unattended. Mine is not a high-security building. The doorman, handy for receiving packages and discouraging low-level muggers and prowlers, is hardly the Maginot Line. There's no closed-circuit TV, no electronic security system, and the locks, while decent enough, are a far cry from state-of-the-art. I had opened this one on several occasions, most recently during a stretch when I wasn't getting along with one of the doormen and refused to use the front entrance when he was on duty. That lasted for a couple of weeks, by which time enough other tenants had complained about him that he'd been let go, and good riddance. But the point is that I was pretty good at zipping through that particular lock, and my sang could hardly have been froider at the prospect of opening it, and why not? A cop who caught me in the act might have given me an awkward moment, but not much more than that; after all, it's not illegal entry when you live there.

I took the elevator to the floor above mine out of an excess of paranoia, walked down a flight, and had a look at my own door. It's not the Maginot Line, either, but I've replaced the original locks and added some refinements over the years, so it's reasonably secure.

But it looked as though someone had had a go at it. There were scratches that looked fresh, and someone had mucked about with the jamb, trying to get a purchase with a pry bar. Nothing will keep a person out who is sufficiently determined to get in—a resourceful housebreaker, confronted with an unbreachable door, will simply go through the wall—but whoever had paid me a visit had been unwilling or unable to carry things that far. I let myself in with my keys, reasonably certain no one had entered in my absence, and locked the locks behind me. I checked everything, including my hidey-hole, just to be sure, and everything was fine.

I drew a tub, soaked in it, got out and dried off and lay down on the bed for a minute. I didn't even realize I was tired, but I must have been gone the minute my head touched the pillow. I don't know how long I slept, because I don't know what time I lay down, but when I opened my eyes it was ten after six, and I was sufficiently disoriented that I had to check my calendar watch to be entirely certain it was still that afternoon, not six the following morning.

I called Carolyn and couldn't reach her at home or at work. I put on clean clothes, tossed some other clothes and sundries into a flight bag from a defunct airline, and rode the elevator to the basement. If it had stopped at the lobby floor I might have been able to get a peek at the man with the newspaper, if he was still there, but he might have been able to get a peek at me at the same time, so I guess it was just as well the trip was nonstop. I let myself out through the service entrance, circled the block to avoid the little reception committee in front of the building, and tried to figure out where to go next.

Was I hungry? I'd had a hot dog and a knish a couple of hours back. I didn't really feel like sitting down to a meal, but I felt like eating something. But what?

Of course. What else?

Popcorn.

SIXTEEN

"I think it's so romantic," Carolyn said. "I think it's just about the most romantic thing I ever heard of."

"It wasn't romantic," I said.

"Oh, come on, Bern, how can you even say that? It's incredibly romantic. Night after night, a man goes to the theater all by himself."

"What do you mean, night after night?"

"Last night and tonight, that's night after night." She shook her head at the wonder of it. "Each time he buys two tickets and saves two seats, always in the same location. Each time he gives one of them to the ticket-taker and tells him that a woman may be joining him later."

"And each time he buys the largest-size popcorn," I said. "Don't forget that. And sits there and eats it all himself. You can't beat that for romance."

"Bern, forget the popcorn."

"I wish I could. I've got a husk stuck between two molars and I can't budge it. I just hope it's biodegradable."

"You're just trying to be cynical to hide how ro-

mantic you are." She made a fist, punched me play-
fully on the shoulder. "You son of a gun," she said,
not without admiration. "I didn't know you were going to the movies tonight."

"I hadn't planned on it."

"You just happened to be there when the movie
was about to start. Just the way I happened to be out
in front when it let out the other night, so I could
just happen to catch a glimpse of Ilona."

"In my case it's almost literally true," I said. "I
couldn't reach you, I didn't know what to do with
myself, and I was five minutes from the Musette
with half an hour until curtain. And I asked myself
if I felt like seeing two more Humphrey Bogart films,
and I had to admit the answer was yes."

"So you bought two tickets because it seemed like
the hardheaded and sensible thing to do."

"Maybe that was romantic," I admitted.

"Maybe?"

"To tell you the truth," I said. "I thought there was
a slight possibility she would show up."

"Honestly?"

"If she wanted to get in touch with me," I said,
"that was the way to do it. Obviously I didn't have to
leave a ticket for her. But I figured I could afford it.
I had twenty bucks from her boyfriend."

"Mike Todd?"

"Mikhail," I said, giving the name the full treat-
ment.

"You're positive that was her in his apartment,
Bern?"

"Not necessarily. She could have been in the next apartment, shouting through a hole in the wall."

"You know what I mean. You're sure it was her?"

"Positive."

"Because a lot of women have accents, especially the ones you find hanging out with guys named Mikhail. I mean, what exactly did you have to go by? It's not as if she said 'Bear-naaard.' "

"No, it's as if she said 'Mikhail,' and I'm positive it was her. Unless it just happened to be someone else with great tits and an Anatrurian accent."

"What tits? You didn't get a look at her, so how do you know what kind of tits she had?"

"I've got a good memory for that sort of thing."

"But the girl in Mikhail's apartment—"

"Was Ilona. Trust me on this, will you? I recognized her voice, the pitch, the inflection, the accent, everything. If she'd come to the door I would have recognized the rest of her, tits and all. Okay?"

"Whatever you say, Bern."

"I think it was brilliant of me not to drop my jaw on the floor when I heard her speak up. I just took his twenty dollars and got the hell out of there."

She frowned. "Bern," she said, "I hope you're not planning on keeping that twenty."

"Why not?"

"You got it under false pretenses."

"I get most of my money under false pretenses," I said. "I felt relatively legitimate for a change. He actually handed me the money. Most of the time I take it out of somebody's strongbox."

"This is different, Bern."

"How do you figure that?"

"That money was a donation. If you keep it, you're not stealing it from Mike Toddsky, or whatever you want to call him. You're actually stealing it from the AHDA."

"The what?"

"The American Hip Dysplasia Association. What's the matter? Why are you looking at me like that?"

"Carolyn," I said carefully, "I made that up. I didn't want to pick some popular disease, because for all I knew somebody else in the building had come collecting for it a couple of days ago. So I picked hip dysplasia, because I figured I was safe. There's no such thing as the American Hip Dysplasia Association."

"There most certainly is."

"Oh, come on."

"What do you mean, 'Oh, come on'? The AHDA is leading the fight against the worst canine crippler around. They're sponsoring some of the most important research going on in veterinary medicine."

"You're serious," I said.

"Of course I'm serious. Look, Bern, I'm in the business, I don't take dog diseases lightly. And I give an annual donation to the fight against hip dysplasia, not a whole lot but as much as I can afford. I mean, there are a lot of worthy causes out there. Look at feline leukemia." She heaved a sigh, while I wondered where I was supposed to look for feline leukemia. "I was just surprised that you know about the AHDA, Bern, seeing that you're not a dog person. But now it turns out you don't know about it after all."

"Well," I said, "I do now."

"You do, and you can give me twenty dollars right now and I'll send it in for you. Unless you want to write a check so you can take it off your taxes."

I found a twenty and handed it over.

"Thanks, Bern. I bet you feel better already, don't you?"

"How much do you want to bet?"

"Well, you will," she said, and tucked the twenty away. "So tell me," she said. "How were the movies?"

"The movies?" I said. "The movies were great. *Virginia City* and *Sabrina*. What's not to like?"

"*Virginia City*," she said. "It sounds like a western. Actually, it sounds like a southern western, if you stop and think about it. What is it?"

"A western."

"Humphrey Bogart in a western?"

"Errol Flynn's the hero," I said. "Bogart's a half-breed bandit."

"Give me a break, Bern."

"With a mustache and sideburns, and it is a sort of a southern western, because it's during the Civil War and Confederate sympathizers in this Nevada mining town are planning to ship a load of gold bullion to Dixie."

"But Errol Flynn saves the day?"

"And Bogie's killed, of course. Flynn won't say where the gold is because he hopes it'll be used to rebuild the South after the war. That's his story, anyway. I figure he wanted a retirement fund for himself. Anyway, Miriam Hopkins pleads for his life and Abraham Lincoln commutes his sentence."

"Who played Lincoln?"

"I missed the credit. Not Raymond Massey, though."

"And *Sabrina*'s with Audrey Hepburn, right? She's in love with Alan Ladd and winds up with Bogart."

"William Holden."

"She winds up with William Holden?"

"Holden's the brother she starts out with, and Bogart gets her in the end."

"Yeah? What happened to Alan Ladd?"

"He must have been off making another picture," I said, "because he sure wasn't in this one."

We were in her apartment on Arbor Court, where I'd gone, flight bag in hand, after the credit crawl at the end of *Sabrina*. No one was home when I got there, unless you want to count Archie and Ubi. I let myself in and played with them and made a pot of coffee, and before I'd drunk half a cup of it she'd come in, relieved to see me.

We were sitting at the kitchen tub-table now, and I'd switched from coffee to Evian water while Carolyn sipped Scotch. "I don't particularly feel like a drink," she said, "but it's not a good idea to miss a day. It's like exercise. If you want to stay in shape, you should make sure you get out there and do something every day. Even if it's just a slow jog around the block or two laps in the swimming pool, at least you're hanging in there."

"I'd join you," I said, "but I might work tonight."

"It's kind of late for it, Bern."

"I know, and I don't think I will, but I might. It's

called keeping my options open. While you're hanging in there, I'm keeping my options open."

"I think it's great the way it looks as though we're just sitting here with glasses in our hands," she said, "when we've each actually got a sound philosophical basis for what we're doing. I was glad to find you here when I got in, Bern. I was a little worried when I didn't hear from you all day."

"I called," I said.

"And we talked? Better bring on the ginkgo biloba, because I don't remember a thing."

"I couldn't reach you," I said. "I tried you here and at the store. Two, three times minimum. You were never at either place."

"Which store, Bern?"

"The Poodle Factory, of course. How many stores do you have?"

"Just one," she said, "but you've got one, too, and that's where I was."

"At my store?"

"Uh-huh."

"Barnegat Books?"

"No. Lord and Taylor. How many stores do *you* have, smartie?"

"I was closed today, Carolyn."

"That's what you think."

"You opened up for me?"

"Well, I had to go in to feed Raffles," she said, "and I got to thinking that somebody might be trying to get in touch with you. Like Tiggy, for instance, or Candlemas, or the other one whose name was mentioned. The fat man. Sarnoff."

"Tsarnoff," I said.

"Whatever you tsay, Bern. I figured nobody could reach you at home, and they didn't know you were staying here, and you don't have an answering machine on either of your phones, so how could they get in touch with you?"

"They can't," I said, "which should make it hard for them to kill me."

"Well, I didn't think anybody would try to kill me, so I figured I'd spend the day in the bookstore. It's not as if I had anything else to do. My store's closed for the weekend."

"So was mine. How did you manage? The bargain table must have been a bitch to move."

"For a small weak woman like me? That's what I figured. I left it inside."

"Really? It's a good draw, it lets people know they're passing a bookstore."

"Bern, I wasn't looking to do big business. I just wanted to be open in case anybody came by with a message for you. I sold some books, but that wasn't the point."

"You actually sold some books?"

"What's so remarkable about that? You sit behind the counter, people bring up a book, you check the price and add the tax and take their money and make change. It's not nuclear physics."

"How much did you take in?"

"I don't know, a little under two hundred dollars. Whatever it was, I left it in the register."

"I'm surprised you didn't send it to the hip dysplasia people."

"I wish I'd thought of it. A lot of your regular customers asked about you. They wanted to know if you were sick. I told 'em you were up till all hours and had a killer hangover."

"Thanks a lot."

"People like hearing that sort of thing, Bernie. It's a humanizing flaw, they identify with you and feel superior to you at the same time. Anyway, I didn't want to say you were sick or they might worry."

"You could have said I had hip dysplasia."

"You think that's funny, but—"

"I know, I know, it's no laughing matter."

"Well, it's not." She poured herself a little more Scotch, hanging in with a vengeance. "Mowgli came by with a shopping bag full of treasures from the Twenty-sixth Street flea market. He said he was sure you'd want them, but I said I couldn't do any buying."

"Is he going to come back?"

"He'll have to. I gave him a ten-dollar advance and got him to leave the books for you to look at. If they're not worth ten dollars—"

"They'll be worth it. You did the right thing, otherwise he'd have taken them to somebody else. Anybody else come in that I should know about?"

"Tiggy Rastafarian."

"Rasmoulian."

"I know, I was being funny."

"You're joking anyway, right? He didn't really come in."

"Sure he did. I think that book confused him, Bern. He didn't know what to make of it. He's a snappy dresser, the way you said, and I guess he's pretty short, but you made him sound like a midget."

"For a full-grown person," I said, "he's not."

"He's taller than I am, Bern."

"That's different."

"How is it different? Because I'm a woman? Why should that make a difference?"

"You're right," I said. "It's a clear-cut case of sex discrimination, and I think there must be a government agency you can call. What did he want?"

"Tiggy? He wouldn't come right out and say, and then he didn't get a chance to say anything, because Ray came in."

"Again? Tiggy must think he lives there."

"That's what Ray seems to think. He comes in and makes himself right at home, doesn't he? He remembered Tiggy, who I guess would be hard to forget, wouldn't he? Ray greeted him by name, but of course he got the name wrong, not that Tiggy bothered correcting him. He just got the hell out of there, which gave Ray a chance to do what he'd wanted to do from the minute he walked in."

"What was that?"

"What he always does. Make short jokes. 'Hey, Carolyn, it does my heart good to see you finally got a boyfriend your own size.' And that was just to get himself warmed up. I happen to be altitudinally challenged. What's the big deal?"

"Well, you know how he is."

"I know what he is, too," she said with feeling, "but I'm not insensitive. You don't see me making asshole jokes every time I'm in the same room with him. He wants you to get in touch with him. He says it's urgent."

"Did he say why?"

"No, and I couldn't get it out of him, but he sounded serious. I told him you were away for the weekend."

"Good thinking."

"I said I didn't know where but you'd mentioned something about New Hampshire. Bern, do you think those were cops hanging around your place uptown? Because he said he knew you hadn't been home, and how else would he know that unless they had the place staked out?"

"Maybe," I said. "They were obvious enough about it. But I don't get it. I can see him dropping in, he does that all the time, and I can even see him leaving a message that it's urgent, even if it's not. But a stakeout? What for?"

"Unless they found out about Hoberman."

"So what if they did? Look, when I ID'd the body, I made sure Ray got the impression I wasn't a hundred percent certain, that I was mostly going through with it to oblige him and be a nice guy. If they finally got a make on Hoberman's prints or something like that, well, yeah, I can see where he'd want to talk with me, at least to get me to rethink the ID. But why would he park a cop in my lobby and two more in an unmarked car out in front?"

"You could call him and ask him."

"How? I'm in New Hampshire."

"You came back ahead of schedule."

"I don't want to come back," I said. "Then he'll want to pull me in, and that's the last thing I want."

She thought about it. "Okay, you're calling him from New Hampshire, because you called me to tell me how beautiful it is up there and I gave you his message. That would work, wouldn't it?"

"Maybe. Until he ran a trace and found out where the call came from."

"Would he do that?"

"He might."

"You want to rent a car and drive up somewhere to make the call? Not New Hampshire, that's too far, but say Connecticut? Then when he traces the call . . . forget I said anything, Bern. That doesn't make any sense."

"I didn't think it did."

"He said you can call him at home anytime. He said you'd have the number."

"He's right, I do. I'll see how I feel about it in the morning. What's this?"

She'd handed me a business card. No name, no address, just a seven-digit number, the first three digits separated from the last four with a hyphen.

"It looks like a phone number," I said.

"Very good, Bern."

"No area code, though." I ran my thumb across the surface. "Raised lettering," I said. "Or should that be numbering? Since there aren't any letters. I don't remember Ray's number offhand, but I'd be willing to bet this isn't it. Unless he had it changed, but this is a little too minimalist for Ray, wouldn't you say?"

"It's not Ray's."

"Where did it come from?"

"A man who walked into the store and asked for you. I said you weren't in."

"You were right about that."

"He said you should call him sometime to discuss a matter of mutual interest."

"Ah, that narrows it down. This is great, I've got a card with a name and no number and another with a number and no name. I wish somebody else would come along and give me one with nothing on it but an address. Ten Downing Street, say, or Sixteen hundred Pennsylvania Avenue."

"Maybe one of those was this guy's. I tried to get his name but you'd have thought it was a state secret."

That rang a muted bell. I said, "I don't suppose he was around six-two or -three, mid to late thirties, short blondish hair, broad shoulders? Handsome guy, might have been wearing black Levi's and an air of contentment."

"Sounds like Mike Todd."

"That's who I was describing. Is that who gave you the card?"

"Nothing like him. This man never wore jeans in his life. He was wearing a white suit."

"Maybe it was Tom Wolfe."

"It wasn't Tom Wolfe. This guy was sixty or sixty-five, around six feet tall, blue eyes, iron-gray hair. Bushy eyebrows, big nose like an eagle's beak, prominent jaw."

"I'm impressed," I said. "All you left out was his weight and the amount of change in his pocket."

"I kept my hands out of his pockets," she said, "so I don't know about the second part. I'd say he weighed somewhere around three hundred and fifty pounds."

I made a sound by snicking the tip of my tongue back from my teeth. "Tssss," I said.

"As in Tsarnoff. That would be my guess, Bern."

"You had a busy day," I said. "You did great, Carolyn."

"Thanks."

"It was a good idea to open the store, and I'd say it was productive. I don't know what they all want from me or what I'm going to give them, but it's good to know they're looking for me. At least I think it is. I'll know more when I make some calls in the morning."

"I don't know what Ray wants," she said. "I guess everybody else wants the documents."

"Whatever they are."

"And wherever they are."

"Oh, I think I know where they are," I said.

"You do?"

"Well, I've got an inkling. Put it that way."

"That's great. And you've got a partner, too. I don't mean me, I mean the mouse."

"The mouse? Oh, Charlie Weeks. I guess we're partners. In that case I hope he takes care of himself."

"Why's that? Oh, if he gets killed you'll have to do something about it."

"You got it," I said, and leaned back and yawned. "I'm beat," I said. "Ray can wait until morning, and so can everybody else. I'm going to bed. Or to couch, if I can persuade you to—"

"Let's not have that argument again. You're not going out? You could have been drinking Scotch after all."

"Somehow," I said, "I don't think I'm going to wake up tomorrow morning and regret that I didn't have anything stronger than Evian this evening."

"Maybe not," she said, "but you can't miss days and expect to stay in shape. That's my theory. You want me to mind the store tomorrow?"

"I'm never open Sundays."

"Is that carved in stone somewhere? It wouldn't hurt anything if I opened up, would it?"

"No, but—"

"Because I found a book there that I was reading, and I might as well finish it before I start something else. And you never know who'll pop in looking for you."

"Well, that's true. What did you find to read?"

"Reread, actually, but it's one I haven't looked at since it came out. It's an early one of Sue Grafton's."

"I didn't think I had anything of hers in stock. Oh, I remember. It's a book club edition, isn't it?"

She nodded. "It's the one about the jazz musician who kills his unfaithful wife by throwing her onto the subway tracks."

"I don't think I ever read that one. What's the title?"

" '*A' Is for Train*," she said. "You can borrow it when I'm done with it."

"Borrow it? It's my book."

"That's okay," she said. "You can still borrow it, but you'll have to wait until I'm finished."

SEVENTEEN

I slept soundly and woke up early, managing to get dressed and out the door without waking Carolyn, who looked so blissful curled up on the couch that I couldn't feel too guilty for taking her bed. I walked across town, pausing at my bookshop only long enough to feed Raffles and give him fresh water, then catching the IRT at Union Square and riding to the Hunter College stop at Sixty-eighth and Lex. I walked six blocks up and two blocks over, stopping en route at a deli for a container of coffee and a bagel. When I got to where I was going I found a good doorway and lurked in it, passing the time by sipping the coffee and gnawing at the bagel. I kept my eyes open, and when I finally saw what I'd come there to see I retraced my steps, but this time I passed up the deli and went straight to the subway station.

I caught another train, this one headed downtown, and got off at Wall Street. There's no more peaceful place in the city on a Sunday morning, when the engines of commerce have ground to a halt. It's never entirely deserted. I saw joggers on training runs, chugging away, and folks wandering around singly and in pairs, intent on enjoying the stillness.

I'd come to use the phone.

There were more convenient phones, including one in the bookstore and another in Carolyn's apartment, but you can never be sure you're not calling someone with one of those gadgets on his phone that displays the number you're calling from. I was reasonably certain Ray Kirschmann wouldn't have anything like that at his home in Sunnyside, if only because he wouldn't want to spend the extra $1.98 a month, or whatever they charge for the service. But he'd have the resources of the New York Police Department, and thus could probably get the folks at NYNEX to trace the call.

If he traced it to a pay phone in the West Village, he'd guess I was at Carolyn's apartment. So I had to go someplace, and Wall Street seemed as good a choice as any. Let him trace the call, and let him race down to the corner of Broad and Wall, and let him wonder if I was planning to knock over the New York Stock Exchange.

Even so, I saved him for last.

My first call was to the fat man, and my first thought was that the card was a phony, or that I'd dialed wrong. Because the man who answered didn't sound fat.

I know, I know. You can't judge a book by its cover (but try to get a decent price for it if it's stained or water-damaged, or, God forbid, missing altogether). Nor can you tell much about a body by the voice that comes out of it, which is a good thing for the phone-sex industry. All that notwithstanding, the voice I heard didn't sound like one that might have come out of a man who weighed three hundred and fifty pounds, had a beak like an eagle, and wore a white suit. It sounded instead as though its owner never got past the sixth grade, moved his lips on the rare occasions when he read something, spent his most productive hours with a pool cue in his hand, and, when not using that cue for massé shots, was skinny enough to hide behind it.

I asked to speak to Mr. Tsarnoff, and he asked me what I wanted.

"Tsarnoff," I said confidently, "and you're not him. Tell him it's the man who wasn't at the bookstore yesterday."

There was a pause. Then a voice—a round voice, a rich voice, a voice that hit every consonant smack on the head and got the last drop of flavor out of every syllable—said, "In point of fact, sir, there is no end of people who were not at that bookstore yesterday. Or at any bookstore, on any occasion."

Now this was more like it. This was the kind of voice I'd had in mind, a voice that could have introduced *The Shadow.*

"I'm obliged to agree with you," I said. "Ours is a subliterate age, sir, and the frequenter of bookstores a rare reminder of a better day."

"Ah," he said. "It's good of you to call. I believe you have found something that belongs to me. I trust you're aware there's a substantial reward offered for its return."

I asked if he could describe it.

"A sort of leather envelope stamped in gold," he said.

"And its contents?"

"Diverse contents."

"And the amount of the reward?"

"Ah, did I not say, sir? Substantial. Unquestionably substantial."

"Sir," I said, "I must say I like your style. Were I in possession of the article you seek, I've no doubt we could come to terms."

There was a pause, but not a very long one. "The subjunctive mode," he said, "would seem to imply, sir, that you are not."

"The implication was deliberate," I said, "and the inference sound."

"Yet one has the sense that there is more to the story."

It was a pleasure having this sort of conversation, but it was also a strain. "It is my earnest hope, sir, to be able to report altered circumstances, and indeed to have it in my power to claim your generous reward."

"Your hope, sir?"

"My hope and expectation."

"I am gladdened, sir, for expectation promises ever so much more than hope alone. When might this hope be fulfilled, if I might ask?"

"Anon," I said.

"Anon," he echoed. "A word that makes up in charm what it sacrifices in precision."

"It does at that. 'Shortly' might be more precise."

"I'm not sure that it is, but I daresay it's a shade more encouraging."

"It is my intention," I said, "to call you later today, or perhaps tomorrow, to suggest a meeting. Will I be able to reach you at this number?"

"Indeed you will, sir. If I am not at home myself, you may leave word with the lad who answers the telephone."

"You'll hear from me," I said, and rang off.

My next call was to my partner, Charlie Weeks. I told him I'd held off calling until he returned from his morning walk.

"You had an ample margin for error," he said. "I'm a creature of habit in my old age, I'm afraid. I wake up at the same time every day without setting a clock. I've got halfway through the Sunday *Times* already."

"The plot thickens," I said. "I think you're right about what happened to Hoberman. I think Candlemas killed him."

"It seems the likeliest explanation," he said, "but leaves us high and dry for the time being, since Candlemas himself seems to have disappeared."

"I have some ideas about that."

"Oh?"

"But this is no time to go into them," I said, "and I wouldn't want to do it over the phone."

"No, I wouldn't think so."

"I wonder if I could come to your apartment. This evening, say? On the late side, if it's all right with you. Eleven o'clock?"

"I'll have the coffee made," he said. "Or will you want decaf at that hour?"

I told him I could handle the hard stuff.

There was nothing for it. I spent another quarter and called Ray Kirschmann's home number in Queens. When a woman answered I said, "Hi, Mrs. Kirschmann. It's Bernie Rhodenbarr. Is Ray in? I hate to disturb him on a Sunday morning, but I'm calling from up in New Hampshire."

"I'll see if he's in," she said, a phrase I've always found puzzling no matter who uses it, a secretary or a spouse. I mean, who are they kidding? Don't they already know if he's in or not, and don't they think I know?

Her reconnaissance mission took a few minutes, and I wished she would shake a leg. I had plenty of quarters left, but I didn't want a recorded operator to cut in and ask me for one. It wouldn't do wonders for my credibility.

But that commodity turned out to be thin on the ground anyway, as it turned out. "New Hampshire," were the first words Ray said, and he invested them with a full measure of contempt. "In a pig's eye, Bernie."

"I was going to stay in Pig's Eye," I told him, "but all the motels were full, so I wound up in Hanover. How'd you happen to know that, Ray?"

"The only thing I know for sure," he said, "is you're no more in New Hampshire than you are in New Zealand."

"What makes you so sure of that, Ray?"

THE BURGLAR WHO THOUGHT HE WAS BOGART 229

"You sayin' so right off the bat, tellin' my wife so's she can pass it on to me. If you was really in New Hampshire, Bernie, that's the last thing you'd do. No, I take that back. It's the second-last thing."

"What's the last?"

"Placin' the call altogether. You'd wait until you got back. You ask me, you spent the night with that sawed-off morphodyke buddy of yours, for all the good either of you could have got out of the experience. An' then you figured you better call me, an' you went someplace out of the way in case I trace the call, which how am I gonna do anyway from my home phone?"

"How you do go on," I said.

"I had to guess," he said, "I'd say you're across the bridge in Brooklyn Heights. Can you see the Promenade from where you're standin', Bernie?"

"Yes," I said. "And it looks lovely in the morning mist."

"It's a beautiful day, an' if there was any mist you missed it, 'cause it burned off hours ago. Anyway, I take it back. There ain't enough background noise for Brooklyn. It's Sunday mornin', right? Be my guess you're down in Wall Street. You can't see the Promenade, but I bet you a dollar you can see the Stock Exchange."

"You're amazing, Ray. I swear I don't know how you do it."

"An' that's to make me think I'm wrong, but I think I'm right, for all the good it does me. You really want to know how I done it, Bernie, it's just a case of us knowin' each other a long time. Not surprisin'

I know you pretty good by now, thinkin' of all we been through."

"The mist hasn't all burned off, Ray. Some of it's in my eyes, to go with the lump in my throat."

"Got you all choked up, huh, Bernie? Maybe this'll unchoke you. Couple of uniforms are walkin' a beat the other day on the Lower East Side, an' one of the neighborhood kids takes 'em to this boarded-up buildin' at the corner of Pitt and Madison. That's Madison Street, not Madison Avenue, by the way."

"That explains what it was doing on the Lower East Side."

"Yeah, but does it explain what they found when the kid showed 'em which board was loose an' how to get in? Three guesses, Bernie."

"Even if I don't guess," I said, "you'll probably tell me."

"A dead body."

"Not mine, thank God," I said, "but it's good of you to voice concern, Ray. I didn't think you cared."

"You want to guess who?"

"If it's not Judge Crater," I said, "it would pretty much have to be Jimmy Hoffa, wouldn't it?"

"The watch an' wallet was gone," he went on, "which you'd expect, seein' as kids an' God knows who else was in an' out of the buildin' all along. But under his clothes the guy was wearin' a money belt, although there wasn't a whole lot of money in it."

"Unless the uniforms helped themselves."

He made that sound with his tongue and his teeth, but I don't think he was trying to say "Tsarnoff." "Bernie," he said, "you got a low opinion

of the NYPD, which you oughta be ashamed of yourself. If they took a dime off the stiff, I got no way of
knowin' about it, so I'll just tell you what they didn't
take. How's that?"

"I'm sure it'll be fascinating."

"First thing was a passport. Had the guy's picture
on it, so you could tell right off he didn't lift it off of
somebody else. Had his name right there, too."

"Passports usually do."

"They'd have to, wouldn't they? Accordin' to the
passport, his name was Jean-Claude Marmotte."

"Sounds French."

"Belgian," he said. "Least he was carryin' a Belgian
passport, only it don't hardly matter what country
gave it to him, on account of they didn't."

"Huh?"

"It was a phony," he said. "A good phony, or so
they tell me, but one thing's sure and that's that the
Belgians never heard of him."

He started to say something else, but the recording cut in, inviting me to deposit more money or
hang up.

"Gimme your number there," Ray said, "an' I'll call
you back."

I gave that the only answer it required, dropping a
fresh quarter in the slot.

"Now why'd you go an' do that, Bernie? I was all
set to call you back. How often do I get to call anybody in Pig's Eye, New Hampshire?"

"How often do I get to hear about dead Belgians
in boarded-up buildings?"

"You didn't ask how he died."

"I didn't even ask who he was. Sooner or later I'll get around to asking why you're telling me all this."

"Sooner or later you won't need to. He died on account of bein' shot once at close range in the side of the head. Entry was through the ear, matter of fact. Slug was a twenty-two. Very professional job, all in all."

"Killed where you found him?"

"Probably not, but that's inconclusive because of the mess the kids made of the crime scene. Wherever he bought it, he was a long ways from Belgium when he died. A long ways from New Hampshire, too, but aren't we all?"

"There's a point here somewhere."

"There is," he agreed, "an' I'm gettin' to it. Nothin' in his pockets but lint. No keys, no subway tokens, no nail clipper, no Swiss Army knife. But he's wearin' this nice tweed suit, an' it turns out there's a secret pocket in the jacket."

"A secret pocket?"

"I don't know what else you'd call it, bein' as it ain't where you'd expect to find a pocket, down near the bottom and around in the back. An' it's hard to spot unless you're lookin' for it, and it zips open an' shut, an' we found it an' unzipped it, an' you want to take a guess what we found?"

"Another passport."

"Mind tellin' me how you happened to know that?"

"You mean I got it right? It was a guess, Ray. I swear it was."

"This one's Italian, and the name on it is Vassily Souslik."

"That doesn't sound Italian," I said. "Spell it." He did, and it still didn't sound Italian. "Vassily's a Russian name, or Slavic, anyway. And Souslik sounds like something you'd order at the Russian Tea Room."

"I wouldn't know," he said, "not goin' to fancy places myself. Anyway, it don't matter, on account of it's a fake, too. The Belgians never heard of Marmotte an' the guineas never heard of Souslik. Same likeness an' description on both of 'em, Bern, an' they match the dead guy to a T. Who knows, maybe it'll remind you of somebody you know. Five-nine, one-thirty, DOB fifteen October 1926, hair white, eyes hazel. That's off the Belgian passport, an' the Italian's close enough. They got his eyes as brown, but maybe they haven't got a word for hazel. Narrow face, little white mustache—this ringing any kind of a bell for you?"

"Not yet. Why should it?"

"Well, that's the thing," he said. "See, once we found the one secret pocket, we checked on the other side, and wouldn't you know there was another secret pocket to match?"

"And to think some people doubt the existence of God."

"An' this one's got a passport in it, too, an' this one's Canadian, an' it's no more legit than the other two. Issued at Winnipeg, it says in good old American English, except it was never issued at all, it was made by somebody with no official standing. Same

234   *Lawrence Block*

face on the photo, though, an' whyntcha see if you can tell me the name on the passport?"

"You tell me, Ray."

"Hugo Candlemas," he said. "Now what do you call that if it ain't a big coincidence? I mean, the average person lives a lifetime without ever meetin' up with a single Hugo Candlemas, an' here I went an' met up with two of 'em, both in the space of a couple of days. An' both of 'em deader'n Kelsey's nuts, too."

"If Ripley were still alive," I said, "and if he were still turning out 'Believe It or Not' . . ."

"This guy don't look a bit like the Candlemas we got on ice, Bernie."

"Not even a faint family resemblance?"

"Not even related by marriage. You want to explain it to me, Bernie? How you took a good long look at the stiff at the morgue and ID'd him as a guy who turned up dead himself the next day?"

The recording cut in again, asking me to deposit more money if I wanted to go on talking. That voice speaks those very same words thousands upon thousands of times every day of the year, and how often does its message come as welcome news? Rarely, I'd have to say, but this was one of those rare occasions.

I glanced at my handful of coins, dropped them back in my pocket. "I'm out of change," I said. "I'll call you back."

"For Christ's sake, Bernie, I know you're not in New Fucking Hampshire. Gimme your number and I'll call you back."

"It's scratched off the dial," I said. "I can't make it

out. Stay right where you are, Ray. I'll get back to you."

He was saying something else, but I didn't wait for NYNEX to cut him off. I hung up on him.

When I called again a little later I didn't get to talk to his wife. Ray answered the phone himself, and he must have been sitting on it. "It's about time," he said, "you son of a bitch."

I didn't say anything.

Neither did he for the longest moment, and then he said, "Hello?" He said it very tentatively, and I let it hang in the air for a beat before I replied.

"Hello yourself," I said, "and aren't you glad to hear my voice? Isn't it suddenly more welcome in your ear than the commissioner's, say, or some nosy parker from the Internal Affairs Division?"

"Jesus," he said.

"I'm sorry it took so long, Ray. You wouldn't believe how long it took to find change of a dollar."

"Well, Wall Street on a Sunday. I knew that's where you were."

"You know me too well," I said. "But getting back to Candlemas—"

"Yeah, let's by all means get back to him."

"You remember I was a little uncertain at the morgue."

"You told me goin' in you don't like to look at dead people. I figured that was it."

"I only made the ID to make your life easier. I let you know I couldn't be sure it was him."

"Hey, Bernie, c'mon. It'd be one thing if it was

238 *Lawrence Block*

close, but these two stiffs couldn't look less alike unless one of 'em was missin' a head. How could you look at the one and said it was the other?"

I'd given myself time to come up with an answer. That's why I'd hung up on him earlier. "I met them both at once," I said. "And they both told me their names at the same time. I wasn't paying that much attention to which name went with which face. To tell you the truth, I wasn't paying a lot of attention to their names. But it was the guy you found at Pitt and Madison that I *thought* was Candlemas, because he was the guy who bought the book from me."

"So at the morgue . . ."

"At the morgue I got a look at him and it wasn't the guy I was expecting to see. But it *was* somebody I recognized, so I figured maybe I got a wire crossed. Maybe I'd been thinking the one man was Hugo Candlemas, while all along it was the other man."

"An' you met both of these winners at your store?"

"That's right."

"An' one of 'em bought a book from you, an' what did the other one do?"

"Nothing."

"They walked in together?"

"I didn't even notice. I don't think they were together, but I could be mistaken."

I just knew he was frowning. I could picture it. "Something smells," he announced. "They're both in your store, they both introduce themselves to you, and they both wind up dead, only miles apart. An' the one who isn't Candlemas winds up in Candlemas's apartment, an' the other one winds up on Pitt

Street with three different fake passports on him. An' one of these Candlemases bought a book from you, an' on the stren'th of that you gave him your touché case to carry it home in. Bernie, I don't know whether to be insulted you think I'd believe such a load of crap or honored you'd take the trouble."

Time to take another tack. "Ray," I said, "when your wife answered earlier, I found myself remembering the time I helped you get a coat for her. Remember?"

"That's changing the subject all to hell an' gone," he said, "but it's a funny thing you should mention it, because I was thinkin' earlier about it myself."

"Really."

"She was sayin' as to how the coat has seen better days, which who hasn't, herself included, only you don't want to try tellin' her somethin' like that. It seems as though they don't last forever, which they damn well ought to, the prices they get for them. Personally I think the only thing the matter with hers is she'd like a new one, but this is gonna be a bitch because she's got a particular style an' color in mind. One of these days, Bernie, the two of us'll have to sit ourselves down an' talk about it."

"Maybe we won't have to," I said.

"What's that supposed to mean?"

"Maybe Mrs. Kirschmann will be able to walk into some place nice, like Arvin Tannenbaum's, say, and buy her own coat."

"Very funny," he said. "The only reason the coat she's got is from Tannenbaum's is that's where you hooked it for her. You think I can let her walk into their showroom an' pick somethin' out? Where am I gonna come up with that kind of dough?"

"Ah," I said. "I thought you'd never ask."

EIGHTEEN

That left me with a couple more phone calls to make, and I made them. Then I got on the East Side IRT and rode uptown once again, riding one stop past Hunter College this time and emerging at Seventy-seventh Street. I walked down a block and found the building where the whole thing started, but I wasn't sure I wanted to call it that. It seemed clear that this business started a long while before the previous Wednesday night, and a long ways away.

But it was Hugo Candlemas's building I was standing in front of now, and he had been more my employer than my partner, but he was dead, too, and it looked as though I was supposed to do something about it. I wasn't sure just where he'd been killed, but there was no question as to where Cappy Hoberman had been stabbed to death, and I felt it was about time for me to return to the scene of the crime.

In the entrance hall, I studied the four buzzers before pushing the top one, marked CANDLEMAS, to save me the embarrassment of walking in on some police lab technicians, themselves returned to the

crime scene in the wake of the second murder. I
didn't really expect there'd be anybody around, and
there wasn't, and when I'd waited long enough to establish that I took out my ring of tools and let myself
into the building.

You'd have thought they were my American Ex-
press card, the way I never left home without them.

Up on the fourth floor, the door to Candlemas's
apartment was secured by a whole lot of that yellow
crime scene tape, along with a couple of large handbills proclaiming the premises to be off-limits to unauthorized persons, sealed by order of the New York
Police Department. To add a little muscle, someone—probably the yutz of a locksmith who'd opened
up for the cops—had mounted a hinged hasp on the
outside of the door and jamb and fastened it with a
shiny new padlock.

None of this looked to be inexpungable. The
stoutest padlock is no match for a brute armed with
a can of freon and a hammer; spray it with the one
and swat it with the other and you've unfastened the
Gordian knot. I had neither of those precision instruments, but I wouldn't need them; I knew this brand
of lock, and they're notoriously easy to pick.

I was more concerned with the paper and plastic.
Anyone could get past them, but not without leaving
traces of one's passage. The ideal, of course, would
be to have a roll of crime scene tape and a couple of
handbills in your hip pocket; instead of trying to re-
store the originals on your way out, you could simply
replace them.

But I was not so equipped. I filed the thought

away for future reference, cast a wistful glance at the padlock, and trotted downstairs.

On my way, I remembered Ray's review of the building's other tenants—the gay couple in the basement, the blind woman on the ground floor, a businessman from Singapore in the Lehrmans' apartment on two, and an unidentified tenant or tenants on the third floor. "The hell with who lives on the third floor," Ray had said. "They're like everybody else, they don't know shit."

In the front hall, I found their buzzer, marked GEARHARDT. I tried them first, hoping that they knew at least to get out of town on a holiday weekend. But no, not long after I poked their buzzer a male voice came over the intercom, asking me who I was.

"My name is Roger," I said cheerfully, "and my friend's name is Mary Beth, and we'd like to talk to you about the state of your immortal soul."

"Whyntcha shove it up your ass?" he suggested.

"Oh!" I said, trying to sound shocked, but I think it was a waste of time, because he'd already broken the connection. I moved on to the buzzer immediately below it, deciding on a different approach for the fellow from Singapore. I couldn't take the chance that he might welcome a visit from a couple of urban missionaries, or be too polite to let on otherwise. I could just pretend I was looking for the Lehrmans.

But I didn't have to, because he didn't answer the bell. I reentered the building—no lockpicking this time, I'd kept my foot in the door—and went up a flight, to confront a door equipped with two excellent locks, one your basic Segal, the other a police lock fitted with one of the new pickproof Poulard cylinders.

Pickproof indeed.

The Lehrmans had a nice place, furnished with a little too much of everything—too many rugs on the floor, too many paintings on the walls, too much furniture crowded together in the rooms. Too many knickknacks on the marble mantel over the fireplace, too many on the whatnot shelf in the corner by the window. A minimalist decorator would have shuddered, and I don't know what a Chinese businessman from Singapore would have made of it, but from a professional standpoint I have to say I was thrilled.

It was a decorative scheme to gladden the heart of a burglar. You'll never catch a burglar proclaiming that less is more. A burglar knows that less is less, and more is more. People who cram their apartment full of stuff, assuming they're not the Collier brothers and the stuff is not old newspapers, are people who *like* things. They're a lot more likely to have something worth taking than a guy who beds down on a futon in a room with nothing else in it but the track lighting on the ceiling.

It would have been fun to have a look around, but who had the time? I walked straight through the apartment to the large bedroom at the rear, moved a bookcase and a large jade plant in a pot that looked like Rockwood, unlocked and raised the bedroom window, and crawled out onto the fire escape. I climbed two flights, past the sullen Mr. Gearhardt and his imperiled soul, and wasted close to ten minutes trying to find a benign way to open the late Mr.

Candlemas's bedroom window. He had casement windows, secured by a lever that you raised and lowered from within. But you couldn't reach it from outside, naturally enough, not unless you could pry the window back from the frame and get the right sort of gizmo in that way. It's not that hard if you've got the tools for it. Just watch an enterprising teenager open a locked automobile in the wink of an eye and you'll get the idea.

This wasn't the identical operation to grand theft auto, but it requires a similar instrument, and I didn't have one on hand. I tried to get in without it and kept coming teasingly close, which in turn kept me trying. It finally dawned on me that I was spending far too much time in plain sight on a fire escape, whereupon I used the glass cutter on my tool ring and cut out one of the window's little panes. I reached in, turned the latch, and let myself in.

I was in there for hours. It was stuffy at first, but I opened a window in the front room, and the pane I'd removed in the rear provided good cross-ventilation. It didn't take me long to find the spot where Cappy Hoberman had lain bleeding. They hadn't outlined the body in tape or chalk. They don't do that anymore, preferring to have the crime scene photographer expose a few rolls of film before they move the body. But they hadn't done anything about the blood, either, and a lot of it had soaked into the carpet.

I stood there and looked at it. He'd died on the Aubusson, and his blood hadn't done a lot for the rug's appearance. Even if you assumed that Candle-

mas had bought the rug from someone other than its
rightful owner, he must have paid a good sum for it.
It looked terrible now, but somebody someday would
be able to get the stains out. They've got all sorts of
chemicals and enzymes available, and nowadays they
can get blood out of anything, even a turnip.

But they couldn't pump it back into Hoberman.

I walked around the apartment, running alternate
scenarios through my mind. Hoberman gives Charlie
Weeks the bone carving of the mouse, cuts his visit
short, and returns to this apartment. By cab, natch,
since he didn't have me along to urge him to walk.
Something he says or does moves Candlemas to kill
him. Candlemas grabs something sharp—this letter
opener, say, or one of these Sabatier knives from the
kitchen, or some other implement even better suited
to dispatching a visitor. Candlemas strikes, Hoberman crumples and falls, and Candlemas slips out
and legs it over to Second Avenue, looking to buy
Hefty bags and a Skilsaw.

Then what?

Earlier, Weeks and I had spun out a theory in
which Candlemas got home, found the cops on the
scene, muttered, "Curses, foiled again!" and stole off
into the night. But his own death put a different
light on things. When he left Hoberman bleeding, he
evidently encountered someone. Maybe he went to
the wrong person for help, or maybe someone was lying doggo, waiting for him.

Maybe it was that person who made the 911 call
that sent the cops to Seventy-sixth Street. In any
case, the cops came. Hoberman, the way I figured it,

was still breathing when Candlemas took a powder. His wounds were mortal, and he was alive but not lively, probably inert and unconscious. Somewhere along the way he rallied and wrote six unfathomable letters on my heretofore blameless attaché case, using his own life's blood for ink. Then, perhaps even as the Keystone Kops were sending out for a locksmith, the valiant captain breathed his last.

It was probably around that time, too, that I was downstairs myself, wondering what had happened to Candlemas and considering a little illegal entry of my own. Even loopy with Ludomir, I'd been able to spot that for a bad idea. A good thing, too, considering what I would have walked in on. I could have saved the city the price of a locksmith's house call, but I'd have had a lot of explaining to do, and my task wouldn't have gotten all that much easier when the attaché case turned out to be mine.

The new scenario was pretty reasonable, I decided, and a substantial improvement over the one Charlie Weeks and I had hatched the previous morning. It made the mysterious telephone call to the police a little less inexplicable, and fit the dying message into a logical time frame.

But it didn't do a whole lot to decode it.

C-A-P-H-O-B. What the hell could it mean?

I thought about it as I ambled to and fro, opening drawers and rummaging around in them, exploring closets, looking inside and beneath and behind this and that and the other thing. I was glad to have something to ponder, because this was the worst way to search a place.

The best way is when you know what you're looking for and where it is. You go in, get it, and get out.
Almost as good is when you know what you're looking for; you go through the place systematically,
checking those locations where it's likely to be, and
as soon as you find it you get to go home.

The next best thing—and probably the most
enjoyable—is when you're not looking for anything in
particular. Missions of this sort are burglary at its
best, and they run the gamut from the meticulously
planned suburban break-in, where you time the
neighborhood security patrol and run rings around
the electronic alarm system, to a completely impulsive crime of opportunity, where you kick the door in
and hope for the best. You don't know what they've
got or where they put it, but you get to be Goldi-
locks, sleeping in all the beds and eating all the por-
ridge, and you never know what you're going to find
until you find it.

And, finally, we have the kind of fool's errand I
was on this lovely Sunday. I didn't know what I
wanted or where he'd stashed it, or even if it existed,
whatever it might turn out to be. I had to look everywhere, because I didn't know how big or small it
was, or if it had to be kept cold or dry or out of
drafts.

And it's terribly frustrating. If you find something,
is that it? Or is there something more waiting to be
found? Conversely, if you don't find anything, do you
keep at it until something turns up? Or should you
go on home because there's nothing there?

You know what it's like? Sex without orgasm. How can you tell when you're supposed to stop?

So I was almost glad to have CAPHOB to think about while I searched. I wouldn't call my musing terribly productive, but I came up with some interesting ideas.

1. Suppose CAPHOB was an acronym. Suppose each letter stood for a word. That would be a good way to compress a lot of information into the number of letters you could fit on the side of an attaché case before your life trickled out of you. Just what the letters stood for was hard to say, but the possibilities were extensive, surely. Can Anyone Pinch Hit Or Bunt? Criminal Activity Pays Horribly On Balance. Cancel Anniversary Party—Having Our Baby! None of these struck me as the sort of thing I'd be likely to choose as my last word to the world, but I hadn't been lying there bleeding, struggling to scribble my barbaric yawp over the roofs of the city.

2. Suppose CAPHOB was upside down. After all, I didn't know how Hoberman had spent the years since his adventures in Anatruria. Maybe he'd devoted some of them to a career selling life insurance, until jotting things down upside down had become second nature to him. To test the hypothesis, I printed CAPHOB and turned the piece of paper upside down, and I got the same meaningless word upside down and backwards. Then I printed the individual letters upside down, and this worked a little better, because four of the letters were unchanged. What I got looked something like CVdHOB, except the V

was really an upside-down A. I suppose I could have taken this a step further and tried to work out what CVDHOB might be an acronym for, but you have to draw the line somewhere.

3. Maybe the most obvious explanation was the real one, and he'd been trying to write his name. This did make a certain kind of sense, actually. There'd been no identification found on his person, which suggested that Candlemas might have taken his wallet from him while he lay dying. Maybe Hoberman had recoiled at the thought of rotting away in an unmarked grave, and wanted to let the world know who he was. When you considered the fact that even now the tag on his toe read "Hugo Candlemas," his concern didn't seem so farfetched. It was a damned unsatisfying dying message, pointing not to the killer but to the victim, but what are you going to do, send it back to Hoberman with a rejection slip?

4. Maybe, as Carolyn had suggested earlier, Hoberman was dyslexic. He'd written the right letters but got them in the wrong order. I switched them around without coming up with anything more promising than HOPCAB. It was true, to be sure, that the Boccaccio (say) was only a short hop away by cab, but could that possibly be the urgent information Hoberman wanted to pass on to whoever found his body? I couldn't see it. If I was ready to say the long goodbye and sleep the big sleep, I'd at least try for something profound, like "Life is a fountain," say, or "Take two and hit to right."

5. Perhaps, startling as it was to entertain the no-

tion, perhaps CAPHOB was a word. It wasn't in the dictionary, nor was anything that started out with those first four letters, but suppose it was a proper name. In fact, suppose it was Candlemas's name. It didn't much sound like a name, but was it that much less plausible than Souslik or Marmotte? What would you think if you saw either of those written in blood on the side of *your* attaché case?

6. Was it possible it was just drivel? Consider Dutch Schultz's famous last words, a great extended monologue duly recorded for posterity as he lay dying. They were words, all right, and some of the sentences even parsed, but the great man had made no sense at all. Suppose the good captain, presented with a small canvas, had managed the neat trick of distilling a whole world of meaninglessness into six meaningless letters.

And so on.

Sometime in the middle of the afternoon I got hungry. I was all set to order Chinese food when I realized it wouldn't work; I couldn't open the door to receive it because of the police seals. By this time I was really in the mood for it, too, so I thought about having it delivered to the Lehrman apartment and waiting for it down there. I don't know what made me think that was a sensible idea. Maybe I'd over-dosed on meditation, using CAPHOB as my mantra. Fortunately I nipped the whole enterprise in the bud and raided the kitchen instead.

What I found was leftover Chinese food, but it had been left too long. You wouldn't want to touch it with a ten-foot chopstick. I toasted a couple of English muffins (the bread was stale) and spread them with peanut butter and jelly (the butter was rancid) and washed them down with black instant coffee (the milk was beyond description). Someday, I thought, when all of this was but a memory, I'd be eating real meals again, hearty coffee-shop breakfasts, overseasoned ethnic lunches with Carolyn, real dinners in real restaurants. For now, though, I seemed destined to grab breakfast on the run, skip lunch or steal it, and make the big meal of the day popcorn. My clothes were neither falling off me nor gripping me too tightly, so I seemed to be getting away with it. But it would be nice to eat like a human being again.

I drank the last of the coffee, rinsed my dishes in the sink, and got back to work.

By the time I was done, I had some calls to make. I sat down in the leather club chair, swung my feet up onto the ottoman, held the receiver to my ear, and decided against it. How did I know who had one of those doohickeys on his phone that displays the caller's number? And how could I be sure that none of the folks I wanted to call would recognize Hugo Candlemas's telephone number?

No point taking chances. I'd left NYPD seals intact, I'd steered clear of tainted General Tso's Chicken. After all that, I didn't want to be hoist on the petard of modern communications technology.

I left the Candlemas residence neat and clean, with no evidence of my visit aside from the peanut butter and jelly I'd scarfed and the fingerprints I'd left behind. (I'd wiped up some after myself, but hadn't been a fanatic about it; they already had all the prints they were ever going to lift from the crime scene.) To protect the place from the elements, I cut a rectangle of cardboard from a corrugated carton, shrouded it in plastic wrap from a drawer in the kitchen, and carried it and a roll of tape out onto the fire escape with me. There I drew the casement window shut, reached in and latched it, then withdrew my arm and taped the cardboard in place of the missing pane. Then I scuttled quickly and quietly past the Gearhardts' window and into the Lehrmans' apartment a flight below.

This would have been rendered more complicated if their houseguest had returned in the interim, but he hadn't. I closed their window after me, repositioned the jade plant and the bookcase—the planter was definitely Rockwood, I decided—and chose a telephone in the front room, where I could keep an eye and ear on the door.

I made my phone calls.

When I was done I treated myself to a tour of the apartment. Aside from a massive Chippendale highboy and a closet they'd cleared out for him, the Lehrman possessions remained essentially undisturbed during their absence. I window-shopped, leaving everything where I found it, and being much more careful about fingerprints than I'd been two flights up.

I left the refrigerator unopened.

And, when I let myself out at last, I locked up after myself and left the little brownstone house without incident. The blind woman on the first floor might have heard my footfall on the stairs, the neighbors across the street might have seen me emerge from the entranceway, even as they might have seen me go in some hours earlier. But I'd given them no cause to note my passage. I'd come and gone, leaving no trace.

In *King of the Underworld,* Bogart plays the title role of Joe Gurney. Kay Francis and John Eldredge play a husband-and-wife team of doctors, Eldredge with a mustache almost as unfortunate as Bogie's in *Virginia City.* Eldredge saves a wounded henchman of Bogart, who enlists him as the gang's doctor. When their hideout is raided, Bogart decides Eldredge must have ratted, and shoots him. Bogart and his men get away, but the cops arrest Kay Francis.

Then, in what I thought was a terrific touch, Bogart kidnaps a writer and forces him to ghost his autobiography, planning to kill him when he's done. First, though, he busts two captured gang members out of jail, gets wounded in the process, and manages to find Kay Francis, who's been trying to dig up evidence that will clear her at the trial. A big help she turns out to be; she tips off the cops, infects Bogart's wound, and blinds him with tainted eyedrops. He's stumbling around the hideout after her and the writer, trying to kill them even if he can't see them, when the cops burst in and gun him down.

I watched this from my usual seat, with my usual

barrel of popcorn on my lap, and what was becoming my usual second ticket in the hands of the ticket-taker. While I was on line to buy the popcorn I'd caught the eye of the tall guy with the goatee and the glasses. He smiled and looked away quickly, not wanting to stare at the poor loser who was all by himself once again. Reflexively he slipped an arm around the barely perceptible waist of his girlfriend, the Pillsbury doughgirl. I guess he wanted to make sure she couldn't get away, lest he wind up like me.

A lesser man than I might have felt sorry for himself.

During the intermission I stayed right where I was. I had plenty of popcorn left, and I didn't need to use the john or duck out for a quick smoke. I stayed put, and after a decent interval the lights went down again and the second feature began.

Beat the Devil. Directed by John Huston, who shared the screenplay credit with Truman Capote. The cast included Gina Lollobrigida as Bogart's wife and Jennifer Jones as a compulsive liar married to a fake English nobleman. Peter Lorre's in it as well, along with Robert Morley and a bunch of great character actors whose names I can never remember.

I settled into my seat, thinking that maybe this time I'd be able to understand what was going on on the screen. I must have seen the movie three or four times over the years and was never able to make head or tail out of it. Everybody was trying to hood-wink everybody else, and when Jennifer Jones prefaced a statement with "in point of fact" you knew for certain she was about to come up with a whopper, but beyond that I could never quite manage to follow the plot. Maybe this time would be different.

Five or ten minutes in, I sensed a presence in the aisle. Without averting my eyes from the screen, where Morley and Lorre had their heads together, I listened hard for approaching footsteps. But I don't know that I actually heard her draw near. It was more a matter of simply knowing, some extrasensory awareness that quickened the pulse and made it hard to breathe.

Then she was settling into the seat beside me. I still couldn't take my eyes off the screen. A leg bumped mine momentarily, then drew away. A hand dipped into the vat of popcorn and brushed my hand before closing around a fistful of popped kernels.

I watched the movie and listened to chewing sounds.

Then came an urgent whisper. "You were right, Bern. This is really dynamite popcorn."

Throats were cleared and programs rustled in the row immediately behind ours. I put a finger to my lips and glanced at Carolyn, who mimed a wordless apology.

And, side by side, we ate the popcorn and watched the movie.

On the way out, the ticket-taker gave me a big smile and the guy with the goatee flashed me a thumbs-up. "They're happy for me," I told Carolyn. "Isn't that nice?"

"It's wonderful," she said. "One of those heartwarming little New York vignettes. Imagine if they knew you spent the past two nights at my apartment."

"Please," I said. "They'd start wondering when I'm going to make an honest woman of you."

Across the street they had tables set up on the sidewalk, and it was a nice enough night to sit at one of them. I ordered cappuccino and Carolyn asked for Caffè Lucrezia Borgia, which sounded as though it might be poisoned but turned out to be the house special, a production number consisting of espresso with a slug of Strega in it and a topping of whipped cream and shaved chocolate. She pronounced it excellent and offered me a taste, but I passed.

"Not even a taste? It's not going to get you drunk."

"Without principles," I said, "where are we?"

"I've got to give you credit," she said. "Of course you're going to be way out of shape by the time all this is over. Anyway, I'm starting to wonder if I'm in better shape than I ought to be."

"What do you mean?"

"Well, I kept the store open until I finished 'A' Is for Train, and I only had one drink at the Bum Rap after I closed up, and I swear I didn't even feel it, and afterward I ate a full meal at the Indian place, but even so I've got to admit I had trouble following the movie tonight."

"No one can follow it," I said. "It's Beat the Devil. I think they must have been making it up as they went along, and I'm positive they didn't have any prissy little rule about not having a drink when they had work to do. No worries about getting out of shape, not on that set."

We talked some about the film, and I gave her a rundown on the first feature, *King of the Underworld,* which she was sorry to have missed. "Except I like it better when he doesn't get killed at the end," she said. "You know me, I'm a sucker for a happy ending."

"In *King of the Underworld,*" I said, "the ending's not happy until he dies. But I know what you mean. Maybe that's why they usually show the older picture first. He tended to be alive at the end of the later ones, when he was a bigger star."

"Makes sense. What's the point in being a star if you're just going to get killed the same as always?" She sipped her fancy coffee. "I brought your flight bag."

"So I see."

"Ray came to the store. He was actually pleasant to me, which made me a little nervous. It was him sitting in your lobby, but I suppose he told you that himself."

I shook my head. "I never asked."

"Well, he won't be sitting there anymore, so I thought you might want to sleep at home. There's stuff in there you might need if you do. But I'm not trying to get rid of you, Bern. If you want to stay downtown, I'll just take the bag home with me. Or we'll go together."

"I've got a late appointment."

"Oh."

"And if Ray was sitting in my lobby, who was in the car outside?"

"I didn't ask about that."

"Maybe it was a couple of other cops. And maybe it was somebody with no interest in me whatsoever." I frowned. "And maybe not."

"So you'll sleep at my place. Why be silly about it?"

I hefted the flight bag, put it on the ground next to me. "It was a good idea to bring this," I said. "I'll hang on to it."

"But you'll sleep at my place, right?"

"Who knows where I'll sleep?"

"Bern . . ."

"There's always a little furnished room on East Twenty-fifth Street," I said. "The accommodations are on the Spartan side, but I know for a fact that the bed's comfortable. Or there's the subway. Or a bench in the park, on a beautiful night like this."

"What are you talking about?"

I tilted my head to one side, took hold of my chin with my thumb and forefinger, and let the words come out of the side of my mouth. "It's like this, sweetheart," I said. "I'll find a place to sleep. You don't have to worry about me."

After I'd settled the check she said, "Caphob, caphob. *Ohmigod.*"

"What's the matter?"

"Is it conceivable? Could it possibly be?"

"Could what possibly be?"

She took my arm. "Don't you think maybe . . . no, you'll just tell me I'm out of my mind."

"I promise I won't."

"Okay, here's what I was thinking. Maybe Caphob is the sled."

"You're out of your mind."

"I know, but at least I got a laugh out of you. Bern, the only thing I really have to worry about is that you've seen too many movies. At any moment you're liable to slip into character. Or do I mean out of character? Out of your own character and into his, that's what I mean."

"Not to worry," I said. "You want a cab?"

"I think I'll take the subway. It's a nice night."

"And you want to enjoy it way down below the pavement?"

"I mean I won't mind the walk from the subway stop. You knew what I meant."

"True. *I* want a cab, though. I have to go across town, and I don't want to be late." I held up a hand and a cab pulled up almost immediately. I asked Carolyn if she was sure she didn't want it, and she said she was. I opened the door and the driver gave me a big smile, his eyes bright with recognition.

"Great to see you," I told him. To Carolyn I said, "Get in. This cab's for you."

"But . . ."

"Come on," I said. "How often do you get a chance to ride with a man who knows where Arbor Court is?" I held the door for her, leaned in, and urged Max to tell her about herbs. "But not about the woman and the monkey," I added.

"Wait a minute," Carolyn said. "What's this about a woman and a monkey? I want to hear this."

I closed the door and the cab pulled away. I hailed another, and asked the Vietnamese driver if he knew how to get to Seventy-fourth and Park.

"I'm sure I'll be able to find it," he said dryly. His name was Nguyen Trang, and he spoke good English and knew the city cold. As we rode across town he told me what a great city it was. "But the fucking Cambodians are ruining it," he said.

NINETEEN

Charlie Weeks was waiting in his doorway when the elevator let me out on the twelfth floor. "Ah, Mr. Thompson," he said. "I'm so glad you could make it." The elevator operator took this for a sign that I was welcome, and closed his door and descended.

Charlie held the door for me, followed me inside. "I thought I'd give them the same name as last time," I told him. "It's less confusing that way."

"Less confusing for me as well," he said. "I met you as Bill Thompson, and it's hard to think of you as anyone else. What do they call you, anyway? Bernard? Bernie? Barney?"

"I'll answer to almost anything. Bill, if you'd rather."

"Oh, I can't call you Bill, now that I know it's not your name." He looked me over carefully. "What's your favorite animal?" he demanded.

"My favorite animal? Gee, I don't know. I never really thought about it."

"Never?"

He made me feel I'd wasted a lifetime thinking

about relativity and quantum theory and dialectical materialism when I should have been selecting a favorite animal. "Well, I guess I must have given it a little thought," I admitted.

"What's your favorite?"

"It depends. For eating I'd go with cows, I guess, or sheep. Tofu's not an animal, is it? No, of course not. It's not even a bird. Uh . . ."

"Not to eat."

"Right. Well, let's see. Different animals for different things, I'd have to say. I have a cat working for me in the store, fine mouser. If you're going to have an animal around a bookshop I don't see how you could do better than a cat. Rabbits are cute, but a rabbit in a bookstore would be a disaster. They, uh, gnaw things. Books, for instance. Now, for swimming in figure eights, well, you can't beat the polar bear I was watching the other day. Eight eight eight eight eight, just like a repeating decimal, you'd have sworn he thought he was the square root of minus something-or-other."

His face held an expression of long-suffering. "The animal you identify with," he said. "The animal you see yourself as."

"Oh." I thought it over. "I guess I've always seen myself as a person," I said.

"If you were an animal, what kind of animal would you be?"

"I guess that would depend on what kind of animal I was. I know, I'm supposed to think hypothetically, but I seem to be having trouble. I'm sorry. Is this important?"

"No, of course not. Let's just forget it."

"No, dammit," I said, "that's not right. I ought to be able to figure this out."

"I was the mouse," he said patiently. "Wood was the woodchuck. Cappy Hoberman was the ram."

"And Bateman was the rabbit and Renwick was the cat."

"Rennick."

"Right, Rennick. So you think I ought to have an animal code name?"

"It's really not important," he said. "I was just making conversation."

"No, I'd be glad to have one," I said, "but maybe it's not the sort of thing a person should pick for himself. If you wanted to pick a name for me . . ."

"Hmmm," he said, and stroked his chin with his fingertips. "Something in the weasel family, I think."

"Something in the weasel family?"

"I would think so. An otter?"

"An otter?"

"No," he said, "I don't think so. Not an otter. The playful quality is there, to be sure, but the otter's altogether too straightforward. I'd say not an otter."

"Good," I said. "Tastes of dog, anyway."

"I beg your pardon?"

"Nothing."

"Something furtive," he said. He put his palms together in front of his chest and made a sort of side-to-side motion. "Something nocturnal, something devious, something predatory. Something, oh, burglarous."

"Burglarous," I said.

"Not a wolverine, that's altogether too rapacious. Nor a mink, I don't believe. A badger?" He looked at me. "Not a badger. Perhaps a ferret."

"A ferret?"

"Not a ferret. You know what? I think a weasel, a plain old garden-variety weasel."

"Oh," I said.

"You're the weasel," he said. He clapped me on the back. "Come on, weasel. Have a seat, make yourself comfortable. There's coffee made."

"Thank God," I said.

The weasel was in the kitchen for a little over a half hour, passing on some facts and guesses to the mouse, drinking coffee, and listening to some reminiscences of skulduggery in the Balkans, circa 1950. It was absorbing and entertaining, and if not everything he told me was a hundred percent factual, well, that made us even.

It was close to midnight when I put down my coffee cup, got to my feet, and grabbed up my Braniff bag. "I'd better be going," I said. "I have a feeling we're getting somewhere, but maybe we shouldn't bother. If Candlemas killed Hoberman, we don't have to worry that he got away with it. He's dead himself. He wasn't my partner, and he forfeited any claim on my loyalties when he became a murderer. It might be interesting to know who killed him, but I can't say it's vitally important to me."

"That's a point."

"Well, we can just take it a day at a time," I said,

"and see what happens. But I'm beat. I want to get on home."

"I'll see you out."

I told him he didn't have to go to the trouble, and he assured me it was no trouble. The next thing I knew we were out in the hall, waiting for the elevator I'd been careful not to ring for.

Hell.

I'd thought of having Carolyn call his number at a predetermined time, then contriving to be out in the hall waiting for the elevator at just that moment. But I'd decided it wouldn't work. For one thing, trying to synchronize something like that is just about impossible. If the phone call comes a minute too early or late, the whole scheme falls flat. For another, his apartment was all the way down the hall, and you probably couldn't hear his phone if you were standing by the elevator shaft.

"Is that thing not coming?" he said, after we'd waited for a few minutes.

"It may be a while. Look, there's no reason for you to stand out here in your robe."

"I'm not going to abandon you," he said firmly. "You know, the same damned thing happened last time you were here." He chuckled. "Maybe you don't know how to ring that thing," he said, and reached to do it himself.

I caught hold of his wrist. "I'll level with you," I said.

"Oh?"

"This is a genuinely difficult building to get into,"

I said, "and now that I'm inside it, I hate to see the opportunity go to waste."

"What do you mean?" He studied me with those see-through-everything eyes of his. "You can't be planning another visit to that apartment on the eighth floor."

I shook my head. "Whatever the guy had down there," I said, "he doesn't have it anymore, and I didn't see anything else terribly exciting in his place. But there's a couple on Nineteen, he's a muni bond specialist in a big brokerage house downtown, and I think she's a Vanderbilt on her mother's side. And I happen to know they're in Quogue for the weekend."

"Ha!" he cried, delighted. "You're the weasel, all right."

"Of course, if they're by any chance particular friends of yours . . ."

"Not at all, weasel, not at all. I don't know anyone on the nineteenth floor, certainly not a huckster of municipal bonds. But you'll be careful, won't you? Isn't it dangerous?"

"It's always dangerous," I said, flashing a raffish grin. "That's what makes it interesting."

"Oh, what a weasel! Can't keep him out of the chicken yard."

"But I'll be careful," I assured him. "I'll be in and out in an hour, and this"—I patted the flight bag—"should weigh a little more then than it does now."

"And then you'll simply head for home?"

"I'll take the stairs this far," I said, "for the elevator

operator's benefit. So if you happen to see me in the hallway an hour or so from now, don't be alarmed."

"I hope to be sleeping soundly by then," he said. "I'll rest easy, secure in the knowledge that the weasel is hard at work six stories above me." He thrust his hand at me. "Good hunting, weasel."

"Thank you, mouse."

"Animal names," he said with satisfaction. "They serve a purpose. Until tomorrow, my good little weasel."

"Until tomorrow," I said, and we shook hands and went our separate ways. His led back to his apartment, mine to the stairwell and, presumably, the nineteenth floor.

Except that's not where I went.

I did climb two flights of stairs for starters, then sat at the fifteenth-story landing for a few minutes working things out in my mind. (Yes, I went up two flights and got from Twelve to Fifteen. You read that right. There's no thirteenth floor at the Boccaccio, which is why the mouse could anticipate my doing the work of a weasel six stories above him.)

He could anticipate it, but that didn't mean it was going to happen.

After a good long moment of uffish thought on Fifteen, I retraced my steps and kept on going clear down past Twelve, where Charlie Weeks would soon be sleeping peacefully, and past Eight, where Mike Todd would be sleeping or not, with or without the enigmatic Ilona Markova. I went all the way down to the fifth floor, where I satisfied myself that the hallway was clear before traversing most of it en route to apartment 5-D. I rang the bell, remembering how I'd very nearly neglected to do so the last time I'd been to the eighth floor. In the present instance I'd have been astonished if anybody had been home, and nobody was. I set down my flight bag, took out my tools, picked the two locks, and let myself in.

For all I knew there was a bond salesman on Nineteen, married to a Vanderbilt and weekending in Quogue. It was entirely possible. And it was unquestionably the case that there were quite a few apartments in the Boccaccio unoccupied that weekend, their tenants in the Hamptons or Nantucket or Block Island, their valuables left behind, easy pickings for a weasel, or any reasonably resourceful burglar.

But I didn't have a clue which apartments they were, or an easy way to find out. What I had managed to learn, by calling a slew of realtors from the Lehrman apartment that afternoon, was that there were at least three Boccaccio apartments currently offered for sale. One of them was occupied at present by its owners. A second was sublet for a handsome monthly fee, and would be available to its purchaser when the sublease expired the end of August.

The third, 5-D, was vacant.

The woman who told me about 5-D was a Ms. Farrante, from the Corcoran Group. As Bill Thompson, I'd made an appointment to see it with her on Wednesday afternoon, but I'd decided I couldn't wait that long. So here I was now.

Once I'd locked up I took a quick tour of the
premises, using my pocket flashlight to supplement
what light came in from the windows. The apartment fronted on Park Avenue, and there were no
drapes or shades or venetian blinds, nothing to be-
dim the view of anyone outside who happened to
look in my direction. I could have switched the lights
on anyway—there's nothing terribly suspicious about
a man pacing around in a completely empty
apartment—but you never know what will prompt
some busybody to dial 911, or walk across the street
and say something to the concierge.

It was as empty as an apartment could be, with
nothing on the floors, nothing on the walls, nothing
in the closets or the kitchen cupboards. The walls
smelled very faintly of paint, and the parquet floors
of wax. The apartment, Ms. Ferrante had assured
me, was in move-in condition, the owners had relo-
cated to Scottsdale, Arizona, and the price was negotiable, but not *very* negotiable. "They've turned down
offers," she said.

They wouldn't get a chance to turn down mine. I
didn't want their apartment. I didn't even want to
burgle it. My entry had been illegal, sure enough, so
I had probably crossed the line into felonious terri-
tory, but my intentions were pure enough.

I just wanted a place to sack out for the next
seven or eight hours.

But what an unwelcoming abode I'd picked! It
would have been nice to sit down in a comfortable
chair, but there were no chairs, comfortable or otherwise. It would have been nice to stretch out in a

canopied four-poster, or a big brass bed, or a sagging couch, but there was nothing of the sort, not even an old mattress on the floor.

It would have been nice to soak in a tub. There were two well-appointed bathrooms, one with a gleaming modern stall shower, the other with a massive old claw-footed tub. I started drawing myself a bath—the water came out rusty for the first twenty seconds, but then ran nice and clear. Then I realized there weren't any towels. Somehow I couldn't see myself having a nice hot bath and then standing around waiting to evaporate to dryness. I had some useful things in the flight bag, clean clothes for the morning, a razor and toothbrush and comb, but I sure didn't have a towel.

I pulled the plug and looked around some more. They'd left toilet paper, thank God, but as far as I could tell that was the only thing that hadn't made the trip to Scottsdale with them.

I didn't feel very sleepy. I might have, given more comfortable surroundings, because Lord knows I'd had a tiring day. But the way I felt I'd be awake for hours.

At least I had something to read. I'd tucked a P. G. Wodehouse paperback into my bag when I'd originally packed it, and neither I nor Carolyn had had occasion to remove it, so it was still there. I could take it to the bathroom and perch on the throne, and with the door closed I'd be safe in turning on the lights.

I did all that, and when I worked the light switch

nothing happened. I tried the other john and got the same result. Well, it figured. Why pay the light bill when nobody was living there? Fortunately I had my pocket flash. It wasn't the world's best reading light, any more than the toilet seat was an ideal library chair, but it would do.

And it did, too, until I was somewhere in the middle of Chapter Six, at which point the beam of my flashlight gradually faded down to a soft yellow glow, a fit illumination for lovemaking, say, but nowhere near bright enough to read by. If I'd been genuinely well prepared I'd have had a couple of replacement batteries in my bag, but I wasn't and I didn't, and that was all the reading I was going to do that night.

So much for that. I went out into another room— the living room, one of the bedrooms, who knew, who cared—and stretched out on the floor. I understand that some floors are harder than others, and that I was lucky to be on wood rather than, say, concrete. That must be true, but you couldn't prove it by me. I can't imagine how I'd have been any less comfortable on a bed of nails.

There were no hangers in the closets—they really did take everything, the bastards—so I hung my slacks and jacket over the rail that would have supported a shower curtain, but for their having taken that along, too. I took off my shoes and slept in the rest of my clothes, using my flight bag as a pillow. It was about as useful in that capacity as the floor was as a bed.

I couldn't afford to oversleep, and of course I

hadn't brought an alarm clock with me. But some-how I didn't think that was likely to be a problem.

Did I really have to do this? Couldn't I pay a visit to some other apartment? It was a holiday weekend, so it stood to reason that a substantial number of Boccaccio residents were out of town until Monday night at the earliest.

Suppose I just picked a likely door and opened it. If nobody was home, I was in business. And even if someone was on the premises, was that necessarily a disaster? I have burgled apartments while the ten-ants slept, even on occasion creeping around in the very room where they were snoring away. No one would call it relaxing work, but there's this to be said for it: you know where they are. You don't have to worry about them coming home and surprising you.

This would be different, but couldn't I sleep on the living-room couch, say, while they were sleeping in the bedroom? I'd make sure I woke up before they did. And if something went wrong, if they found me dozing in front of the fireplace, wasn't it the sort of thing I could talk my way out of? Drunk, I'd say, shrugging sheepishly. Got the wrong apartment by mistake, just dumb luck my key fit in the lock. Ter-ribly sorry, never happen again. I'll go home now.

Was that so utterly out of the question? I could pull that off, couldn't I?

No, I told myself sternly. I couldn't.

I squirmed around, trying to find the most com-fortable position, until I realized with dismay that I'd found it early on and it wasn't going to get any better. I heaved a sigh and closed my eyes. I was as snug as a bug on a bare floor, and there's a reason that metaphor has not become part of the language.

It was going to be a long night.

It was a long night.

Every hour or so I would wake up, if you want to call it that, and look at my watch. Then I would close my eyes and go back to sleep, if you want to call it that, until I woke up again.

And so on.

At six-thirty I gave up and got up. I splashed water on my face, dried my hands with toilet paper, and put on the slacks and shoes I'd taken off. I had a clean shirt and socks and underwear in my bag, but I was saving them until I had a clean body to put them on.

It was light out, so I could read again. I went back to Bertie Wooster, and everything he did and said made perfect sense to me. I took this for a Bad Sign.

At seven-thirty I checked the hall, and there were two people in it, waiting for the elevator. I eased the door silently shut. Two minutes later I tried again, and they were gone but someone else had taken their place. It seemed like a lot of traffic for a luxury building early on a holiday morning, but evidently the residents of the Boccaccio were an enterprising lot, not given to lazy mornings in bed. Or maybe they'd spent the night on the floor, too, and were as eager as I to be up and doing.

When I cracked the door a third time there was yet another person in the hall, but she looked to be a cleaning woman who'd just emerged from the ele-

vator and was headed for an apartment at the far end
of the hallway. I stepped out and drew the door shut,
unwilling to lock up after myself as I usually do, not
with so much traffic all around me. The empty
apartment would have to spend the next little while
guarded only by the spring locks, which meant anybody with a credit card could steal inside and make
off with the toilet paper.

So be it. I walked to the stairwell, setting a brisk
pace, and its fire door closed behind me without my
attracting any attention.

So far so good.

I climbed seven flights of stairs, telling myself that
people paid good money to do essentially the same
thing on a machine at the gym. I'll admit I paused a
couple of times en route, but I got there.

At the twelfth-floor landing, I waited until I'd
caught my breath, which took longer than I'd prefer
to admit. Then I opened the door about an inch and
a half and looked out. I'd picked the right stairwell,
and from where I was I had a good if narrow view of
his door.

I hunkered down, which for years I thought was
something people only did in westerns. It turns out
you can do it anywhere, even in a ritzy building on
Park Avenue. It was less tiring than holding a fixed
upright position for a long period of time, and I was
less likely to be seen; people do most of their looking
at eye level, and my own eyes, lurking behind a
slightly ajar door all the way at the end of the hall,
wouldn't be as noticeable if I kept them half their
usual distance from the floor.

I checked my watch. It was seventeen minutes to eight. It seemed to me that should give me plenty of leeway, but I hadn't been there five minutes before I started to worry that I'd missed him.

According to him, he was a creature of habit, leaving the house at the same time and taking the same walk every morning. The previous morning I'd been loitering in a doorway across the street, drinking bad coffee from a Styrofoam cup and waiting for him to make his appearance. He'd done so at ten minutes after eight, and if he stayed on schedule today he'd leave his apartment sometime between a quarter to eight and eight-thirty.

Unless he didn't.

If he was later today than yesterday, I could just wait him out. It's not as though I had a train to catch, or a longstanding appointment at the periodontist. But if he was earlier, more than twenty-seven minutes earlier, say, then I'd get to see him return while I was still waiting for him to leave.

Not good.

If you ever start thinking you're a long ways from being neurotic, just spend a little time squinting at a closed door waiting for it to open. I couldn't get my mind to shut up. I'd made a big mistake, I told myself, staying as long as I had in the empty apartment. Suppose I'd missed him. Suppose the apartment was magnificently empty right now, while I squatted there like a constipated savage. I should have been in place by seven-thirty at the latest. Seven o'clock would have been better, and six-thirty would have been better still.

On the other hand, how long could I perch at the stair landing without someone turning up to ask me what the hell I thought I was doing there? It did not seem unlikely that the stairs would see a certain amount of casual traffic, whether of tenants or building staff. I didn't expect a whole lot of coming and going, but all it would take was one mildly curious individual and the best I could hope for was a summary exit from the premises.

The time crawled. I asked myself what Bogart would do, and right away I knew one thing he'd have done. He'd have smoked. By ten minutes after eight (his departure time yesterday, so where the hell *was* he?) the floor would have been littered with butts and cigarette ash. He'd have tapped cigarettes out philosophically, ground them out savagely, flicked them unthinkingly down the stairs. He'd have smoked like crazy, the son of a gun, but when it came time to take action, by God he'd have taken it.

What if I just went over there and rang his goddam bell? Now, without waiting for any more time to pass. If he'd left early, I'd be able to get in there now instead of wasting the whole day. And if he was still home, if he hadn't left yet, and he answered the bell, well, I would just think of something.

Like what?

I was trying to think of it when his door opened, and I'd been staring at it so hard for so long that it barely registered. Then he emerged, looking quite dapper in flannel trousers and a houndstooth jacket, and wearing the hat he'd been wearing that first night, when he opened the door for Captain Hoberman and blinked in surprise to see me there as well.

He had what seemed like a long wait for the elevator, but he waited patiently, and I tried to follow his example. A young couple emerged from the E or F apartment just as the elevator door opened, and the man called for them to hold the door while the woman locked up. Then they joined Weeks in the elevator and away they all went.

I let out my breath, looked at my watch. It was fourteen minutes after eight.

Three minutes later I was inside his apartment.

TWENTY

I figured I had an hour before he was likely to return. If I wanted to play it safe, all I had to do was
be out of there by nine o'clock.

As it turned out, it didn't take me anywhere near
that long to do what I wanted to do. I was out of his
apartment by twenty to nine, out of the building
shortly thereafter.

I probably would have had time for a shower.

You know, I thought about it. I could have
shucked my clothes, treated myself to a minute and
a half under a spray of hot water, then rubbed myself
speedily dry with one of his fluffy mint-green towels.
I could have stuffed the towel in my flight bag, carrying the evidence away with me. He'd never have
missed it.

But I didn't. Nor did I sneak a cup of the leftover
coffee. He probably wouldn't have missed that, either, and God knows I could have used it, but I was
a good little burglar and left it untouched.

I got in, I got out. When I hit the street I looked
around, and he was nowhere to be seen. I caught a
cab, gave the ethnically indeterminate driver my ad-

dress, and sat back with my Braniff bag cradled on
my lap. I felt grimy and grubby and I couldn't stop
yawning.

I didn't see the suspect car in front of my building,
and I wasn't worried I'd find Ray Kirschmann in the
lobby, but it seemed a bad time to leave anything to
chance. I got the driver to circle the block and let
me off around the corner in front of the service entrance. I'd just finished paying the tab when a fellow
in a glen plaid suit and a horrible tie came out of the
very door I was planning on opening. "Hold it!" I
sang out, and he did, and I was inside my building
without having to pick any locks.

Now isn't that a hell of a thing? I'd never seen this
clown before, so it was odds-on he'd never laid eyes
on me, and here he was letting me through a door
that was supposed to be kept locked.

I very nearly had a word with him about it. I've
been known to do that. After all, I live in the building; the last thing I want is unauthorized persons
roaming its halls and imperiling its tenants, one of
them myself. I've bluffed and smiled and sweet-
talked my way into any number of buildings. I know
how it works, and I'd just as soon nobody worked it
on the place where I live.

But I held my tongue. I'd talk to the fellow another time. For now, I had other things to do.

First a shower and a shave, neither of which could
possibly have been called premature. Then, clad in
fresh clothes, I took the subway downtown and ate a
big breakfast at a Union Square coffee shop. It was

another beautiful day, the latest in a string of them and a fitting finale for Memorial Day weekend. I treated myself to a second cup of coffee, and I was whistling as I walked to my store.

I got a royal welcome from Raffles, who was trying to see how much static electricity he could generate by rubbing against my ankles. I fed him right away, more to keep him from getting underfoot than because I felt he was in great danger of starvation. Then I dragged my bargain table outside—I've thought of putting wheels on it, but I just know if I did some moron would roll it away and I'd never see it again. I wanted the bargain table out there not for the trade it would bring but because I needed the space it otherwise occupied. If all went according to plan, I was going to have a full house this afternoon.

The first person through the door was Mowgli. "Whoa!" he said. "You trying to get rich, Bernie? Man, it's a holiday. Why aren't you at the beach?"

"I'm afraid of sharks."

"Then what are you doing in the book business? I'm surprised to find you here, is all. First Carolyn was here to keep the place open yesterday and the day before, and now you're here in person. You get a chance to look at those books I left for you?"

I hadn't, of course, and didn't really have time to look at them now, but I found the sack of them behind the counter and gave its contents a fast look-through. It was good stuff, including a couple of early Oz books with the color frontispiece illustrations intact. We agreed on a price of seventy-five dollars, less the ten bucks Carolyn had advanced him, and I found four twenties in the cash drawer and held them out to him.

"Haven't got change," he said. "You want to give me sixty and owe me five, or can I owe you the fifteen? That's what I'd rather do, but maybe you don't want to do it that way."

"I'll tell you what," I said. "Help me move some furniture and you won't owe me a dime."

"Move some furniture? Like move it where, man?"

"Around," I said. "I want to create a little space here, set up some folding chairs."

"Expecting a crowd, Bernie?"

"I wouldn't call it a crowd. Six, eight people. Something like that."

"Be a crowd in here. I guess that's why you want to move some stuff around. What's on the program, a poetry reading?"

"Not exactly."

"Because I didn't know you were into that. I read some of my own stuff a while back at a little place on Ludlow Street. Café Villanelle?"

"Black walls and ceiling," I said. "Black candles set in cat-food cans."

"Hey, you know it! Not many people even heard of the place."

"It may take a while to find its audience," I said, trying not to shudder at the memory of an evening of Emily Dickinson sung to the tune of "The Yellow Rose of Texas" and a lifetime supply of in-your-face haiku. This wouldn't be a poetry reading this afternoon, though, I added. It was more of a private sale.

"Like an auction?"

"In a way," I said. "With dramatic elements."

He thought that sounded interesting, and I told him he could hang around and sit in if he wanted. He helped me bring some chairs up front from the back room, and about that time Carolyn turned up. She had a couple of folding chairs at the Poodle Factory, and Mowgli went with her to fetch them.

Right after they left I got a phone call, and when they came back I made a phone call, and then I actually got a couple of customers, one of whom asked about an eight-volume set of Defoe and actually pulled out his wallet when I agreed to knock fifteen dollars off the price. He paid cash, too, and left me to wonder if I'd been making a mistake all these years, closing up on Sundays and holidays.

At twelve-thirty Carolyn went around the corner to the Freedom Fighter Deli and brought back lunch for all three of us. We each got a Felix Dzerzhinsky sandwich on a seeded roll and a bottle of cream soda, and we sat on three of the chairs I'd set up and pushed two of the others together to make a table. Afterward I repositioned the chairs and stood back to survey the result.

Carolyn said it looked good.

"That's the easy part," I said. "But do you figure anybody will show up?"

Mowgli put his hands together and made a little bow. "If you build it," he announced, his voice unnaturally deep and resonant, "they will come."

And, starting an hour later, they did just that.

* * *

The first arrivals were two men I'd never laid eyes on before, but even so I knew them right away. One was tall and hugely fat, with a big nose and chin and impressive eyebrows. He was wearing a white suit and a white-on-white shirt with French cuffs, the links made from a pair of U.S. five-dollar gold pieces. A black beret looked perfectly appropriate on top of his mane of steel-gray hair.

His companion was rain-thin, with a weak chin and not nearly enough space between his shifty little eyes. He had the kind of pallor you could only acquire by sleeping in a coffin. A lit cigarette burned unattended in one corner of his sullen mouth.

The fat man looked us over. He acknowledged Carolyn with a polite nod, checked out Mowgli and me, and guessed correctly. "Mr. Rhodenbarr," he said to me. "Gregory Tsarnoff."

"Mr. Tsarnoff," I said, and shook his hand. "It's good of you to come."

"We seem to be early," he said. "Punctuality is a fault of mine, sir, and the lot of the punctual man is perennial disappointment."

"I hope you won't be disappointed today," I said. "I haven't met your uh friend, but I believe we spoke on the telephone."

"Indeed. Wilfred, this is Mr. Rhodenbarr."

Wilfred nodded. He didn't extend his hand, nor did I offer mine. "A pleasure," I said, as sincerely as I could. "Uh, Wilfred, I'm afraid I'll have to ask you to put out the cigarette."

He gave me a look.

"The smoke gets in the books," I said. And in the

air, I might have added. Wilfred glanced at Tsarnoff, who nodded shortly. Wilfred then took the cigarette from his lips. I thought he was going to drop it on my floor, but no, he opened the door and flicked it expertly out into the street.

"A deplorable habit," Tsarnoff said, "but the young man has other qualities which render him indispensable to me. I should find it as hard to forgo his services as he to abjure Dame Nicotine. But are we not all slaves to something, sir?"

I couldn't argue with that. I steered him to my desk chair, saying I thought he'd find it the most comfortable of the lot, and he eased his bulk into it. The chair bore the load well. Wilfred, not a whit less sullen without the cigarette, took a folding chair over to the side.

"I wonder," Tsarnoff said. "Might we make lemonade of the sour fruit of punctuality? I am here, sir, and you are here. What do you say we do a deal and leave the latecomers out in the cold?"

"Ah, I wish I could."

"But you can, sir. You have only to act on the wish."

I shook my head. "It wouldn't be fair to the others," I said, "and it would leave some important points unaddressed. Besides, people will be arriving any minute now."

"I daresay you're right," he said, and nodded at the door, where a woman with her arms full of packages was trying to get a hand free to reach for the knob.

It was the flower matron, Maggie Mason, breathless with anticipation. "I never thought you'd be open

today," she said. "How's Raffles? Is he working too,
or did you give him the day off?"

"He's always on the job," I said. "But as a matter
of fact I'm not. The store's closed."

"It is?" She looked around. "That's curious. It *looks*
as though you're open. You have people in the store."

"I know."

"Yes, of course, you would have to know that,
wouldn't you? But your Special Value table is outside."

"That's because there's no room for it in the store
this afternoon," I said. I reached for the CLOSED sign
and hung it in the window. "We're having a private
sale this afternoon. We'll be open regular hours tomorrow."

"A private sale! May I come?"

"I'm sorry, but—"

"I'm a wonderful impulse buyer, really I am. Remember the last time I was here? I just came in to
talk to Raffles, and look at all the books I went home
with."

I remembered it well, as who in my business
would not? A two-hundred-dollar sale, completely
out of the blue.

"Please, Mr. Rhodenbarr? Pretty please?"

I was tempted, I have to tell you. For all I knew
she'd sit there starry-eyed, ready to outbid everybody,
and when the dust had settled she'd own a dozen
more art books and that leather-bound set of Balzac.

"I'm sorry," I said reluctantly. "It really is by invitation only. But next time I'll put you on the invitation
list. How's that?"

It was good enough to send her on her way. I turned back to my guests and had started to say something when Mowgli caught my eye and gave me the high sign. I went to the door and opened it to admit Tiglath Rasmoulian.

This time he was wearing a belted trench coat, and the shirt under it was either persimmon or pumpkin blush, depending which mail-order catalog you prefer. He had the same straw panama, but I could swear he'd changed the feather in its band to one that matched his shirt. "Mr. Rhodenbarr," he said, smiling as he crossed the threshold. Then he caught sight of the man in the white suit and the spots of color on his cheeks looked on the point of spontaneous combustion.

"Tsarnoff," he cried. "You Slavic blot! You foul corpulence!"

Tsarnoff raised his eyebrows, no mean task given the bulk of them. "Rasmoulian," he purred, investing the name with a full measure of malice. "You Assyrian guttersnipe. You misbegotten Levantine dwarf."

"Why are you here, Tsarnoff?" He turned to me. "Why is he here?"

"Everybody's got to be someplace," I said.

This left him unmollified. "I was not told he would be here," he said. "I am not happy about this."

"While I on the contrary am delighted to see you, Tiglath. I find your feculent presence enormously reassuring. How good to know you're not somewhere else, causing unimaginable trouble."

They looked daggers at each other, or possibly scimitars, even yataghans. Rasmoulian's hand slipped into his trench-coat pocket, and across the way young Wilfred matched this escalation by sliding a hand inside his Milwaukee Brewers warm-up jacket.

"Gentlemen," I said inaccurately. "Please."

Across the way, Carolyn seemed to be looking around for a place to hide when the shooting started. Mowgli, standing beside her, showed less alarm. Maybe he was just blasé, considering what he had to be used to in the abandoned buildings he called home. Or maybe he thought these were a couple of book collectors about to lose their heads over something from the Kelmscott Press, and that Wilfred had been reaching for a cigarette, and Rasmoulian for a handkerchief.

For a moment nobody moved, and the two of them kept their agate eyes fastened on one another. Then, in unison, as if in response to some high-pitched tone no human ear could detect, they brought their empty hands into view.

I'll admit it, I breathed easier. I didn't want them shooting each other, not in my store. Not this early in the game, certainly.

The next to arrive was Weeks.

He stood at the door, eyeballed the CLOSED sign, turned the knob, and came on in. He was wearing the same outfit I'd seen him leave the apartment in that morning, houndstooth jacket, flannel slacks, brown-and-white spectator wing tips, and that cocoa hat of his. It was quite a crowd for headwear, with Tsarnoff's beret, Rasmoulian's panama, and Weeks and his natty homburg. I hadn't seen this many hats all at once outside of the Musette Theater, where on some evenings the screen was dark with them.

Tsarnoff and Rasmoulian still had their hats on, but Weeks took his off when he caught sight of Carolyn. His ever-watchful eyes scanned the room, and a smile spread on his face.

"Gregorius," he said. "How nice to see you again. And Tiglath. Always a pleasure. I'd no idea you two gentlemen would be here." As if we hadn't discussed the two of them at great length. He smiled happily at Wilfred, who stared hard at him in return. "I don't believe I've had the pleasure," he said. "Gregorius, won't you introduce me to your young friend?"

Tsarnoff said, "Charles, this is Wilfred. Wilfred, this is Charles Weeks. Mark him well."

Weeks did a double take. " 'Mark him well,' eh? Whatever could you mean by that, Gregorius?" To Wilfred he said, "My pleasure, son," and extended his hand. Wilfred just looked at the hand and made no move to take it.

"For Christ's sake," Weeks said, disgusted. "Shake hands like a man, you wretched toad-sucking little maggot. That's better." He wiped his hand on his pants leg and turned to me. "Weasel," he said warmly. "Introduce me to these nice people."

I made the introductions. Weeks bowed over Carolyn's hand, brushing it with his lips, then shook hands with Mowgli and asked him if he'd really been raised by wolves. First raised, then lowered, Mowgli told him.

I said, "Have a seat, Charlie."

"Why, thank you," he said. "Yes, I think I will." He

took a moment to make his choice, finally selecting the chair two to the left of Tsarnoff, placing his hat on the chair that separated them. "Mowgli's from Kipling's *Jungle Book,* but of course you would know that, wouldn't you, Gregorius?" Tsarnoff rolled his eyes at the question. "Were your parents great Kipling fans, son? Or did you choose the name yourself?"

We weren't to find out, because the door opened before Mowgli could answer. I knew who it was, I'd caught a glimpse of her as she'd crossed the sidewalk in front of the store, and I didn't want to watch her come in. I wanted to watch them watching her, but I couldn't help myself. When she was in a room, that's where my eyes went.

And she did it again.

So I said it again, and out loud for a change. "Of all the bookstores in all the towns in all the world," I said, "she walks into mine."

TWENTY-ONE

Of course she remembered the line. Her eyes brightened with recognition, and she smiled that smile of hers, the one that made her look like the Mona Lisa who swallowed the canary. "Bernard," she said, except of course that wasn't how she said it. "Bear-naard"—*that's* how she said it.

I said, "It's good to see you, Ilona. I've missed you."

"Bear-naard."

"Are you alone? I thought you'd be in company."

"I wanted to come in alone first," she said. "To make sure that . . . that the right people are here."

"Look at these people," I said. "Don't they look right to you?"

Now I managed a look at the rest of them, and they were a sight to see. Charlie Weeks, already bareheaded, sprang to his feet and smiled his little smile. Tsarnoff didn't stand, but snatched off the black beret and held it with both hands in his lap. He looked at Ilona as if trying to decide the best way to prepare her for the table. Rasmoulian took his hat off, held it for a moment, then put it back on his head. His eyes were full of hopeless longing, and I knew just how he felt.

I couldn't read Wilfred's look. His hard little eyes took her in, sized her up, and didn't show a thing.

God knows what Ilona thought looking at that crew, but she evidently found nothing to put her off stride. "I will be right back," she said, and ducked out the door, returning moments later with Michael Todd in tow. He was wearing a gray sharkskin suit and, while he was bareheaded, his tie sported a dozen or more colorful hats floating on a red background.

"Michael," she said (it came out as a sort of cross between Michael and Mikhail), "this is Bernard. Bernard, I would like you to meet—"

"But we have met," Michael cut in. "Only the name was not Bernard. It was—" He searched his memory. "Bill! Bill Thomas!"

"Thompson," I said, "but that's still pretty impressive. I didn't think you were paying any attention."

"He came to the door," he told her. "The other morning. He was collecting for a charity." His eyes narrowed. "He *said* he was collecting for a charity."

"The American Hip Dysplasia Association," I said, "and that's where your money went, so don't worry about it. It's a hell of a worthy cause, and if you'd like I'm sure Miss Kaiser would be happy to tell you more than you could possibly want to know about it."

"But you are not Mr. Thompson? You are Mr. Bernard?"

"Mr. Rhodenbarr," I said, "but you can call me Bernie. Why don't you have a seat, Your—" I stopped myself. "And you too, Ilona. I thought a third person would be coming along with the two of you. Actually he was supposed to pick the two of you up, and I'm a little surprised that you happened to get here without him. I hate to start before he gets here, so perhaps we can—"

"Perhaps we can," Ray Kirschmann said from the doorway. He shouldered his way into the store, cast a cold eye on the assembled company, and propped an elbow on a convenient bookshelf. He was wearing another costly if ill-fitting suit, and damned if he didn't have a hat on, and a fedora at that. I happen to think all plainclothes policemen should wear hats, just like in the movies, but they mostly don't in real life, and I couldn't recall ever seeing Ray in a hat before. It looked good on him.

"What I am," he said, "is I'm touched, Bernie. The idea you'd wait for me. You want to innerduce me to these folks?"

I went around the circle, naming names, and then I got to Ray. "And this is Raymond Kirschmann," I said, "of the New York Police Department."

There were some interesting reactions. Charlie Weeks's eyes brightened and his smile took up a little more of his face. Tsarnoff looked unhappy. Rasmoulian had an air of resignation; the introduction couldn't have come as a surprise to him, since he'd already met Ray twice before, and even Ray's presence was probably something less than a shock, given Ray's propensity for turning up whenever Tiggy paid a visit to Barnegat Books.

Wilfred didn't seem surprised, either, and I figured

it was because he'd made Ray the minute he walked in. Wilfred struck me as the sort of fellow who could spot a cop a block away. On the other hand, I don't suppose his face would have changed expression if I'd introduced Ray as a first vice president at Chase Manhattan, in charge of repairing broken automatic teller machines. Wilfred wasn't much on changing expressions, or of showing one in the first place.

Anyway, the big reaction came from Ilona and Mike, who mumbled and stammered something to the effect that they'd thought Ray was affiliated not with the police at all but with the Immigration and Naturalization Service.

"Now that's innarestin'," he allowed, "an' I can see where you would get the impression, an' maybe I even went an' made a slip of the tongue, sayin' INS when I meant NYPD. It's one batch of initials or another, an' it coulda come out AFL-CIO just as easy. But Bernie here is right, what I am is a cop, an' just for form I prob'ly oughta read you all this here." He held up a little wallet-size card and read, " 'You have the right to remain silent,' " and went all the way to the end, Mirandizing the hell out of everybody.

"I don't understand," Tsarnoff said. "Am I to take it, sir, that we have been placed under arrest?"

"Naw," Ray said. "Why'd I wanna go an' arrest anybody? I don't see nobody breakin' no laws. An' even if I did, I ain't in no hurry to make an arrest. You arrest somebody nowadays, you're lookin' at twelve, fifteen hours of paperwork by the time you're done. Why, on my way in here I saw a young fellow take a

book off of Bernie's outside table, an' do you think I
was gonna arrest him for that?"

"Probably not," I said.

"Of course not. So if anybody in this room should
happen to be carryin' a concealed weapon, with or
without you got a permit for it, as long as it don't see
the light of day you got nothin' to worry about. Or if
there's a person here with outstandin' warrants, well,
put your mind at rest. That ain't what I'm here for."

"And yet you read us our rights," Tsarnoff per-
sisted.

"That's just a contingency procedure," Charlie
Weeks said. "Figure it out, Gregorius. From this
point on, anything anybody says is admissible as evidence. At least that's the supposition. I don't know
what a lawyer would make of it, or a judge."

"A lawyer would make a buck," Ray said, "bein' as
they generally do. An' nobody ever knows what a
judge'll make of anything. An' the real reason I read
the Miranda card is so we'll all take this seriously,
even though it ain't official an' I'm just here to see
what my old friend Bernie's gonna pull out of his hat.
He's done this before, an' I got to admit he generally
comes up with a rabbit."

That was my cue, and I hopped to it. The line that
came to me was *I suppose you're wondering why I
summoned you all here,* and I'll admit it's one I've
used to good effect in the past, but it didn't really
apply this time. They weren't wondering. They knew,
or at least thought they did.

"I want to thank you all for coming," I said. "I

know you're all busy people, and I don't want to take up too much of your time. So I'll get right to it."

I would have, too, but some clown picked that moment to stick his head in the door. "The sign says you're closed," he said, sounding peeved.

"We are," I said. "There's a private sale going on. We'll be keeping our usual hours tomorrow."

"But you got a table outside," he said, "plus your door's not locked."

"I'll fix that," I said, and closed it in his face, and thumbed the catch to lock it. He gave me a look and turned away, and I turned back to my guests.

"Sorry," I said. "Mowgli, if anybody else tries to come in—"

"I'll take care of it," he said.

"Thanks. Where was I?"

"You were getting right to it," Charlie Weeks said.

"So I was," I said, and found a bookcase to lean against. "I want to tell you a story, and I may have to jump around a little, because this story starts in a few different places at a few different times. It has its roots deep in the nineteenth century, when nationalist sentiments began to stir throughout the lands administered by the Austro-Hungarian and the Ottoman empires. One of those Balkan nationalisms precipitated the outbreak of the First World War, when a young Serb shot the Austrian archduke. By the time that war ended, self-determination of nations was a catchphrase throughout the western world. Independence movements flowered across Europe. Among the presumptive nations to declare their independence was the sovereign nation of

Anatruria. It was designated as a kingdom, and its monarch was to be King Vlados the First."

This couldn't have been news to any of them, except for Ray and Mowgli, and possibly Wilfred. But they all paid close attention.

"The Anatrurians did what they could to add substance to their proclamation of sovereignty," I went on. "An extensive series of stamps was printed at Budapest, and some were actually used postally within the borders of Anatruria. Some pattern coins were struck and distributed to friends of the new nation, although a general issue was never produced for circulation. There were a few medals issued as well, bearing the new king's likeness and presented to some men who had been the mainstay of the independence movement."

"Scarce as hen's teeth, all of them," Tsarnoff declared. "And about as eagerly sought in the collector market."

"Anatrurian hopes were dashed at Versailles," I went on, "when Wilson and Clemenceau remade the map of Europe. What would have been Anatruria was parceled up among Romania, Bulgaria, and Yugoslavia. King Vlados and Queen Liliana lived out the remainder of their lives in exile, still serving as a rallying point for those who continued to believe in the Anatrurian cause. But the movement died down."

"The flame flickered," Ilona murmured. "But it was never extinguished."

"Maybe not," I said, "but there was a time when it would have taken it a long time to bring a kettle to the boil. Then, during World War Two, the Anatrurian partisans had an active role."

"They were opportunists," Tsarnoff put in, "switching allegiance as it served their interests. One day they'd be fighting side by side with Ante Pavelic's Croatian Ustachi, murdering Serbs, and the next thing you knew they'd be on the Serbian side, sacking Croat villages. Were they for Hitler or against him? It depended when you asked the question."

"They were for Anatruria," Ilona said. "Every day, every week, every month of the year."

"They were for themselves," Tiglath Rasmoulian said. "As who is not?"

"When the war ended," I went on, "national borders in that part of the world remained essentially unchanged, but governments were in upheaval. The Soviet Union's span of influence quickly took in all of Eastern Europe, and Truman had to draw a line in the sand to keep Greece and Turkey this side of the Iron Curtain. Several American intelligence agencies, at least one of them an outgrowth of the wartime OSS, sought to even the balance in that strategically vital area of the world." I frowned, annoyed at the tone I was taking. In spite of all the films I'd seen lately, I was managing to sound like an Edward R. Murrow voice-over for a documentary.

"Among the clandestine missions dispatched to the region"—damn, I was still doing it—"was a group of five American agents."

I hesitated for an instant, and Charlie Weeks read my mind. "Oh, they were all Americans, all right. Hundred percent red-blooded nephews of their Uncle Sam. No wretched refuse of your teeming shores in the Bob and Charlie Show, not on your life."

"Five Americans," I said quickly. "Robert Bateman and Robert Rennick. Charles Hoberman and Charles Wood. And Charles Weeks."

"Charles Weeks?" Ray said. "This fellow here?"

"This fellow here," said Charlie Weeks.

I told how, for convenience' sake, the Roberts had become Bob and Rob respectively, the Charleses Cappy, Chuck, and Charlie. "And," I said, "they all had animal names."

Mowgli said, "Animal names? I'm sorry, Bernie, I didn't mean to interrupt, but I want to make sure I heard you right."

"Animal names," I said. "You heard me right. Code names, really. Bateman was the cat and Rennick was the rabbit."

"Actually," Weeks put in, "it was the other way around. Not that it matters much, at this late date."

"I stand corrected. Cap Hoberman was the ram. Charlie Weeks was the mouse."

"Squeak squeak," said Charlie Weeks.

"And Chuck Wood's totem, perhaps inevitably, was the woodchuck. His was the only one which was a play on words rather than a reference to some per-ceived personal characteristic, and I mention that because it's relevant. I'm guessing now, but I'd say that Wood selected the name for himself."

"Ha!" said Weeks. He looked up and to the left, reaching for the memory. "You know," he said, "I think you're right, weasel."

Carolyn said, "Weasel?"

I let it pass. "Five Americans," I said, "each with an animal for a code name, undercover in the Balkans. Working together and with partisans and dissidents of every description, all with the aim of destabilizing . . . Yugoslavia? Romania? Bulgaria?"

"Any one would do," Weeks said dreamily. "Or all three. Be nice, wouldn't it? Real feather in the collective cap for Hannibal's Animals." He winked at me. "Another name we had for ourselves. I didn't tell you about that one, did I? After the old man in Adams-Morgan who was running us. *His* code name was Hannibal, don't ask me why, and the name we made up for him was the elephant." He put his fingertips together. "But don't get me started, weasel. It's your party, yours to tell the tale."

I said, "One possible lever they found was the movement for Anatrurian independence. Causes don't die out in that part of the world, they just go dormant for a generation or two. King Vlados was well up in his seventies, a widower living on the Costa de Nada with a succession of housekeepers, his social life the same endless round of drinks and cardplaying with other once-crowned heads that had been sustaining him for the past forty years. He was a valuable symbol of Anatrurian greatness, but you couldn't expect him to march in the van of a renewed patriotic movement. The last thing he was going to do was give up the Spanish sun for some back-room rallies in the Anatrurian hills."

"Mountains," Ilona said.

"But Vlados and Liliana had a son. *L'aiglon,* the

French would say. The eaglet, the crown prince, the heir apparent."

"The colt," Weeks put in. "We called the old man the stallion, you see. Just among ourselves, mind you. He had that mouthful of horse teeth, and then he had retired to stud, hadn't he? So that made his son the colt."

"Todor was his name. Todor Vladov, because that's how Anatrurian names work, with a Christian name and a patronym. His father was Vlados, so his last name was Vladov. Even as your name"—I nodded at Ilona—"is Ilona Markova. You father's name would have been Marko."

"Except for what?" Tiglath Rasmoulian demanded. "You say the man's name *would* have been Marko. What prevented it from being Marko? And what was it in fact?"

"It is still Marko," she said indignantly. "Marko Stoichkov. He has never changed it. He would never do such a thing."

We got that straightened out, though you don't want to know how, believe me.

"Todor Vladov was a toddler when his father accepted the Anatrurian crown. He was in his early thirties when the Bob and Charlie Show took up the cause of Anatrurian independence."

"Time and tide, sir," Tsarnoff said. "They wait for no man, and the bell tolls for us all."

"What does he mean by that?" Rasmoulian snapped. "Why does he not speak that he may be understood?"

"If your cognitive ability had not been arrested

along with your physical development," the fat man said, "perhaps you might be able to follow a simple sentence."

"You glutton," Rasmoulian said. "You gross Circassian swine."

"You rug-peddling justification for the Turkish genocide."

"It is on such a rug that your mother lay with a camel when she got you."

"Yours rolled in the dirt with a boar hog, sir, for her husband ran off with the rug to sell it."

Then they both said several things I couldn't make out. It sounded as though each was speaking a different language, and I don't know that either could entirely understand what the other was saying. But they must have gotten the gist of it, because Rasmoulian's hand went into his trench-coat pocket even as Tsarnoff's gunsel was reaching inside his baseball jacket.

"Let's hold it right there," Ray said, and damned if he didn't have a revolver in his hand, a big old Police Special. I couldn't guess how long it had been since he'd heard a shot fired in anger, or even for practice, and the gun he was holding might very well blow up in his hand if he ever pulled the trigger, but they didn't know that. Tiggy tossed his head and sank deeper into his trench coat, but withdrew his hand from its pocket. Wilfred also showed an empty hand, but otherwise stayed his endearingly expressionless self.

"Back to Anatruria," I said quickly. "Old King Vlados may have given up dreams of a Balkan kingdom, but his son Todor found the idea intoxicating. Contacted by the American agents, he entered Anatruria surreptitiously and had a series of meetings with potential supporters. The stage was set for a popular uprising."

"Never would have stood a chance," Charlie Weeks mused. "Look what the Ivans did in Budapest and Prague, for Christ's sake. But look what a black eye they got for their troubles in the world press." He sighed. "That was all we were after. We were getting the Anatrurians to rise up just so the Russkies could cut them down." He flashed a rueful smile at Ilona, who looked horrified by what he'd just said. "Sorry, Miss Markova, but that was the job they handed us. Stir something up, make some mischief, embarrass the comrades. Like Werner von Braun with his rockets. His job was to get them off the ground. Where they came down was somebody else's department. He wrote an autobiography, *I Aim for the Stars.*" He winked. "Maybe so, Werner, but you sure hit London a lot."

"The Anatrurian rising never did get off the ground," I went on. "There was a betrayal."

"The woodchuck's doing," Weeks said. "At least that was what we always thought."

"The Americans scattered," I said, "and left the country separately. Government authorities swooped down on the Anatrurians and took the heart of the movement into custody. There were some long prison sentences, a few summary executions. According to rumor, Todor Vladov got a bullet in the back of the neck and a secret burial in an unmarked grave. In point of fact he slipped through a border checkpoint just in time and never again returned to Anatruria."

Ray wanted to know how old he'd be now.

"He'd be close to eighty," I said, "but he died last fall."

"And the treasury," Tsarnoff said. "What becomes of the treasury upon Todor's death?"

"The treasury?"

"The war chest," Rasmoulian said, impatient. "The Anatrurian royal treasury."

"Old Vlados's backers were grabbing with both hands when the Austrian and Ottoman empires were falling apart," Tsarnoff explained. "When they found themselves disappointed at Versailles, they packed their bags and hied themselves to Zurich, where they established a Swiss corporation and shunted everything they had into it. The corporation's liquid assets went into a numbered account, everything else into a safe-deposit box."

"Much must be worthless," Rasmoulian said, from deep within the shelter of his trench coat. "Czarist bonds, deeds to property expropriated by dictatorships of the left and right. Shares of stock in defunct corporations."

"The Assyrian is correct, sir. Much would indeed be worthless, but that which is not worthless could very well be priceless. Valid deeds, shares in firms which have thrived. And, while the bonds and currencies of fallen regimes would be of value only as curiosities, instruments of title to business and real property seized by the communists are worth another look now that communism has itself gone obsolete."

"There is no telling what it's all worth," Rasmoulian said, his spots of color glowing.

"Indeed, sir. There is no telling what money remains in that numbered account, or what assets the corporation retains. What could old Vlados have drained off? And what about his son, of blessed memory? No one goes through capital like a pretender trying to maintain a pretense."

"Vlados had an income," Weeks said. "Remember, the people who chose him for the throne didn't pick him off a dunghill. He was a shirttail cousin of the king of Sweden and claimed descent on his mother's side from Maria Theresa of Austria. Queen Liliana was some kind of grandniece of Queen Victoria. They weren't rich enough to buy the Congo from Leopold of Belgium, but Liliana never had to shop at Kmart either. They had an income and they lived within it."

"And Todor?"

"Same story for the colt. We didn't get him back to Anatruria by dangling some dough in front of him. He worked for a living, fronting an investment syndicate based in Luxembourg, but he was comfortable." He grinned. "We hooked him by the ego. He figured he'd look good with a crown on his head."

"He was a patriot," Ilona said. "That is not ego, to go to the aid of your people. It is self-sacrifice."

"How would you know so much about it, little lady? He was long gone from Anatruria before you were born."

He didn't sound as though he expected an answer, and she didn't give him one. I said, "Let's flash-forward to the present, okay? I'd like to tell you about a man named Hugo Candlemas. That's an un-usual name, and he was an unusual man, erudite and personable. Earlier this year he came to New York and took an apartment on the Upper East Side. And a matter of days ago he came into this store and introduced himself to me. He persuaded me to break into an apartment a few blocks away from his and steal a leather portfolio."

"You, Bernie?" The question came from Mowgli, who may have been the only person in the room who didn't know what I did when I wasn't selling books. "Why would he think you'd be up for something like that?"

"At the time," I said, "I thought he'd heard my name years ago from a man he mentioned as a mu-tual acquaintance, a gentleman named Abel Crowe." Both Rasmoulian and Tsarnoff started at the name, which didn't much surprise me. "Until he died, Abel Crowe was at the very top of his profession, which happened to be the receiving of stolen goods."

"He was a fence, all right," Ray Kirschmann agreed. "An' you gotta hand it to him, he was the best wide receiver in the business."

"And I was a burglar," I said. Mowgli, wide-eyed at this news, remained silent, probably because of the elbow Carolyn dug into his ribs. "But I've changed my mind about that. I don't think Abel would have bandied my name about."

"Abel was discreet," Tsarnoff said.

"He was," I agreed, "and even if my name did come up, how would Candlemas remember it years later when he happened to need a burglar? I don't think that's how it happened."

"He must have looked in the Yellow Pages," Charlie Weeks suggested.

"I don't think so," I said. "I think he followed Ilona."

"A couple of weeks ago," I said to her, "you walked into my store. I tried to figure out how you got here, because I couldn't believe it was coincidence. But at the time there was nothing for it to coincide with, was there? I'd never met Candlemas or heard of any of the people in this room. I didn't know Anatruria from God's Little Acre.

"And you were just looking for something to read. You picked out a book, and we got talking and found out we shared a passion for Humphrey Bogart. There was a Humphrey Bogart film festival just getting underway, and you knew about it, and we arranged to meet at the theater that night. Before we knew it we were going every night, watching two movies together, eating popcorn from the same container, then going our separate ways."

I looked into her eyes, and I thought of Bogart and tried to borrow a little nobility from him. "You're a beautiful woman," I said, "and I could have gone for you in a big way if you'd ever given me the slightest encouragement, but you never did. It was clear from the start that you had someone else. And that was okay. I liked your company, and I guess you liked mine, but what we both liked was up there on the screen."

There was gratitude in her eyes now, and a touch of relief, and something else as well. Wistfulness, maybe.

"I don't know if Candlemas was on your tail when you came into the bookstore," I said. "Probably not. But if he followed you at all he could hardly help running into me, because we were spending seven nights a week at the movies. He'd want to know who I was, and it wouldn't have been hard for him to find out. The kind of people he'd have asked would have known about my sideline as a burglar."

"It's the booksellin' that's a sideline," Ray put in.

I ignored that. "Candlemas needed a burglar," I said, "and he probably did know Abel Crowe, who spent the war in a concentration camp and knocked around Europe for a few years before he came over here. He would have learned I was a good burglar——"

"The best," Ray said.

"——and he had a name to drop to establish his bona fides. He sounded me out, and when the address he wanted me to burgle didn't ring a bell, he knew Ilona hadn't told me about the man who lived there."

"And who was that?" Ray wanted to know.

"The man in her life," I said. "The man, too, whom Candlemas had pursued to New York. He's right here. Mr. Michael Todd."

"*Around the World in Eighty Days*," Mowgli said. "Great flick. But didn't his plane go down?"

"Michael Todd," I said. "You speak good unaccented English, Mike, so why shouldn't your name be just as American as your speech? But you anglicized it along the way, didn't you? Why don't you tell them what it was before you changed it?"

"I'm sure you'll tell them," he said.

"Mikhail Todorov," I said. "The only son of Todor Vladov, the only grandson of Vlados the First. And, if there is such a thing, the rightful heir to the Anatrurian throne."

TWENTY-TWO

I guess we're all suckers for royalty. Half the house must have known or suspected Mike's place in the scheme of things, but all the same a hush fell over the room, and it hung there until Carolyn broke it. "A king," she said. "I can't believe it. In my store."

"Your store?"

"Well, it's almost my store, Bern. Who kept it open over the weekend? Uh, speaking of my store, Your Majesty, I don't suppose you have a dog that needs washing, but if you ever do—"

"I'll most certainly think of you," he said, whereupon Carolyn looked almost glassy-eyed enough to drop a curtsy. "Mr. Rhodenbarr, I haven't said anything until now, but perhaps I should. This business of an Anatrurian throne makes me quite uncomfortable. My grandfather's moment of glory occurred ages ago, and my father's little adventure took place before I was born, and very nearly cost him his life. That my family had a tentative claim on a putative crown was interesting, even amusing, something to impress a girl or enliven a social gathering. I have my own life, with a small amount of capital and a career in international finance and economic development. I don't spend time nostalgic for a royal past or dreaming of a royal future."

"And yet you came to New York," I said gently.

"To get away from Europe and its talk of thrones and crowns."

"And you brought a gold-stamped leather portfolio."

He sighed heavily. "When my father lay dying," he said, "he called me to his side and turned over to me the portfolio of which you speak. Until then I did not know of its existence."

"And?"

"He had scarcely spoken to me of Anatruria. You must understand that none of our family had ever lived there. My grandfather was chosen to be king of the Anatrurians, but he was not previously Anatrurian himself. Now, on his deathbed, my father spoke of his deep love for this small mountainous nation, of the loyalty our family commanded there and the responsibility which consequently devolved upon us. I thought he was raving, affected by the drugs his doctors had given him. And perhaps he was."

"He was a great man," Ilona said.

"I would say so, but then he was my father. Middle-aged when I was born, often absent while I was growing up, but surely a great man in my eyes. With his dying breath he told me of my duty to Anatruria, and passed on the royal portfolio."

"What did it hold?"

"Papers, documents, souvenirs. Shares of stock in a Swiss corporation."

"Bearer shares," I said.

"Yes, I believe so."

"Like bearer bonds," Charlie Weeks said. "The Swiss are nuts about that sort of thing. When they change hands, there's no need to go through any paperwork to record the transfer. They're like cash, they belong to whoever is in possession of them."

"And with them in your hands," I said, "you could take possession of all the assets of the corporation."

Todd—Mikhail? The king?—shook his royal head. "No," he said.

"No?"

"You need the account number *and* the shares," he said. "Believe me, I went to Zurich, I consulted bankers and attorneys there. This corporation was set up in an unusual fashion, and one must be in possession of the bearer shares and know the number of the account in order to lay hands on any of the corporation's assets. My father passed on the shares, which he had received from his father, but neither he nor his father had been entrusted with the account number."

"Out with it, man," said Tsarnoff. "Who has it?"

"Probably no one," Todd said.

"Ridiculous! Someone must know."

"Someone must have known once, some leader of the Anatrurian movement. Perhaps several people knew. You have already said that my father was lucky to get out of Anatruria with his life. Others were not so lucky. So many were taken from their families, only to receive a bullet in the back of the neck and burial without ceremony in an unmarked grave. I would guess that many secrets were buried along with those men, and that the number of the Swiss account was one of those secrets."

He sighed again. "I remember sitting at a café after my last meeting with a lawyer and a banker, sitting with a glass of wine and wishing my father had taken the portfolio to the grave with him as some Anatrurian had taken the account number. But instead he'd entrusted it to me. In a sense, he'd pressed a crown on my head, and it was not so easy to lay it aside. I told you how I had never thought of Anatruria. Now I could scarcely think of anything else."

"Who could even say how much the wealth might be?" This from Rasmoulian, his eyes wide at the possibilities. "It could be nothing. It could be millions."

"The money is the least of it," the king said. "What am I to do? That is the only question of any importance."

Ray didn't understand, and said so.

"For decades," the king said, "the world's few reigning kings have been anachronisms, while uncrowned royals have been little more than a joke. But all of a sudden this is not so. There are monarchist movements throughout all of the old Eastern Bloc. Portions of portions of nations are all at once reaching out and achieving sovereignty. If Slovenia and Slovakia can join the United Nations, is an independent Anatruria such an impossibility? If Juan Carlos can be king of Spain, and if men can seriously urge a Romanov restoration in Russia—the Romanovs! in Russia!—"

"Not entirely out of the question," Tsarnoff allowed.

"—then who is to say Anatruria cannot have a king? And who am I to deny my people if indeed they want me?" He smiled suddenly, and now the resemblance was unmistakable—to Ilona's photograph of Vlados, to Mikhail's own photo of his father resplendent in uniform. "And so I came to New York," he said, "to get away from Europe, and to decide what I shall do next."

"It looks as though Hugo Candlemas followed you here," I said. "As I said, he picked me to steal the portfolio from you, although I didn't know what I was stealing or whose apartment I was taking it from."

"Not like you, Bernie," Ray said.

"I know," I said. "It wasn't. I don't know why I went for it, and all I can come up with is a combination of his charm and all those Bogart movies I was watching. He made the proposition one afternoon, and the following night I was with a man named Hoberman, on my way to . . . excuse me, but what do I call you? Your Highness? Your Majesty?"

" 'Michael' will be fine."

"I was on my way to Michael's apartment."

"Hoberman," Ray said. "That's a name you mentioned before, Bernie."

I nodded. "Cappy Hoberman was the ram, one of the five agents in Anatruria. Candlemas paired me with him because Hoberman could escort me into the high-security building where Michael lives. He could go there on the pretext of visiting another tenant in the building."

"Which is where I come in," Charlie Weeks said.

"Interesting," Tsarnoff said. "Of all the buildings in all the cities in America, the young king moves into yours."

The line had a familiar ring to it. I had an answer, but Weeks got there first. "No coincidence at all," he said. "Michael gave me a call as soon as he got to New York. He'd never met me, of course, but I'd kept in touch with Todor ever since I helped him get out of Anatruria two steps ahead of the KGB. Michael needed a place to stay, and I knew there was an owner in the building looking to sublet, and he liked the place and moved in right away."

"As it turned out," I said, "I didn't steal the portfolio. I'll admit I tried, Michael, but I couldn't find it."

"There was one night last week when I took it from the apartment," he said. "Ilona thought a friend of hers should see one of the documents."

"I must have just missed it. Meanwhile, Cappy Hoberman went back to Candlemas's apartment, where somebody stabbed him to death."

"Wait a minute," Ray said. "That's the guy? Hoberman?"

"Right."

"Cap Hob," he said, staring hard at me. "Cap Hob. Captain Hoberman."

"Right."

"But why in the hell would he—"

I held up a hand. "It's complicated," I said, "and it's probably easier all around if I just tell it straight through. Cappy Hoberman was stabbed to death in the Candlemas apartment. But he lived long enough to leave a message. He printed C-A-P-H-O-B in block capitals on the side of a handy attaché case."

"Which happened to belong to a certain burglar we all know," Ray said.

"Didn't it," I said sourly. "He died, and left a dying message that didn't make sense to anyone. Meanwhile, Hugo Candlemas disappeared."

"So this Candlemas killed him," Ilona said.

"It seems obvious, doesn't it? But who was Candlemas? Well, he was someone who knew Hoberman and Weeks, someone who was familiar with Anatrurian history and had come over from Europe to keep tabs on Michael here. And he was someone with a lot of fake ID, because in addition to forged identification in the name of Hugo Candlemas, he also had high-quality counterfeit passports in the names Jean-Claude Marmotte and Vassily Souslik. That gives it away. I should have known before, but—"

"The last name you mentioned," Tsarnoff said. "Say it again, sir, if you please."

"Vassily Souslik."

"Souslik," he said, and chuckled. "Very good, sir. Very good indeed."

"What is so good?" Rasmoulian demanded. "It is good because he has a Russian name? I do not understand."

"Now that you mention it," Ray said, "neither do I.

I'm the one told you about those names, Bernie, and
they didn't mean a thing to me, an' if they meant
anything to you I never heard a peep out of you
about it. What in hell's a sousnik, anyway?"

"A souslik," I said. "Not a sousnik. And it's a Russian word, which is why Mr. Tsarnoff understood it
and why the rest of us didn't, although you'll find it
in some English dictionaries and encyclopedias. And
it means a large ground squirrel indigenous to Eastern Europe and Asia."

"Well, for Christ's sake," Ray said, "that explains
everything, don't it? A big fat squirrel. That cracks
the case wide open, all right."

"What it does," I said, "is identify Candlemas for
us. So does his French alias, because a marmot is
pretty much the same thing as a souslik. But I
should have known earlier on if I'd been paying attention to what he called himself this time around.
Candlemas is a church festival commemorating the
purification of the Virgin Mary and the presentation
of the infant Christ in the temple. But it's celebrated
on the same date every year like Christmas, not tied
to the lunar calendar like Easter."

Someone asked the date.

"February second," I said.

They met this with mystified silence and shared
the silence like Quakers through whom God had, for
the moment, nothing to say. Then Wilfred, silent
skulking Wilfred, said, "My favorite holiday."

Everybody looked at him.

"Groundhog's Day," he said. "Second of February.
Most useful holiday of the year. He pops out, he

don't see his shadow, you got yourself an early spring. Bright sunny day, he sees his shadow, forget about it. Six more weeks of winter."

I said, "The groundhog, the souslik, the marmot. All names for—"

"The woodchuck," said Charlie Weeks, smiling his tight little smile. "Alias Chuck Wood, alias Charles Brigham Wood. Disappeared into Europe after the balloon went up in Anatruria. Some people thought he was killed. The rest of us figured he was the one who sold us out."

I let that last pass. "Candlemas was the woodchuck," I agreed. "I guess he kept tabs on people from afar. He knew where Michael was living, and he knew that his old friend the mouse was in the same building. But he couldn't approach the mouse himself."

"I'd had enough of him in Anatruria," Weeks said.

"So he used Hoberman as his cat's-paw," I said, and frowned at the metaphor, an inappropriate one among all these rodents.

"And when Cappy had served his purpose," Weeks said, "the woodchuck killed him."

"In his own apartment?"

"Why not?"

"And on his own rug? Candlemas might sacrifice an old friend, but why throw in a valuable rug?"

"How valuable?" Ray wanted to know. I couldn't tell him, and Tsarnoff suggested dryly that we consult the rug peddler in our midst for an evaluation.

"Stop that!" Rasmoulian said. "Why does he do

that? I am not an Armenian. I know nothing about carpets. Why does he say these things about me?"

"The same reason you call me a Russian," Tsarnoff said smoothly. "Willful ignorance, my little adversary. Willful ignorance founded on malice and propelled by avarice."

"I shall never call you a Russian again. You are a Circassian."

"And you an Assyrian."

"The Circassians are legendary. The women are exquisite whores, and the males are castrated young and make great gross eunuchs."

"The Assyrians at their height were noted chiefly for their savagery. They have dwindled and died out to the point where the few in existence are wizened dwarves, the genetically warped spawn of two millennia of incestuous unions."

We were making progress, I was pleased to note. For all the verbal escalation, neither Rasmoulian's hand nor Wilfred's had moved so much as an inch toward a concealed weapon.

"Candlemas didn't kill Hoberman," I said. "Even if he didn't care about the rug, even if he had some dark reason to want Hoberman out of the picture, the timing was all wrong. Would he risk having a corpse on the floor when I got back with the royal portfolio?"

"He'd kill you, too," Weeks said.

"And write off another rug? No, it doesn't make sense that way. It's a shame, too, because Candlemas makes a very convenient killer."

"That's the truth," Ray said. "Tell 'em why, Bernie."

"Because he's dead himself," I said, "and can't argue the point. He died within hours of Hoberman,
but he took longer to turn up. The cops found him
in an abandoned building at Pitt and Madison."

"That's the place to find one," said Mowgli, as one
who knew. "A corpse or an abandoned building. Or
both."

"How was he killed?" Tsarnoff wanted to know.

"He was shot," Ray said. "Small-caliber gun fired
at close range."

"Two different killers," Tiglath Rasmoulian suggested. "This woodchuck stabbed the ram, and was
shot by someone else."

"If this happened in Anatruria," Ilona said, "you
would know that the woodchuck was shot by a son
of his victim, or perhaps a brother. Even a nephew."
She shrugged. "But you would not inquire too
closely, because this would not be a police matter. It
is merely blood avenging blood, and honor requires
it."

"There's no honor here," I said. "And a good thing,
too. There was only one killer. He followed
Hoberman when he left the Boccaccio, tagged him
to the woodchuck's apartment a few blocks away,
and stabbed him right off. Then he abducted Candlemas, took him down to Pitt Street—"

"Pitt Street," Mowgli said. "You're down there, you
might as well be dead."

"—and killed him when he'd learned all he could
from him. Or maybe he took him somewhere else,
killed him after interrogating him, and took the dead
body to Pitt Street."

"Coals to Newcastle," Mowgli said.

"Then someone was watching my building," Michael said.

"No."

"You mean this Hoberman was under surveillance all along?"

I shook my head. "The ram was visiting his old friend, the mouse. They hadn't seen each other in years. And when the mouse told me about that visit, he made a real point of saying how the ram was in a hurry to get out of there."

"Ah," Charlie Weeks said. "You mean he was going to meet somebody on his way back to the woodchuck's place."

"No," I said. "That's not what I mean."

"It's not?"

"It's not," I said. "What I mean is that you wanted me to know that Hoberman was hardly in your apartment for any time at all. That way it wouldn't occur to me that you had plenty of time to get him settled in with a cup of coffee and excuse yourself long enough to make a quick phone call."

"Why would I do that?"

"Because you knew something was up. You didn't know what, but you were the mouse and you smelled a rat. You couldn't tag along with Hoberman. He'd be on guard. But you could call a confederate and stall Hoberman long enough for the man you called to post himself within line of sight of the Boccaccio's front entrance. Whether or not he knew Hoberman by sight, you could supply a description that would make identification an easy matter."

"Oh, weasel," Charlie Weeks said. "I'm disappointed in you, coming up with a wild theory like that."

"You deny it, then."

"Of course I deny it. But I can't deny the possibility that somebody followed Cappy home. It seems a little farfetched to me, but anything's possible. Thing is, I don't see how you're going to guess who it was."

"And if you had called someone, I'd just be guessing as to his identity, wouldn't I?"

"Since I didn't call anyone," he said, "the question's moot. But we can say that you'd just be taking a shot in the dark."

"Wait a minute," Carolyn said. "What about the dying message?"

"Ah, yes," I said. "The dying message. Could Hoberman have left a clue to his killer? We know what his message was." I walked over to my counter and reached behind it for the portable chalkboard I'd stowed there earlier. I propped it up where everybody could see it and chalked CAPHOB on it in nice big block caps. I let them take a good long look at it.

Then I said, "Cap hob. That's what it looks like. That's because we're in America. If we were in Anatruria it would look entirely different."

"Why's that, Bernie?" Ray asked. "Have they got their heads screwed on upside down over there?"

"I could show you in the stamp catalog," I said. "The Anatrurians, like the Serbs and the Bulgarians, use the Cyrillic alphabet. This is an important matter of national identity over there, incidentally. The

Croats and Romanians use the same alphabet we do, while the Greeks use the Greek alphabet."

"It figures," Mowgli said.

"The Cyrillic alphabet was named for St. Cyril, who spread its use throughout Eastern Europe, although he probably didn't invent it. He did missionary work in the region with his brother St. Methodius, but they didn't name an alphabet after St. Methodius."

"They named an acting technique," Carolyn said. "After him and St. Stanislavski."

"The Cyrillic alphabet is a lot like the Greek," I said, "except that it's got more letters. I think there's something like forty of them, and some are identical in form to English letters while some look pretty weird to western eyes. There's a backward N and an upside-down V and one or two that look like hen's tracks. And some of the ones that look exactly like our own have different values."

Carolyn said, "Values? What do you mean, Bern? Is that like how many points they're worth in Scrabble?"

"It's the sound they make." I pointed to the blackboard. "It took me forever to think Cappy's dying message might be in Cyrillic," I said, "and for two reasons. For one, he was an American. Early on I didn't know the case had an Anatrurian connection, or that he'd ever been east of Long Island. Besides, all six of the letters he wrote were good foursquare red-blooded American letters. But it so happens they're all letters of the Cyrillic alphabet as well."

"I do not know this alphabet," Rasmoulian said carefully. "What do they spell in this alphabet?"

"The A and the O are the same in both alphabets," I said. "The Cyrillic C has the value of our own S. The P is equivalent to our R, just like the rho in the Greek alphabet. The H looks like the Greek eta, but in Cyrillic it's the equivalent of our N. And the Cyrillic B is the same as our V."

In a proper chalk talk, I'd have printed a transliteration of the Cyrillic on the slate. Instead I gave them a few seconds to work it out for themselves.

Then I said, "Mr. Tsarnoff, I don't know which alphabet Circassians favor, but certainly you've spent enough time in the former Soviet Union to be more familiar than the rest of us with Cyrillic. Perhaps you can tell us what message the gallant Hoberman left us."

Tsarnoff stayed in his chair, but just barely. His face was florid and his eyes bulged; if Charlie Weeks wanted an animal name for him, you'd almost have to go with bullfrog.

"It is a lie," he said.

"But what does it say?"

"S-A-R-N-O-V," he said, pronouncing each letter separately and distinctly, as if pounding nails into a coffin. "That is what it says, and it is a lie. It is not even my name. My name is Tsarnoff, sir, T-S-A-R-N-O-F-F, and that is not at all what you have written there, in Cyrillic or any other alphabet known to me."

"And yet," I said, "it strikes one as an extraordinary

coincidence. I suppose you would pronounce it Sarnov, and—"

"That is not my name!"

"Tsue me," I said. "It's not that far off."

"I never met your Captain Hoberman! Until this moment I never heard of him!"

"I'm not sure that last is true," I said, "but we'll let it go. The point you're trying to make is that you didn't kill Hoberman, and you can give it a rest, because I already know that."

"You do?"

"Of course."

"Then why did Hoberman write his name?" Ray asked.

"He didn't," I said. "He didn't write a damn thing. That's a dying message, whether you pronounce it Caphob or Sarnov, and Hoberman was doing the dying, and it was his blood that formed the letters and his forefinger that traced them. I don't know if Hoberman even knew Cyrillic after so many years away from the region, but it certainly wasn't second nature to him, and what he'd automatically turn to in his haste to name his killer before his life drained out of him."

"Then who left the message?" Carolyn wanted to know. "Not what's-his-name, the groundhog—"

"The woodchuck. No, of course not. The killer left the message as a diversionary tactic. He probably chose Cyrillic because he knew little about his victim beyond the fact that he was somehow connected to Balkan politics. He wrote what he did because he wanted to implicate you, Mr. Tsarnoff, and he mis-

spelled your name because his familiarity with Cyrillic was tenuous. So what do we know about our
killer? He is not Anatrurian, he did not know his vic-
tims from the days of the Bob and Charlie Show, and
he has a murderous antipathy toward Mr. Tsarnoff."

"Piece of cake," said Ray Kirschmann. "Gotta be
Tigbert Rotarian, don't it? Only thing, if he's in the
rug business, why's he want to ruin a good carpet
like that?"

Rasmoulian was on his feet, his face whiter than
ever, his patches of color livid now. He was protest-
ing everything at once, insisting he was not in the
rug trade, he had killed no one, and his name was
not whatever Ray had just said it was.

"Whatever," Ray said agreeably. "I'll make sure I
got the name right when we get down to Central
Booking. Main thing's did he do it or not, an' I think
you still got your touch, Bernie. Tigrid, you got the
right to remain silent, but I already told you that, remember?"

Rasmoulian's mouth was working but no sound
was coming out of it. I thought he might go for a
gun, but his hands stayed in sight, knotted up in little fists. He looked like a kid again, and you got the
sense that he might burst into tears, or stamp his
foot.

The whole room was silent, waiting to see what
he'd do. Then Carolyn said, "For God's sake, Tiggy,
tell 'em it was an accident."

Jesus, I thought. What could have induced her to
come out with a harebrained thing like that?

"It was an accident," Tiglath Rasmoulian said.

TWENTY-THREE

I t was unquestionably an accident, he explained.
He had never meant to harm anyone. He was not
a killer.

Yes, admittedly, he had been armed. He had outfitted himself that evening with a pistol and dagger
as well, although it was never his intention to use either of them. But this was New York, after all, not
Baghdad or Cairo, not Istanbul, not Casablanca.
This was a dangerous city, and who would dream of
walking its streets unarmed? And was this not even
more to be expected if one was of diminished stature
and slightly built? He was a small person, if not the
dwarf that a certain hideously obese individual was
wont to label him, and he could only feel safe if he
carried something to offset the disadvantage at
which his size placed him.

And yes, it was true, he had received a telephone
call from Mr. Weeks, with whom he had had occasional business dealings over the years. At Mr.
Weeks's bequest, he'd driven to the Boccaccio and
parked across the street with the motor running.
When Hoberman emerged from the building he

watched him flag a cab and tailed him a short distance to what would be the murder scene. He entered the brownstone's vestibule just as Hoberman was being buzzed in and caught the door before it closed, following his quarry upstairs to the fourth-floor apartment. But evidently his activities had not gone unnoticed; he was standing in the hallway, trying to hear what was going on inside and deliberating his next move, when the door opened suddenly and Hoberman grabbed him by the arm and yanked him inside.

He had no time to consider the matter. His response was automatic and unthinking; in an instant the dagger was free of its sheath and in his hand, and in another instant it was in Hoberman's body. He did not know who the man was, nor had he any knowledge of the identity of the other man, the slender white-haired fellow in the suit and checkered vest. He did not know anything of the pursuit in which the two were engaged. All he knew was that he had just killed a man. Reflexively, of course, and in self-defense, to be sure, but the man was dead and Tiglath Rasmoulian was in trouble.

The white-haired man, the one they now seemed to be calling the woodchuck, was far too slow to react. He just stood there, staring in shock, and before he could do anything Rasmoulian was holding a gun on him. He put him against a wall with his hands in the air while he went through the pockets of the man he'd killed until he came up with a wallet. He stuffed it in his own pocket to examine at leisure.

And, while he was kneeling by the unfortunate

man's body, yes, something came over him, some hostility to an old foe. He took hold of the poor man's hand, dipped the forefinger in the blood, and wrote that foe's name on a convenient surface, which happened to be the side panel of an attaché case. And if his Cyrillic was imperfect, well, he'd come close enough. It was a barbaric alphabet anyway.

Then came the tricky part. Down the stairs and all the way to where he'd parked the car, he covered Candlemas with one hand in his pocket gripping the pistol; he was ready to fire through his own coat if he had to, and it was a good coat, the very one he was wearing today. It was late and the streets were empty; he waited for an opportune moment, then forced Candlemas to climb into the trunk. He locked the trunk, got behind the wheel, and drove downtown.

And yes, he knew the streets of the Lower East Side, and knew he and his prisoner would be undisturbed in one of the abandoned buildings to be found down there. He had asked Candlemas many questions, and had obtained some answers, but by no means managed to get the whole story. He knew that a bookstore proprietor had been engaged to steal some very valuable documents from an apartment in the building Hoberman had emerged from, and he got my name from Candlemas, and the name of the store. He knew there was an Anatrurian connection, and that was about all he knew.

He might have learned more, but there was another accident. Candlemas tricked him, pretending to cooperate fully, lulling him into inattention, then making a bid to escape. Once again Rasmoulian's reflexes sprang unbidden into action, and Candlemas, trying to get away, was shot dead. A single bullet had snuffed out the man's life.

Accidents, two of them. What else could you call what had occurred? It was tragic, he regretted it deeply, he was a man who had always deplored violence. Surely he could not be held accountable for the violence that had taken place in spite of all he had done to prevent it?

"Yeah, well, accidents'll happen," Ray said. "Guy who got stabbed, I looked at him lyin' there and I knew I was lookin' at one hell of an accident. You see a guy with four stab wounds in him, you know right off he's been in a real bad accident."

"My reflexes are good," Rasmoulian said.

"I guess they are. Candlemas, now, down there on Pitt Street, was tryin' to escape when he got hisself cut down. I got to say, though, he wasn't very good at it, because there were powder burns on his ear, so he couldn't have escaped more than a foot or so from the gun that killed him. Guy like that, he better not set up shop givin' people escape lessons."

There was a stretch of silence, broken by Charlie Weeks, who leaned back in his chair and crossed his legs first. "There are accidents and accidents," he said.

"Can't argue with that," Ray allowed.

"It was an accident, for instance, that I myself played an unwitting part in Cappy Hoberman's death. I'm less inclined to regret Chuck Wood, considering the little stunt he pulled in Anatruria."

I'd let that pass once, but enough was enough. "I don't think so," I said.

"I beg your pardon, weasel?"

"Let's ease up on the 'weasel' routine," I said. "You can call me Bernie. What I don't think is that the woodchuck sold out the good guys in Anatruria."

"Really? That's what we all thought."

"I think it was the mouse," I said. "I think you must be proud of it, too, or you probably wouldn't hang on to that letter of commendation from Dean Acheson."

"Now how could you possibly know about that?" Weeks said. "If I had a letter like that I'd certainly keep it in a locked drawer, wouldn't I? And you've never been in my apartment that I wasn't constantly in the same room with you."

"It's puzzling, all right," I said.

He seemed to shrink under the combined gaze of Ilona and Michael, melting away like the water-soaked Wicked Witch of the West. "It was a strategic decision made at a high level," he said. "I had no part in the decision and no choice but to implement it."

"And the good sense to see that it was the woodchuck who got blamed for it, and not the mouse."

"It happened over forty years ago. I won't apologize for it now, or explain the justification. I was a young man then. I'm an old man now. It's done."

"And the two men Rasmoulian killed?"

"I never thought that would happen," he said. "I wanted to know what the hell was going on. Cappy

Hoberman called up, came to see me on the flimsi-
est of pretexts, and was eager to be on his way almost immediately. It never occurred to me he was
running interference for a burglar. I thought he
wanted something, or was setting me up somehow.
For all I knew he'd tumbled to the way it all went
kerblooey in Anatruria, and he had some curious no-
tion of revenge." He shrugged. "The whole point is I
didn't know. I needed to call someone who could tag
him and report back. And the redoubtable Assyrian
tagged him a little more forcefully than any of us
would have preferred."

"It is unfair," Ilona said.

"Life's unfair, honey," Charlie Weeks said. "Better
get used to it."

"It is unfair that you get away with this, while
Tiglath Rasmoulian pays the penalty."

"There should be no penalty," Rasmoulian said.
"An accident, an act of self-defense—"

"I got to tell you," Ray Kirschmann said. "We got
us a problem here."

Another silence. Ray let it stretch for a bit, then
broke it himself.

"Way I see it," he said, "I got enough to arrest Mr.
Ras—" He broke off, made a face. "What I'm gonna
do is call you TR," he told Rasmoulian, "which is
your initials, and also stands for Teddy Roosevelt,
who it just so happens was police commissioner of
this fair city before he got to be president of the
United States."

"Thank you very much," Rasmoulian said.

"I got enough to arrest TR," Ray said, "an' I

wouldn't be surprised if there's enough to indict him. He confessed to a double homicide after bein' Mirandized one or two times, dependin' how you calculate it. So his confession ain't admissible, since nobody wrote it down an' got him to sign it, or had the presence of mind to tape it. But anybody here could testify that he confessed, same as a cellmate can rat out a defendant, sayin' he confessed, except in this case it happens to be the truth. TR here did confess, an' we all heard him."

"So?"

He glared at me. "So I can arrest him, an' as far as the trial's concerned, well, who knows what'll happen, because you never know. What I can promise you, though, is he'll get bail. Was a time nobody made bail on a murder charge, but now they do, an' my guess is TR here'll have to post something like a quarter mil max and he's on the street. And once he's on the street, citizen of the world that he is, all he's gotta do is bail out, if you follow me."

"Bail out?"

"Skip the country, forfeit the bond, and go about his business. And what's even more of a shame is me and my fellow officers'll be makin' life hard for all the rest of you, even with TR here off the hook and out of the country. Takin' testimony from Mr. Weeks, inquirin' into the source of Mr. Sarnoff's income—"

"Tsarnoff, officer."

"Whatever. Makin' sure everybody's papers are legit. An' of course there'll be reporters crawlin' up everybody's ass, poppin' flash bulbs at the king an' queen of Anna Banana—"

"Anatruria."

"Whatever. Be more important for you people to remember the name of the country, bein' as they'll probably wind up sendin' you back to it. Not Mr. Weeks, though, on account of he's an American citizen, an' they'll most likely want to keep him around so Congress can ask him some questions."

He went on in this vein, probably longer than he had to. After all, these people were professionals. They'd played the game before, in the Balkans and the Middle East.

Weeks said, "Officer . . . Kirschmann, is it?" He picked up his homburg, balanced it on his knee. "You know, I got a speeding ticket a couple of years ago in the state of Montana. They had to pass a speed limit there, and in order to qualify for federal highway funds it had to be a max of sixty-five on the interstates and fifty-five everywhere else."

"That a fact," Ray said.

"It is," Charlie Weeks said. "Now, Montana's too large and too sparsely settled for those limits to make any sense. And the federal government could make them pass that law, but they couldn't regulate how they enforced it. So Montana assigned only four state troopers to speed limit enforcement, and you know how large the state is."

"Prolly as big as Brooklyn and Manhattan put together."

Weeks's smile spread across his face. "Very nearly," he said. "The federal government couldn't establish penalties for violating the speeding laws, either, so Montana set the fine at five dollars per violation. If one of the state's four traffic cops nails you for doing a hundred and twenty-five miles an hour in a fifty-five zone, it costs you five bucks."

"Reasonable," Ray said.

"Very reasonable, but here's the point I'm trying to make. Just so no one's grossly inconvenienced, neither the motorist nor the arresting officer, the fine may be collected on the spot. You pull me over, I give you five dollars, and I go on my way."

"An' everybody's happy," Ray said.

"Exactly. And the state's best interests are served. Admirable, wouldn't you say?"

"In a manner of speakin', yeah."

"Officer," Gregory Tsarnoff said, "if the Assyrian is only going to forfeit bond, perhaps he could post it directly, without going through the usual channels."

"I'll tell you this," Ray said. "It's irregular."

"But expedient, surely."

"I don't know about that," he said, "but it'd get the job done."

"Tiglath," Charlie Weeks said, "how much dough have you got on you?"

"You mean money?"

"No, I'm thinking about starting a bakery. Yes, I mean money. You came here thinking you'd have a chance to bid on those bearer shares. How much did you bring?"

"Not so much. I am not a rich man, Charlie. Surely you know that."

"Don't dick around, Tiggy, it's late in the game for that. What are you carrying?"

"Ten thousand."

"That's U.S. dollars, I hope. Not Anatrurian tschirin."

"Dollars, of course."

"What about you, Gregorius?"

"A little more than that," Tsarnoff said. "But can you possibly be suggesting that I help raise bail money for the Assyrian? He wrote my name in blood!"

"Yeah, but credit where it's due, Gregorius. He spelled it wrong. Do I think you should kick in? Yes, I do." He frowned. "You know what else I think? I think there's too many people in the room. We need a private conference, Gregorius. You and me and Tiggy and Officer Kirschmann here."

"And Wilfred."

"If you prefer, Gregorius."

"An' Bernie," Ray said.

"And the weasel, to be sure."

I steered everybody else to my office in the back. That didn't seem fair to Ilona and Michael, but they didn't seem to mind, Ilona smiling her ironic smile while the king looked as though he'd suffered a light concussion. Between them they were less irritated than Carolyn and Mowgli, who were unhappy to be missing the next act.

I left them admiring the portrait of St. John of God, the patron saint of booksellers, and got back in time to hear Weeks explaining that he had the bearer shares. "Michael's a nice fellow," he was saying, "but that family was never loaded with smarts. After I heard about the burglary attempt, I told him I wanted to check the portfolio. I haven't given it back to him yet, and when I do the shares won't be in it."

Tsarnoff stroked his big chin. "Without the account number—"

"Without the number the shares are just paper, but who's to say there's no one alive who knows the number? For that matter, who's to say you can't create a hairline fissure in the rock-solid walls of the Swiss banking system? If the three of us threw in together . . ."

"You and I, sir? And the Assyrian?"

Weeks was smiling furiously. "Be like old times," he said. "Wouldn't it, now?"

"Well, now," Ray said, and there was a knock on the door. I looked up, and the knock was repeated, louder. I gave a dismissing wave, but the large young man at the door refused to be dismissed. He knocked again.

I went to the door, cracked it a few inches. "We're closed," I said. "Private meeting, not open for business today. Come back tomorrow."

He held up a book. "I just want to buy this," he said. "It's off that table there, fifty cents, three for a buck. Here's a buck."

I pushed the money back at him. "Please," I said.

"But I want the book."

"Take the book."

"But—"

"It's a special," I said. "Today only. Take it, it's free. Please. Goodbye."

I closed the door, turned the lock. I turned back to the five of them and found they'd made their deal.

Rasmoulian had taken off his trench coat and was hunting under his clothes for a money belt. Wilfred handed a manila envelope to his employer, who opened it and began counting hundred-dollar bills. Weeks drew a similar stack of bills from his pocket, removed a rubber band, licked his thumb, and began counting.

"I wish I knew why the hell I was doing this," Weeks said. "I've got all the money I need. What the hell do you think it is, Gregorius?"

"You miss the action, sir."

"I'm an old man. What do I need with action?" No one had an answer, and I don't think he wanted one. He finished counting his bundle, collected bundles from the other two, weighed all three in his cupped hands. I gave him a shopping bag from behind the counter and he dropped all the money into it. A few hours ago that bag had contained books, the ones I'd bought from Mowgli for seventy-five dollars. Now it was full of hundred-dollar bills.

Four hundred of them, according to Weeks, who held it out toward Ray.

"I don't know," Ray said, and shot a quick glance my way. I moved my head about an inch to the left and an inch to the right. Ray registered this, widened his eyes. I met his eyes, then raised mine a few degrees toward the ceiling.

"Thing is," he said, "there's a lot's gotta be done, a bunch of police personnel gotta be brought in on this. Seems to me forty grand's gonna spread too thin to cover it all."

"Well, I'll be a son of a bitch," Charlie Weeks said. "I thought we had a deal."

"Make it fifty an' we got a deal."

"That's an outrage. We'd already agreed on a figure, for Christ's sake."

"Put it this way," Ray said. "You got yourself a real good deal when that trooper stopped you out in Montana. But you ain't in the Wild West this time around. This here's New York."

TWENTY-FOUR

"It doesn't seem right," Carolyn said. "Tiggy murdered both of those men. And he winds up getting away with it."

It was around four-thirty and we were around the corner at the Bum Rap. Carolyn was staying in shape with a glass of Scotch on the rocks; I was getting back into shape gradually, nursing a beer.

"Mrs. Kirschmann needs a new fur coat," I said.

"And she gets it, and Tiggy gets away clean. But when does justice get served?"

"Justice gets served last," I said, "and usually winds up with leftovers. The fact of the matter is there would never have been enough evidence to convict Rasmoulian, even if he didn't skip the country in advance of trial. He'd never wind up in prison, and this way at least he winds up out of the country, and so do the rest of them."

"Tsarnoff and who else?"

"Wilfred, of course. Getting Wilfred and Rasmoulian out of the country means a saving of untold lives. They're a pair of stone killers if I ever saw one."

"And now they'll be working together."

"God help Europe," I said. "But there's always the chance that they'll kill each other. Charlie Weeks is on his way out of the country, too. He'll be catching the Concorde as soon as he makes arrangements to close his apartment at the Boccaccio. Between the three of them, they think they've got a chance of coming up with the Swiss account number and looting the long lost treasury of Anatruria."

"You figure they'll get hold of the number?"

"They might."

"And do you think there's an Anatrurian treasury left for them to loot?"

"If they ever get that account number," I said, "I think they're in for the greatest disappointment since Geraldo broke into Al Capone's vault. But what do I know? Maybe the cash is gone, depleted by banking fees over the past seventy years. Maybe the stuff in the safe-deposit box is nothing but czarist bonds and worthless certificates. On the other hand, maybe whoever gets in there will be sitting on a controlling interest in Royal Dutch Petroleum."

She thought about it. "I think the important thing for those three is to be in the game," she said. "It doesn't really matter who wins the hand, or how much is in the pot."

"I think you're right," I said. "Weeks even said as much. He wants to play."

She picked up her drink, shook it so that the ice cubes clinked pleasantly. "Bern," she said, "I was really glad I could be around for most of it at the end there. I never met a king before."

"I'm not sure you met one today."

"Well, that's as close as I expect to come. Mowgli was impressed, incidentally. He said he was seeing a whole new side of the book business today." She sipped her drink. "Bern," she said, "there's a few things I'm not too clear on."

"Oh?"

"How'd you know it was Tiggy?"

"I knew it was somebody," I said. "When Rasmoulian turned up at the bookstore, I assumed Candlemas had told him about me. When it turned out Candlemas was dead all along, I figured he must have done some talking before he died, probably to the man who killed him. Rasmoulian knew me by name, not by sight, so he hadn't followed Candlemas or Ilona to my store, or spotted me with Hoberman and followed me home."

"And you knew Charlie Weeks had called him. How did you know that?"

"When I called Weeks and went over to his apartment," I said, "he didn't know what the hell I wanted. He really did think I was some guy named Bill Thompson who'd come up on the elevator with Cappy Hoberman. When I said I wanted to talk to him, he probably thought I'd heard something about Hoberman's death, but not that I had anything to do with the burglary."

"But if Tiggy told him . . ."

"Tiggy told him Candlemas had admitted hiring a burglar to break into the king's apartment. But Weeks didn't know that burglar was the guy who'd said two words to him in the hallway. Then, once we started talking, he put two and two together."

"And?"

"And he tried to keep what he knew to himself, but he made a slip. When I said how Rasmoulian had known my middle name, he said, 'Grimes.' Now where did that come from?"

"Maybe you told him."

I shook my head. "When it was time to leave," I said, "he was still calling me Bill Thompson, pretending he didn't have a clue that wasn't my real name. If he knew the Grimes part, he'd know about the Bernie and the Rhodenbarr, too. So he knew more than he should, and for all his talk about joining forces he was keeping what he knew to himself. I played along, but I knew then and there that he was more than an old friend of Hoberman's and a ticket into the building. He was involved clear up to his hat."

"And when did you know Candlemas was the woodchuck?"

"Not as soon as I might have. The names on the passports did it for me. Not Souslik, I had to check some reference books before I found out what a souslik was, but I recognized the word 'marmot' even if Candlemas did give it a French-style ending on his fake Belgian passport. Then I looked up 'Candlemas' and found out it was just Groundhog's Day with hymns and incense."

"Wilfred's favorite holiday."

"Yes, and wasn't that a revelation?" I transferred some beer from my bottle to my glass, then from the glass to me. "I should have guessed earlier. On my first visit to Candlemas's apartment, one of the knickknacks I noticed was what I took for a netsuke."

"What kind of a rodent is that, Bern?"

"You know, those little ivory carvings the Japanese collect. They originally functioned something like buttons for securing the sash on a kimono, but for a long time now they've made them as objets d'art. I didn't look close at the one Candlemas had, but I figured it was ivory, and that it was supposed to be a beaver but the tail was broken off."

"And actually it was a woodchuck?"

"It was still there yesterday," I said, and took a little velvet drawstring bag from my pocket, and drew Letchkov's bone woodchuck from it. "If I'd been paying attention I would have known it wasn't a beaver. It's a perfect match for Charlie Weeks's mouse—the bone's yellowed in just the same way. You know, when Charlie showed me the mouse, I got a little *frisson.*"

"*That's* a rodent, right?"

I gave her a look. "It's a feeling," I said. "I knew there was something familiar about the mouse, but I couldn't think what it was. Anyway, Candlemas was the woodchuck, and he kept his carved totem all those years. I guess he had the mouse, too, and gave it to Hoberman to pass on to Weeks."

"Why did he need Hoberman? If he was the woodchuck, he knew Weeks as well as Hoberman did. Why couldn't he sneak you into the Boccaccio himself?"

"I'm not positive," I said. "He may have been afraid of the reception he'd get from Weeks. Remember, Weeks had spread the story that Candlemas had sold out the Anatrurians. Candlemas knew he hadn't, but he couldn't afford to find out if Weeks really believed it. Either way, he might not get a warm reception from the mouse."

"So he figured he'd be safer using Hoberman."

"But not safe enough," I said.

She had more questions and I had most of the answers. Then she started to order another round and I caught her hand on the way up. "No more for me," I told her.

"Aw, come on, Bern," she said. "It's been weeks since we had drinks together after work, and on top of that it's a holiday. Get in the spirit of it, why don't you?"

"We're supposed to remember the war dead," I said, "not join them. Anyway, I've got somewhere to go."

"Where's that?"

"Guess," I said.

In *The Big Shot*, Humphrey Bogart plays Duke Berne, a career criminal who's trying to go straight because a fourth felony conviction will put him in prison for life. But he can't stay away from it, and goes in on the planning of an armored-car heist. The head of the gang is a crooked lawyer, and the lawyer's wife is Bogart's old sweetheart. *She* won't let Bogie risk his life, and keeps him from participating in the robbery by holding him in his room at gunpoint. A witness picks him out of a mug book anyway, which strikes me as questionable police work, but that's my professional point of view showing.

The lawyer's jealous, and screws up Bogie's alibi, and he winds up going down for the count. There's a prison break, and Bogie gets away, but one thing after another goes wrong, until finally Bogie hunts down the rat lawyer and kills him. He's shot, though, and dies in the hospital.

That was the first picture, and I'd never seen it before. I got caught up in it, too, and maybe that was why I didn't eat much of the popcorn, or it may have been because I'd been munching peanuts at the Bum Rap. Either way, I had more than half a barrel left at intermission. I had to use the john—beer's like that—but I went and came back without hitting the refreshment counter.

I didn't feel like seeing the guy with the goatee, or any of the other regulars I'd gotten to know by sight. I just felt like sitting alone in the dark and watching movies.

The second picture was *The Big Sleep*, and whoever put the program together had been having fun, combining two pictures with near-identical titles. But of course this was the classic, based on the Chandler novel with a screenplay by William Faulkner, starring Bogie and Bacall and featuring any number of good people, including Dorothy Malone and Elisha Cook, Jr. I won't summarize it for you, partly because the plot's impossible to keep straight, and partly because you must have seen it. If not, well, you will.

Ten minutes into the picture, at a moment when I was really immersed in what was happening on the screen, I heard the rustle of cloth and got a whiff of perfume, and then someone was settling into the seat beside me. A hand joined mine in the popcorn barrel, but it wasn't groping for popcorn. It found my hand, and closed around it, and didn't let go.

We both watched the screen, and neither of us said a word.

When the movie ended we were the last ones to leave the theater, still in our seats when the credits ended and the house lights came up. I guess neither of us wanted it to be over.

On the street she said, "I bought a ticket. And then the man told me to get my money back. He said you left a ticket for me."

"He's a nice man. He wouldn't lie to you."

"How did you know I would come?"

"I didn't think you would," I said. "I didn't know if I would ever see you again, sweetheart. But I thought it was worth a chance." I shrugged. "It was just a movie ticket, after all. It wasn't an emerald."

She squeezed my hand. "I would take you to my apartment, but it is not mine anymore."

"I know. I was there."

"So you will take me to yours."

We walked, and neither of us spoke on the way. Inside, I offered to make drinks. She didn't want one. I said I'd make coffee. She told me not to bother.

"This afternoon," she said. "You said we went to

the movies together, but that we were no more than friends."

"Good friends," I said.

"We went to bed together."

"What are friends for?"

"Yet you did not let anyone know we went to bed together."

"It must have slipped my mind."

"It did not slip your mind," she said with cool certainty, "nor will it ever slip from mine. I will never forget it, Bear-naard."

"It made such an impression on you," I said, "that you emptied out your apartment and moved right out of my life."

"You know why."

"Yes, I guess I do."

"He is the hope of my people, Bear-naard. And he is my destiny, even as Anatrurian independence is my life. I came here to be with him, and to . . . to strengthen his commitment to our cause. To be a king, to have a throne, all that is nothing to him. But to lead his people, to fulfill the dreams of an entire nation, that stirs his blood."

Play the song, I thought. Where the hell was Dooley Wilson when you needed him?

"And then you came along," she said, and reached out a hand to touch my face, and smiled that smile that was sad and wise and rueful. "And I fell in love with you, Bear-naard."

"And once we were together . . ."

"Once we were together we had to be apart. I could be with you once and keep you as a memory to warm me all my life, Bear-naard. But if I had been with you a second time I would have wanted to stay forever."

"And yet you came here tonight."

"Yes."

"Where do you go from here, Ilona?"

"To Anatruria. We leave tomorrow. There's a night flight from JFK."

"And the two of you will be on it."

"Yes."

"I'll miss you, sweetheart."

"Oh, Bear-naard . . ."

A man could drown in those eyes. I said, "At least you won't have Tsarnoff and Rasmoulian and Weeks getting in your way. They'll be off playing hopscotch with the gnomes of Zurich, trying to find a way into a treasure your guy already gave up on."

"The real treasure is the spirit of the Anatrurian people."

"You took the words right out of my mouth," I said. "But it's a shame you don't have much in the way of working capital."

"It is true," she said. "Mikhail says the same thing. He would like to raise funds first so we will have money on which to operate. But the time is now. We cannot afford to wait."

"Hang on a minute," I said. "Just wait here, okay?"

I left her on the couch in the living room and paid a quick visit to my bedroom closet. I came back with a cardboard file folder.

"Weeks had these," I said. "He slipped them out of the portfolio along with the bearer shares, and I scooped them up this morning when I was in his apartment. I figured it was safe to take these because I don't think he paid much attention to them. His whole orientation is politics and intrigue. As far as he's concerned, these were just a propaganda device."

She opened the folder, then nodded in recognition. "The Anatrurian postage stamps," she said. "Of course. King Vlados received a complete set and passed them on to his son, and they have come down to Mikhail. They are pretty, aren't they?"

"They're gorgeous," I said. "And this isn't a set, it's a set of full sheets."

"Is that good?"

"They're a questionable issue from a philatelic standpoint," I said, "or else they'd be damn near priceless, considering their rarity. As it is, they're still valuable. They're unpriced in Scott, but Dolbeck prices provisional and fantasy issues, and the latest Dolbeck catalog has the full set at twenty-five hundred dollars."

"So these stamps are worth over two thousand dollars? That is good."

"If you're selling," I said, "you generally figure on netting two-thirds to three-fourths the Dolbeck value."

"Two thousand, then. A little less."

"Per set."

"Yes," she agreed. "That is very nice."

"It's nicer than you realize," I said. "The stamps are printed fifty to a sheet, so you're holding fifty sets. That's somewhere around a hundred thousand dollars."

She stared. "But . . ."

"Take it before I change my mind," I said. "There's a man at Kildorran and Partners who specializes in this kind of material. He'll either buy it from you or arrange to sell it for you. He's in London, on Great Portland Street, and his name and the firm's address are written down on the inside of that folder you're holding. I don't know if you'll get a hundred grand. It may be more, it may be less. But you'll get a fair price." I extended a forefinger, chucked her under the chin. "I don't know how your flight's routed tomorrow night, but if I were you I'd change things and take a day or two in London. You don't want to wait too long with those things. You might make a mistake and use one to mail a letter."

"Bear-naard, you could have kept these."

"You think so?"

"But of course. No one knew you had them. No one even knew they were valuable."

I shook my head. "It wouldn't work, sweetheart. The hopes and dreams of a couple of little people like you and me don't add up to a hill of beans next to the cause you and Michael are fighting for. Sure, I could use the money, but I don't really need it. And if I ever do I'll go out and steal it, because that's the kind of man I am."

"Oh, Bear-naard."

"So pack them up and take them home with you," I said. "And I think you'd better go now, Ilona."

"But I thought . . ."

"I know what you thought, and I thought so too. But I went to bed with you once and lost you, and I don't want to go through that again. One time is a good memory. Twice is heartbreak."

"Bear-naard, I have tears in my eyes."

"I'd kiss them away," I said, "but I wouldn't be able to stop. So long, sweetheart. I'll miss you."

"I'll never forget you," she said. "I'll never forget Twenty-fifth Street."

"Neither will I." I took her arm, eased her out the door. "And why should you? We'll always have Twenty-fifth Street."

TWENTY-FIVE

I t was a full week before I got around to telling Carolyn about that final evening in Ilona's company. I don't think I ever made a conscious decision to keep it from her. But it turned out to be a busy time for both of us. I kept my usual hours in the bookstore, and put in some overtime as well, riding the Long Island Rail Road to Massapequa one evening to appraise a library (for a fee; they didn't want to sell anything), and spending another evening at a book auction, bidding on behalf of a customer who was shy about attending those things himself.

Carolyn had a busy schedule herself, with a kennel club show coming up that meant a lot of dogs for her to pretty up. And there were a lot of phone calls and visits back and forth when Djinn and Tracey got back together again, and Djinn accused Tracey of having an affair with Carolyn, which was what Djinn had done after a previous breakup. "Pure dyke-o-drama," Carolyn called it, and eventually it blew over, but while it lasted there were lots of middle-of-the-night phone calls and phones slammed down and loud confrontations on street corners. When it finally cleared up, she plunged with relief into the new Sue Grafton novel she'd been saving.

So we had lunch five days a week and drinks after work, and then on Tuesday, a week and a day after Memorial Day, we were at the Bum Rap after work and Carolyn was telling a long and not terribly interesting story about a Bedlington terrier. "From the way he acted," she said, "you'd have sworn he thought he was an Airedale."

"No kidding," I said.

She looked at me. "You don't think that's funny?"

"Yeah, it's funny."

"I can see you think it's a scream. I thought it was funny."

"Then why aren't you laughing?" I said. "Never mind. Carolyn, there's something I've been meaning to tell you." And then I signaled Maxine for another round of drinks, because this was going to be thirsty work.

I told her the whole story and she listened all the way through without interrupting me, and when I was done she sat and stared at me with her mouth open.

"That's amazing," she said. "And you didn't say a word about it for a week and a day. That's even more amazing."

"I just kept forgetting to bring it up," I said. "You know what I think it was? I must have wanted a little time to digest it."

"Makes sense. Bern, I'm amazed. I don't want to work the word to death, but I am. I'll tell you this, kiddo. It's the most romantic story I ever heard in my life."

"I guess it's romantic."

"What else could it be?"

"Stupid," I said. "Real stupid."

"You gave away a hundred thousand dollars."

"Something like that."

"To a woman you'll probably never see again."

"I might see her on a stamp," I said. "If Anatruria makes the cut. But no, I'll probably never see her again."

"She didn't even know about the stamps, did she? That you had them, or that they were worth anything."

"Tsarnoff or Rasmoulian would have known what they were worth, or at least known they were worth plenty. Candlemas might have known—he had a collector's orientation. The others didn't think in those terms. And no, nobody knew I had them, least of all Ilona."

"And you gave them to her."

"Uh-huh."

"And you got to make the famous hill-of-beans speech."

"Don't remind me."

"Why'd you do it, Bern?"

"They needed the money," I said. "I can always use money, but I can't pretend I had a genuine need for a hundred thousand dollars. They needed it."

"Hell, Bern, the hip dysplasia people need it, too, and it was all I could do to get twenty bucks out of you."

"The stamps came from Anatruria," I said.

"I thought they came from Hungary."

"You know what I mean. They were issued in the cause of Anatrurian freedom, and if they were worth all that money after all those years, then the money belonged to the cause. If there is such a cause, or if there even is such a country." That was confusing, and I stopped and took a sip of my drink and started over. "If she hadn't shown up at the Musette," I said, "I don't know what I would have done. I meant to call the king and give him the stamps, and maybe I would have done it, but maybe not. I just don't know.

"But the point is she *did* show up. I bought that extra seat, and I swear I wasn't all that surprised when she wound up sitting in it."

"And once she did . . ."

"I held her hand, fed her popcorn, took her home, gave her a fortune in rare stamps, and sent her on her way."

"With the hill-of-beans speech echoing in her cute little ears."

"Forget the hill-of-beans speech, will you?"

"Schweetheart, the hopes and dreams of a couple of little shitkickers like you and me don't amount to a hill of beans when you pile 'em up next to the Anatrurian Alps, and—"

"Dammit, Carolyn."

"I'm sorry. You know what happened to you, don't you?"

"I think so."

"All those movies."

"That's what I was going to say."

"You watched Bogart do the noble self-sacrificing thing one time too many, and when the opportunity came your way, you didn't have a prayer. Poor Bernie. Everybody made something out of this business but you. Ray was the big winner. What did he wind up with, forty-eight grand?"

"He had to spread that around a little. The official story now is that Candlemas killed Hoberman, then went down to the Lower East Side to cop some dope."

"Right, he was your typical junkie."

"And got shot when the deal went sour. I would guess somewhere between twenty-five and thirty-five thousand dollars'll wind up in Ray's pocket."

"And of course he insisted you take some of the money."

"It must have slipped his mind."

"Not fair, Bern. After all, you solved the whole case. He just stood there."

"He doesn't just stand. He looms."

"Good for him. He gets the money, Ilona and the king get the stamps, and the three mouseketeers get the bearer shares and go chasing after the lost treasure of Anatruria. And what about you? You didn't even get laid."

"Maybe that was dumb, too," I said. "But all she's going to be for me is a memory, and I didn't have to repeat the experience to be sure I'd remember it. I'm in no danger of forgetting."

"No."

I picked up my drink, held it to the light. "Anyway," I said, "it's not as though I wind up empty-handed."

"How do you figure that, Bern?"

"I got the bone woodchuck from Candlemas's apartment, remember?"

"Wow, Bern."

"And when I stopped by Charlie Weeks's place, the stamps weren't all I swiped. I got the mouse carving Hoberman gave him."

"Gee, you can just about retire when you sell those two little beauties, can't you?"

"No, I think I'll hang on to them as souvenirs. My real profit comes tomorrow night."

"What happens tomorrow night?"

"A man named Sung-Yun Lee goes to see *The Chink in the Armoire*."

"Is that a show?"

"On Broadway, at the Helen Hayes. Very hot ticket. I got a pair from a scalper and it cost me perilously close to two hundred bucks."

"All in the interests of getting him out of the house," she guessed. "But who the hell is he, and what house do you want to get him out of? Oh, *wait* a minute. The people downstairs from Candlemas, but I forget their names."

"The Lehrmans."

"And he's in their place on an exchange program. Right?"

I nodded. "And they'll be gone for another month, and their place is absolutely overflowing with good stuff, and you couldn't ask for a better setup. The security is nothing, the locks are child's play, and the

guy who's living there won't have a clue that anything's missing, because it's not his stuff. He'll go on
being careful not to look in their closets or poke
around in their drawers, and everything I take will be
converted into cash long before they're even back in
the country."

I went on, telling her about some of the items I'd
noticed on my brief passage through the Lehrman
apartment. When I stopped she said, "I'll tell you
something, Bern. I'm relieved."

"What do you mean?"

"You're your old self again. Bogart's great on the
screen, but all that Noble Loser stuff is no way to go
through life. I'm glad you're getting ready to steal
something. It's tough on the Lehrmans—"

"Oh, I'm sure they're insured."

"Even if they're not, I'm happy for you." She
frowned. "That's tomorrow, right? Not tonight?"

"No, why? Oh." I brandished my glass. "No, it's tomorrow. You know I don't drink when I'm working."

"That's what I was wondering."

"Anyway," I said, "I've got something else planned
for tonight. In fact, you might want to come along,
but we'll have to go straight from here."

"I don't know," she said. "I'm about halfway into
the new Sue Grafton and I'm kind of anxious to get
back to it. It's really something."

"Well, you always like her work."

"One of the things I like is she never repeats herself, and this one's kind of shocking."

"Really?"

She nodded. "Sadism and perversion," she said.

"Roman orgies, incest. Toga parties. I've got to tell
you, it's a whole lot kinkier than what Kinsey usually
gets herself mixed up in."

"Gee, maybe you were right about Kinsey."

"I know I'm right, but she doesn't do anything wild
herself. Everybody else does, though."

"What's it called, anyway?"

"*'I' Is for Claudius.*"

"Catchy," I said. "But you can stay home and read
anytime. Come on and keep me company."

"Where, Bern?"

"A movie."

"The Bogart festival's over, Bernie. Isn't it?"

"Over and done with. But down at the Sardonique
in Tribeca they're starting an Ida Lupino film festival."

"Bern, I got a question. Who cares?"

"What have you got against Ida Lupino?"

"Nothing, but I never knew you were such a big
fan. What's the big deal about Ida Lupino?"

"I always liked her," I said. "But tonight's movies
are kind of special. *They Drive by Night* and *High Sierra.*"

"I'm sure they're both terrific, but . . . wait a minute, Bern. I know *High Sierra*. It's not an Ida Lupino
movie."

"It most certainly is."

"She may be in it, but that doesn't make it her
movie. It's a Humphrey Bogart movie. He's trapped
on a mountain peak with a rifle, and they kill him."

"Why'd you have to ruin the ending for me?"

"Come on, Bern, you know the ending. You've seen the movie."

"Not recently."

"What's the other one? *They Drive by Night?* Who's in that, if you don't mind my asking? Besides Ida Lupino."

"George Raft," I said. "And I think Ann Sheridan."

"And?"

"And Bogart. He plays a one-armed truck driver. They showed *High Sierra* at the Musette, but on a night I couldn't go. I was stuck at that auction. And *They Drive by Night* never played the Musette."

"Maybe for a good reason."

"Don't be silly," I said. "I'm sure it's great. What do you say? Do you want to go? I'll buy the popcorn."

"Oh, what the hell," she said. "But one thing, Bern. Can we get one thing straight?"

"What's that?"

"This is entertainment," she said. "These are not training films. Is that understood?"

"Of course."

"Good," she said. "Don't forget, sweetheart."